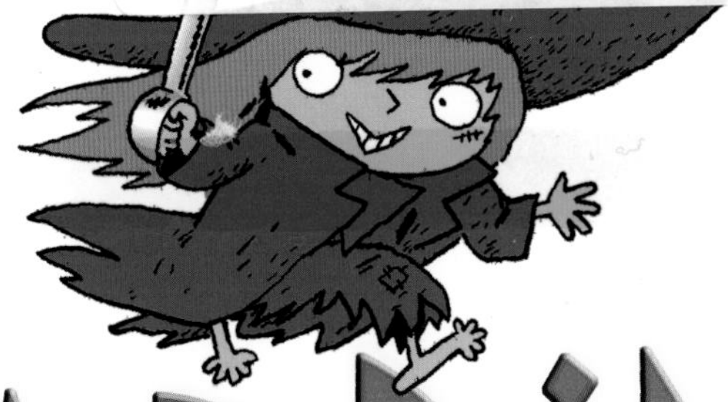

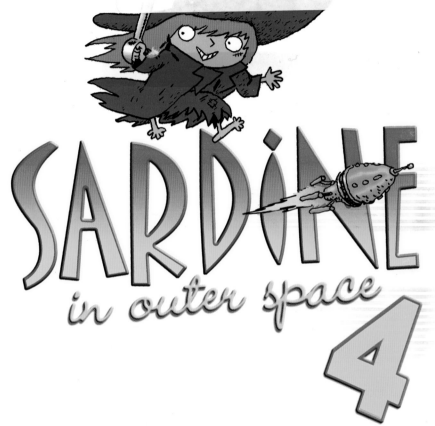

# SARDINE in outer space 4

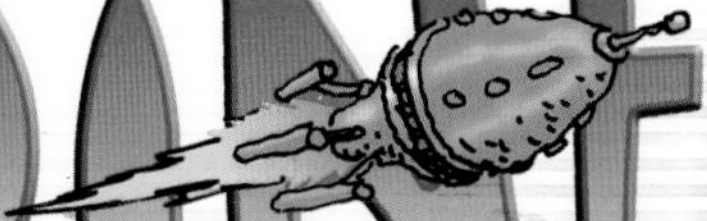

# SARDINE 4
## in outer space

Stories by Emmanuel Guibert
Pictures by Joann Sfar
Color by Walter Pezzali
Translation by Edward Gauvin

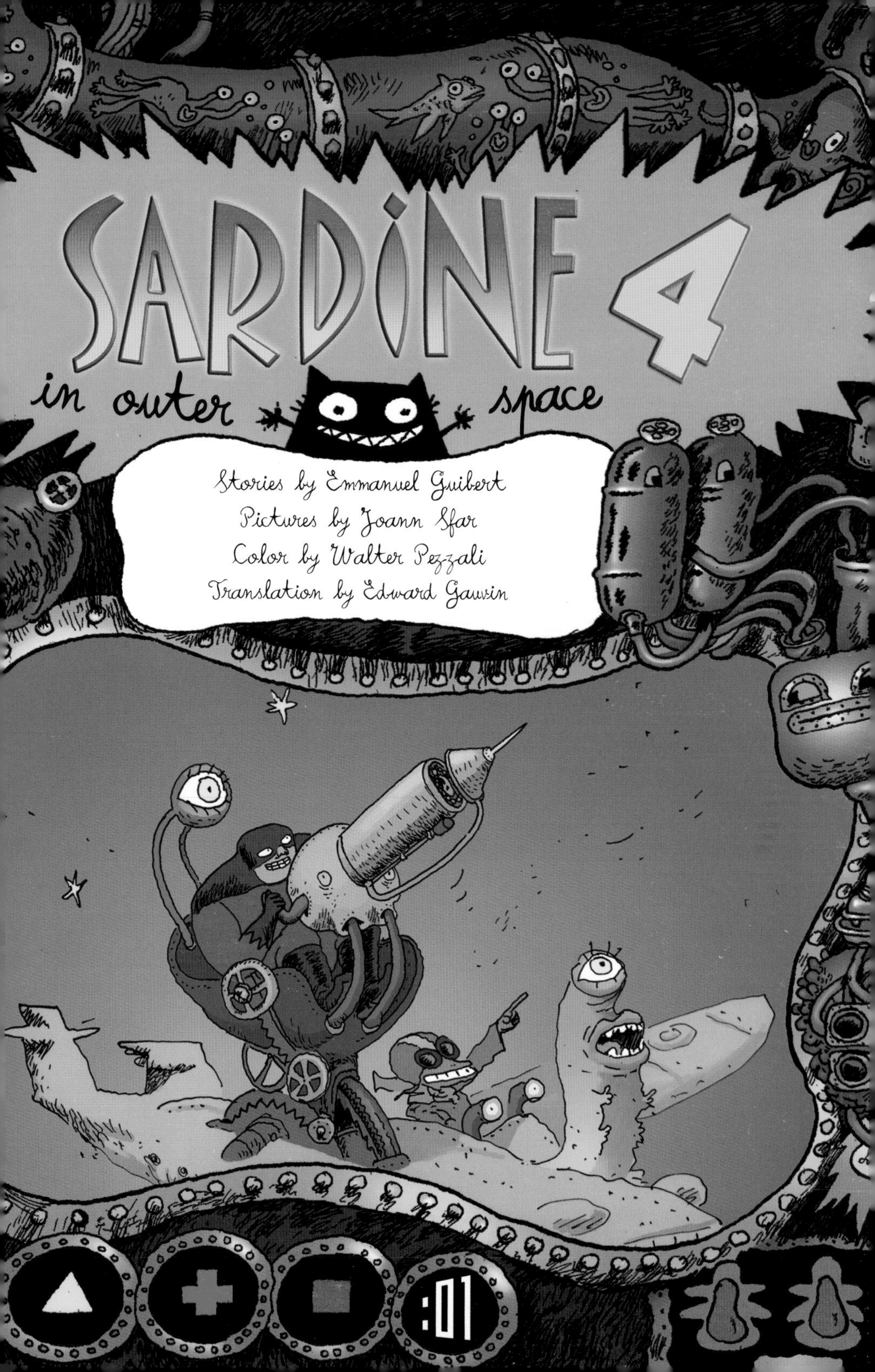
:01

# Contents

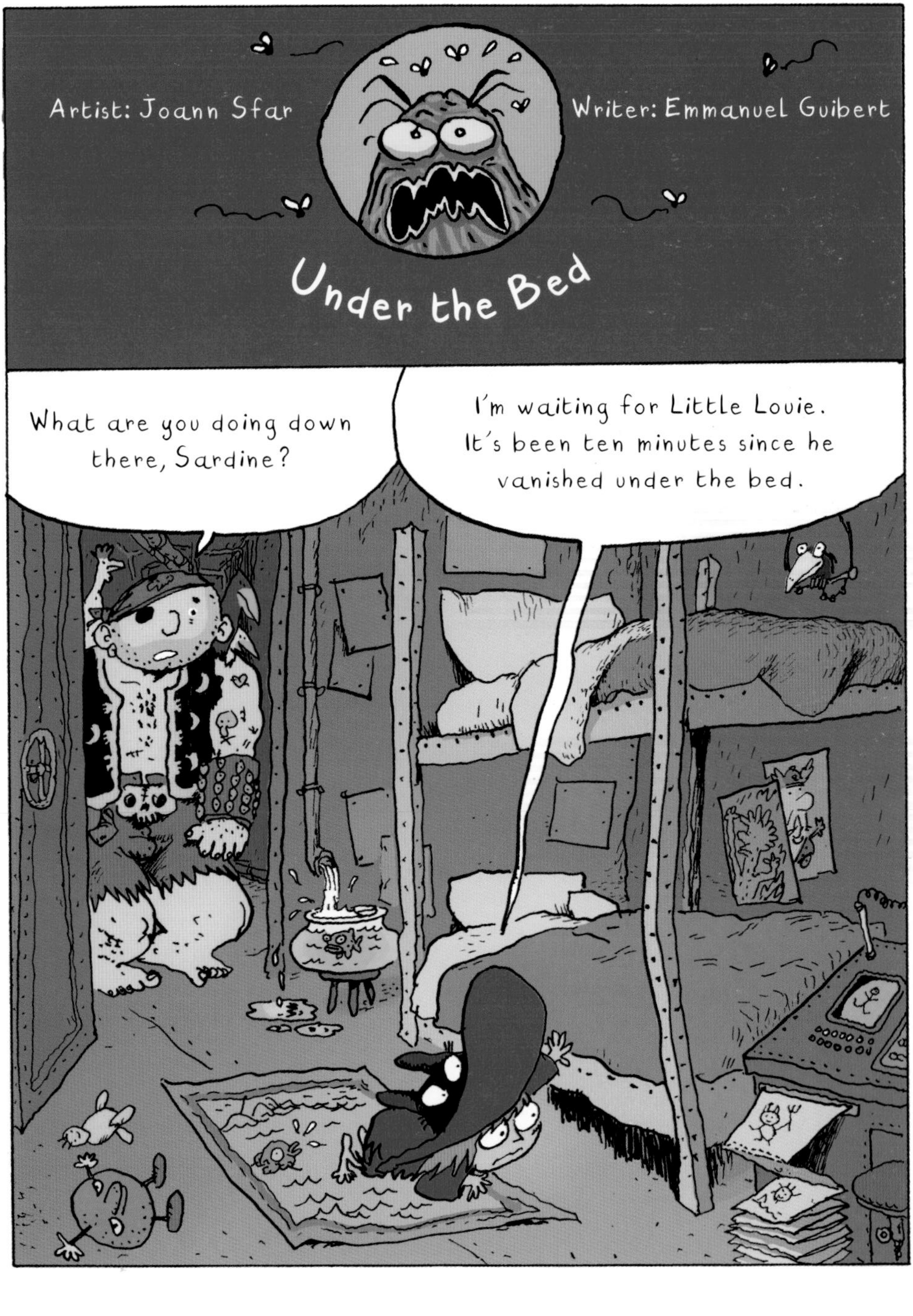
Artist: Joann Sfar
Writer: Emmanuel Guibert
Under the Bed
What are you doing down there, Sardine?
I'm waiting for Little Louie. It's been ten minutes since he vanished under the bed.

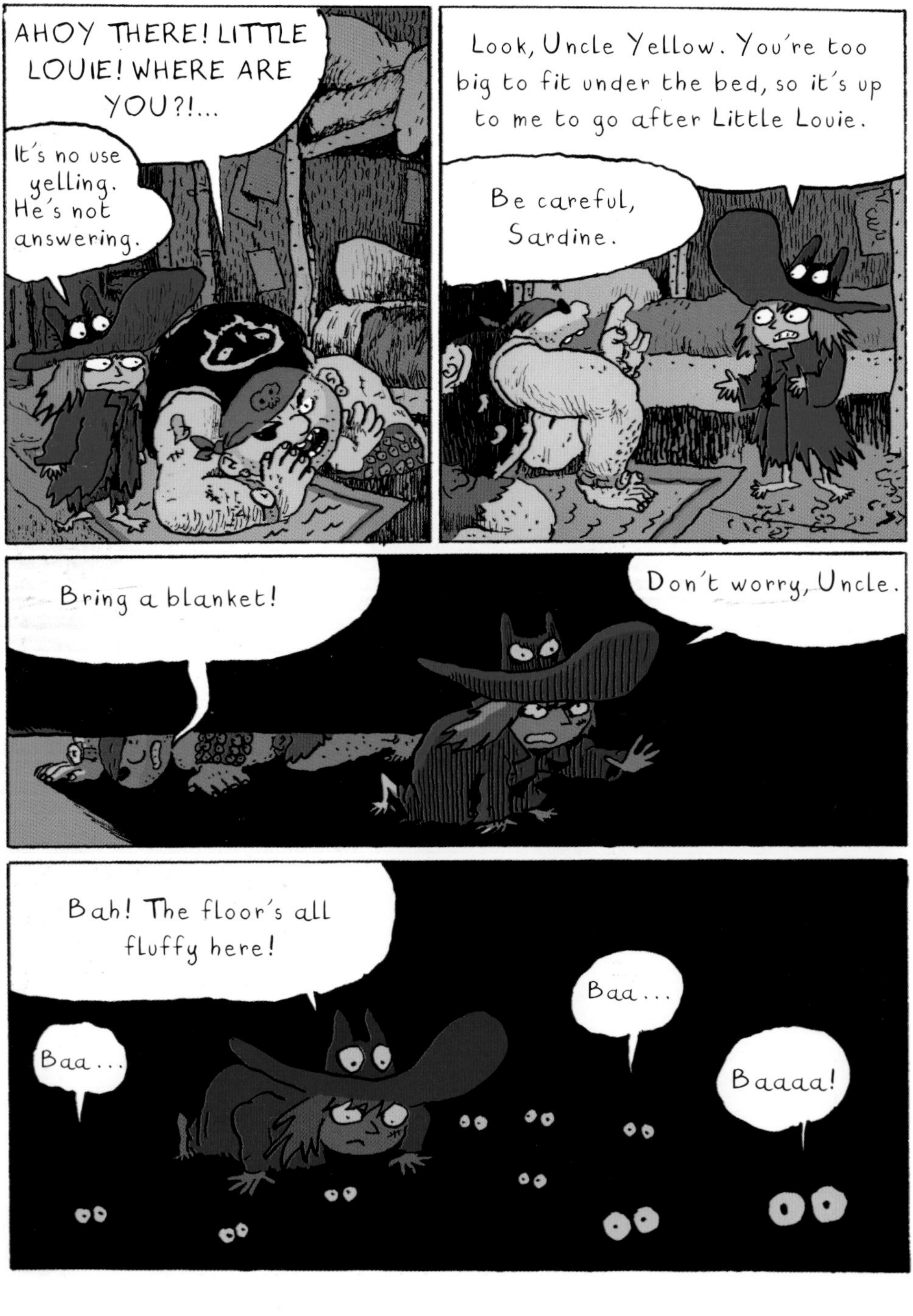
AHOY THERE! LITTLE LOUIE! WHERE ARE YOU?!...
It's no use yelling. He's not answering.
Look, Uncle Yellow. You're too big to fit under the bed, so it's up to me to go after Little Louie.
Be careful, Sardine.
Bring a blanket!
Don't worry, Uncle.
Bah! The floor's all fluffy here!
Baa...
Baa...
Baaaa!

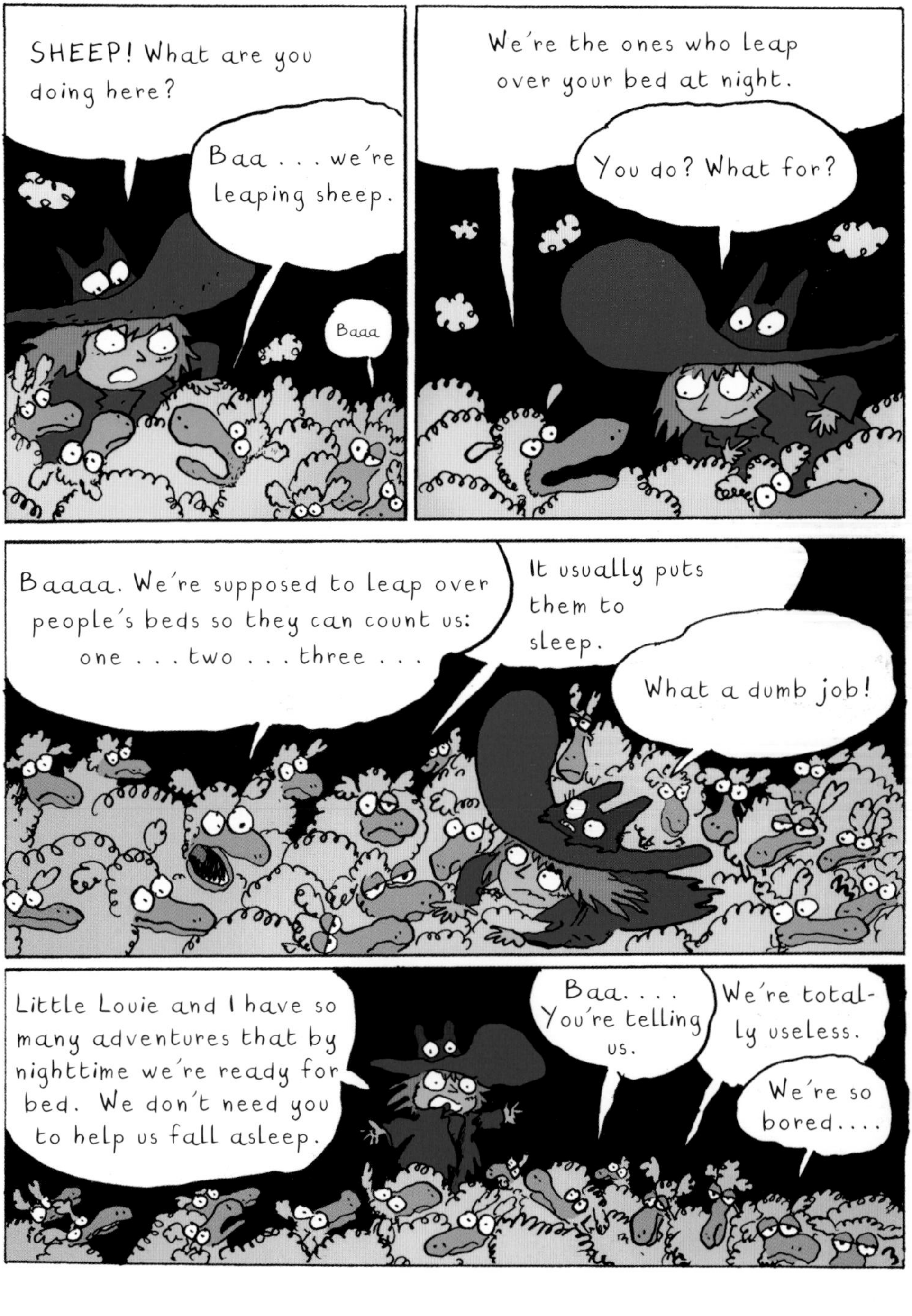
SHEEP! What are you doing here?
Baa . . . we're leaping sheep.
Baaa
We're the ones who leap over your bed at night.
You do? What for?
Baaaa. We're supposed to leap over people's beds so they can count us: one . . . two . . . three . . .
It usually puts them to sleep.
What a dumb job!
Little Louie and I have so many adventures that by nighttime we're ready for bed. We don't need you to help us fall asleep.
Baa. . . . You're telling us.
We're totally useless.
We're so bored. . . .

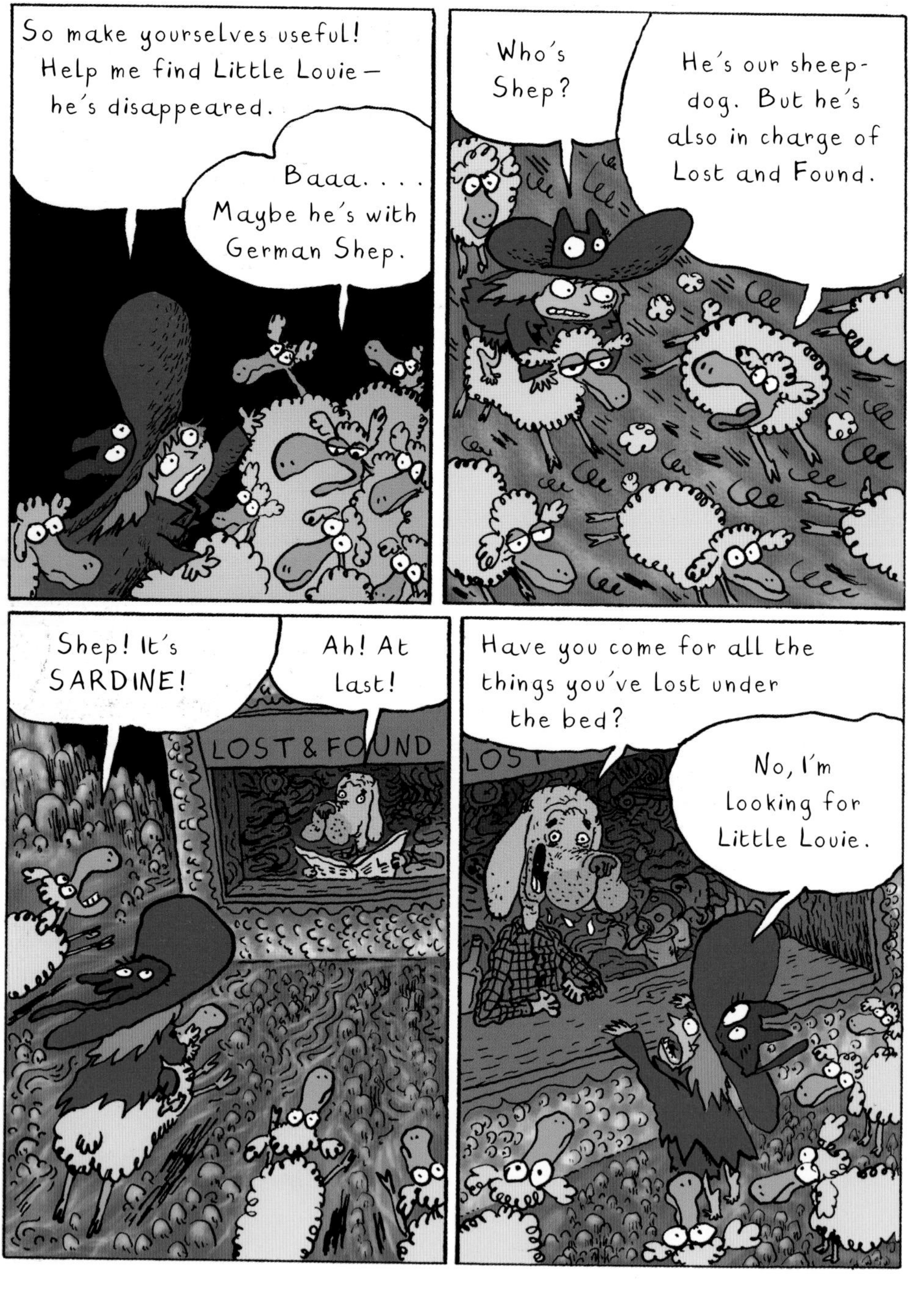
So make yourselves useful! Help me find Little Louie—he's disappeared.
Baaa. . . . Maybe he's with German Shep.
Who's Shep?
He's our sheep-dog. But he's also in charge of Lost and Found.
Shep! It's SARDINE!
Ah! At last!
LOST & FOUND
Have you come for all the things you've lost under the bed?
No, I'm looking for Little Louie.

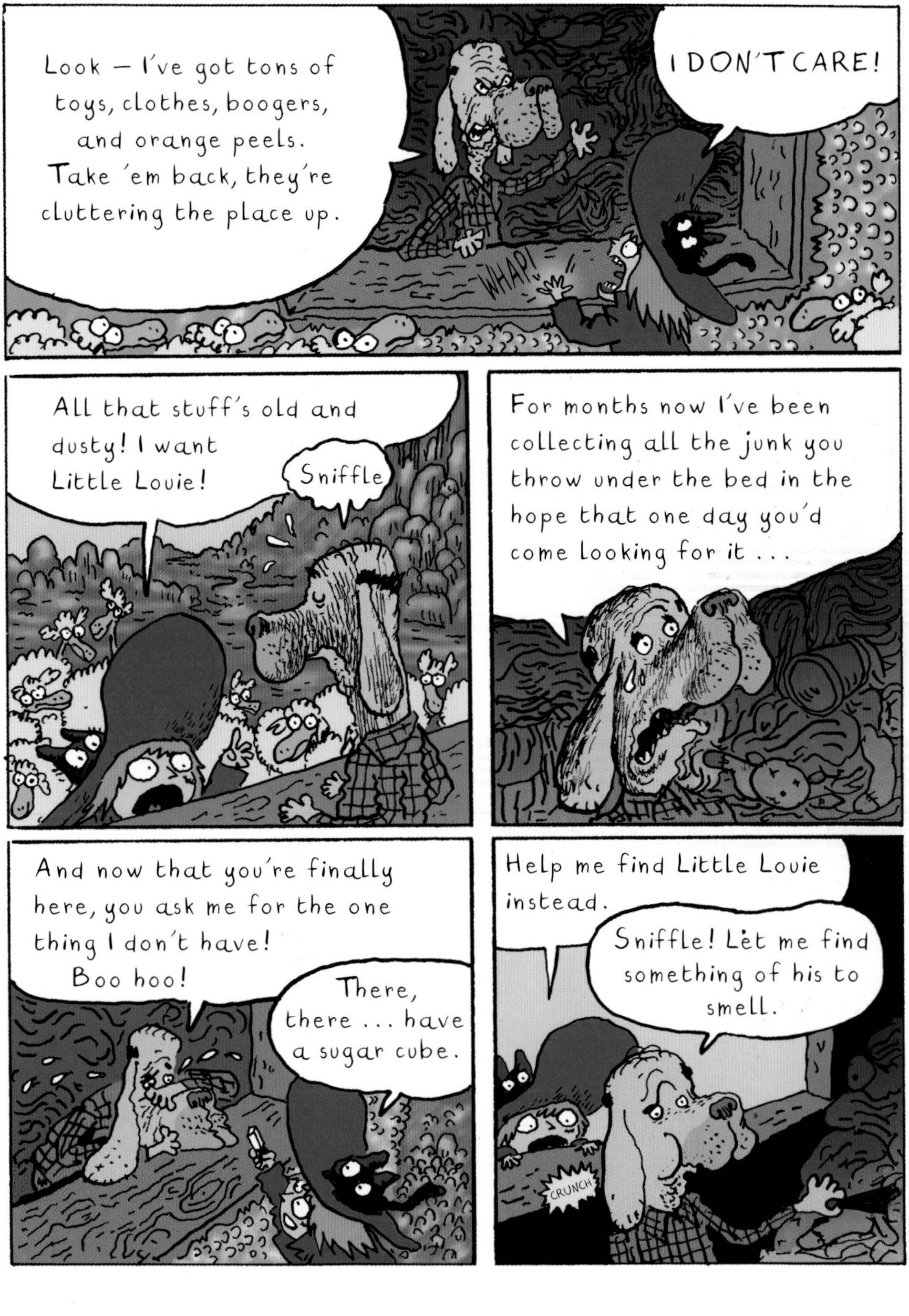

Look — I've got tons of toys, clothes, boogers, and orange peels. Take 'em back, they're cluttering the place up.
I DON'T CARE!
WHAP!
All that stuff's old and dusty! I want Little Louie!
Sniffle
For months now I've been collecting all the junk you throw under the bed in the hope that one day you'd come looking for it . . .
And now that you're finally here, you ask me for the one thing I don't have!
Boo hoo!
There, there . . . have a sugar cube.
Help me find Little Louie instead.
Sniffle! Let me find something of his to smell.
CRUNCH

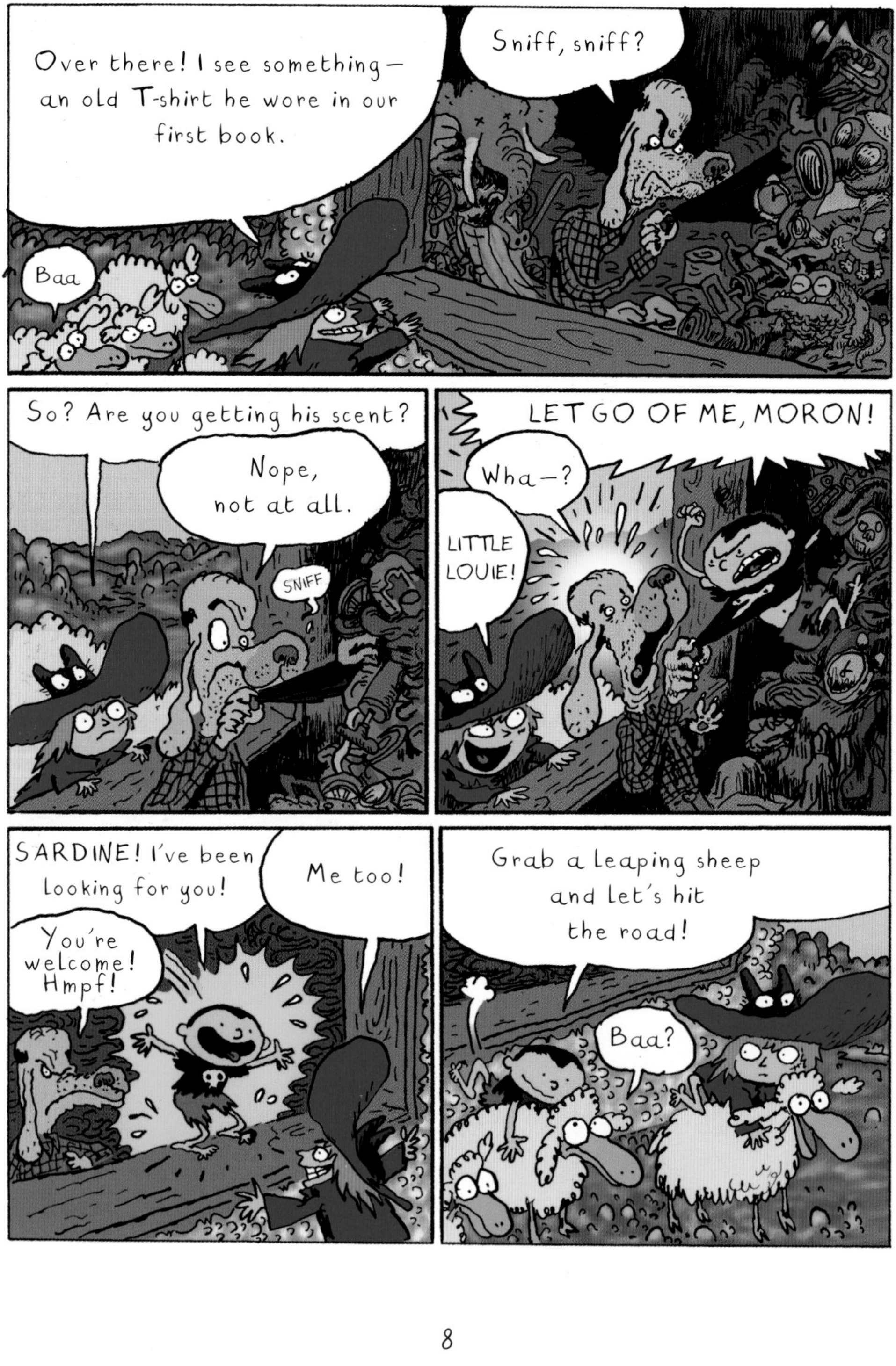
Over there! I see something—an old T-shirt he wore in our first book.
Baa
Sniff, sniff?
So? Are you getting his scent?
Nope, not at all.
SNIFF
LET GO OF ME, MORON!
Wha–?
LITTLE LOUIE!
SARDINE! I've been looking for you!
Me too!
You're welcome! Hmpf!
Grab a leaping sheep and let's hit the road!
Baa?

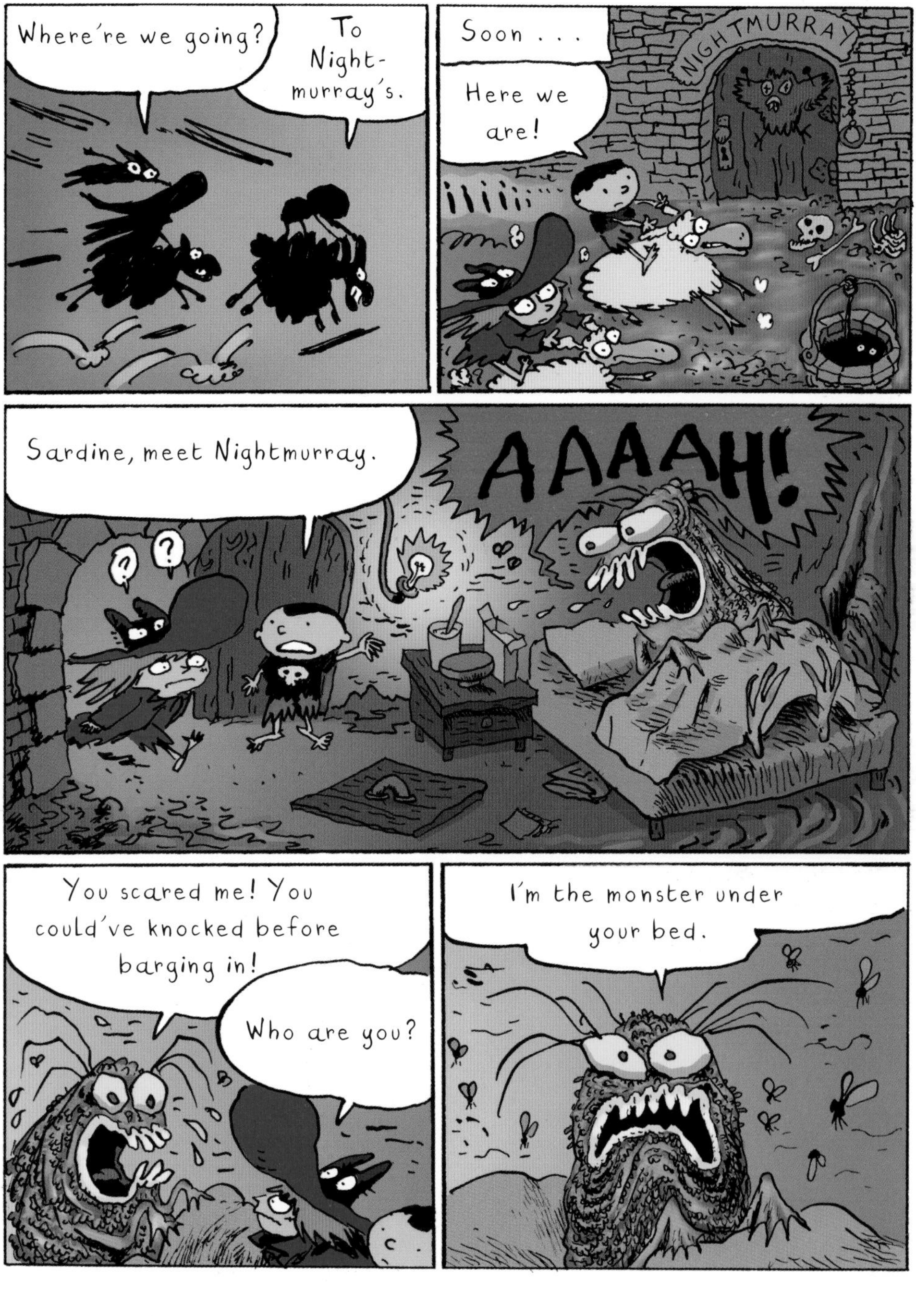
Where're we going?
To Night-murray's.
Soon . . .
Here we are!
NIGHTMURRAY
Sardine, meet Nightmurray.
AAAAH!
?
?
You scared me! You could've knocked before barging in!
Who are you?
I'm the monster under your bed.

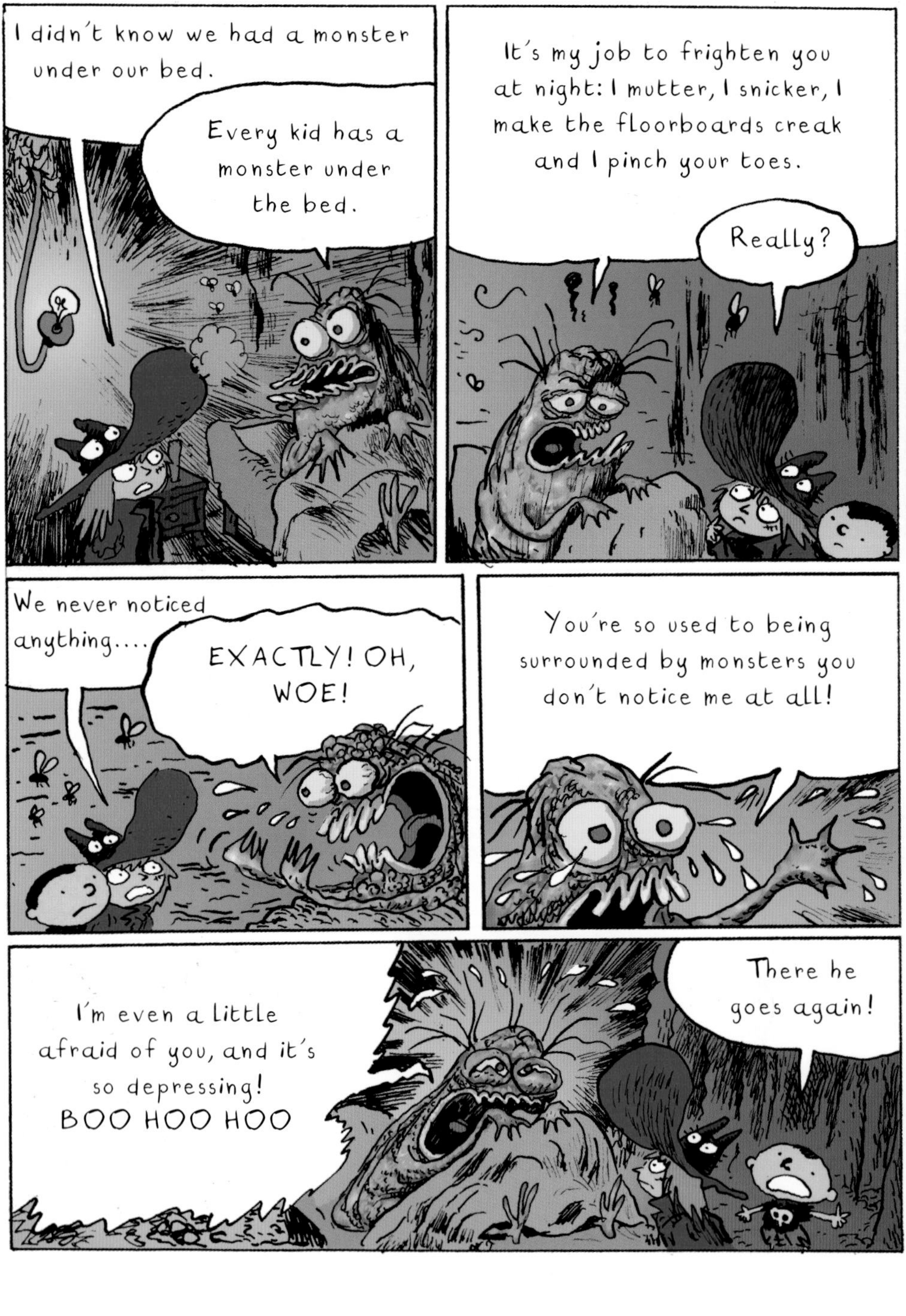

I didn't know we had a monster under our bed.
Every kid has a monster under the bed.
It's my job to frighten you at night: I mutter, I snicker, I make the floorboards creak and I pinch your toes.
Really?
We never noticed anything....
EXACTLY! OH, WOE!
You're so used to being surrounded by monsters you don't notice me at all!
I'm even a little afraid of you, and it's so depressing! BOO HOO HOO
There he goes again!

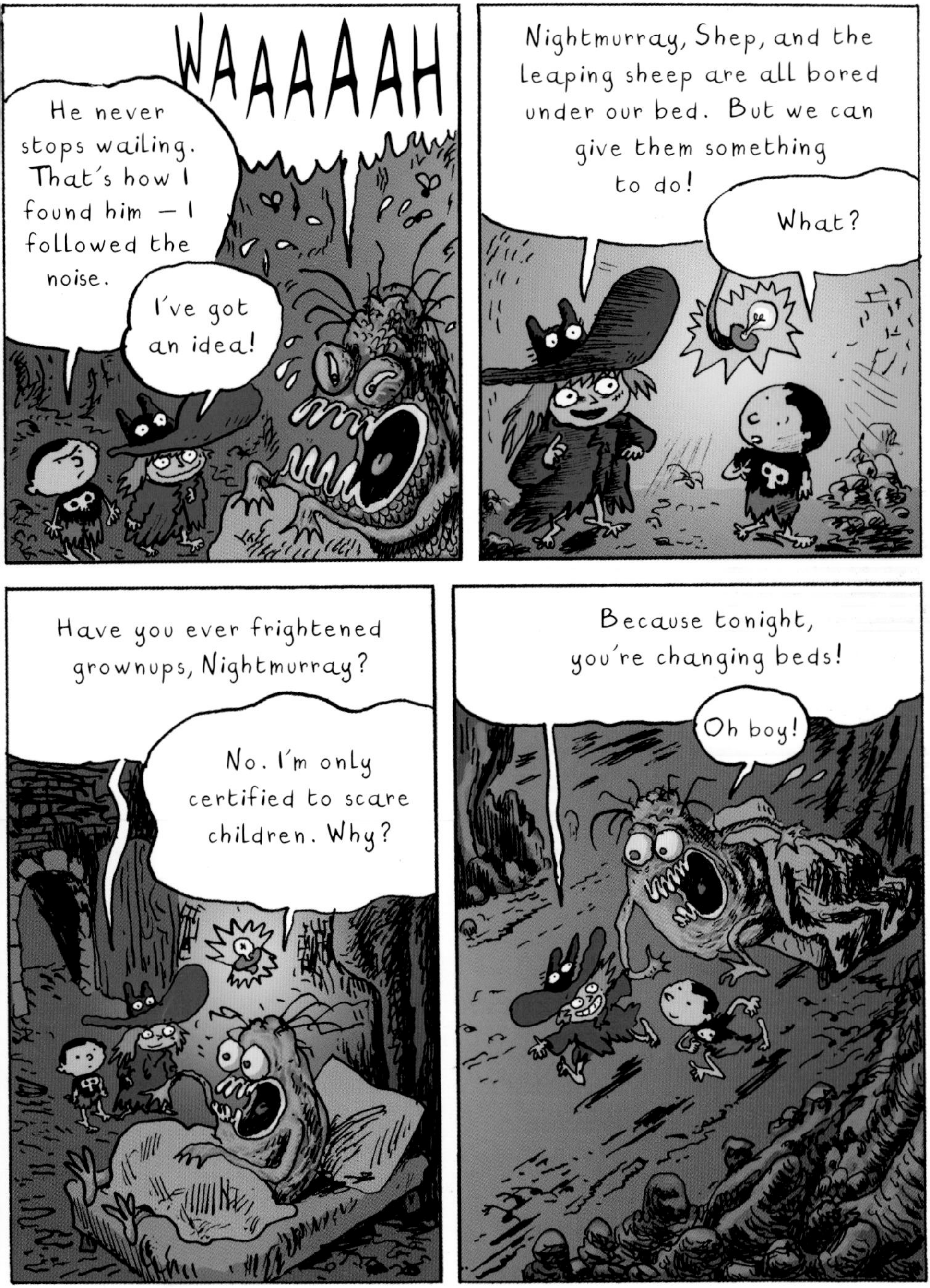
WAAAAAH
He never stops wailing. That's how I found him — I followed the noise.
I've got an idea!
Nightmurray, Shep, and the leaping sheep are all bored under our bed. But we can give them something to do!
What?
Have you ever frightened grownups, Nightmurray?
No. I'm only certified to scare children. Why?
Because tonight, you're changing beds!
Oh boy!

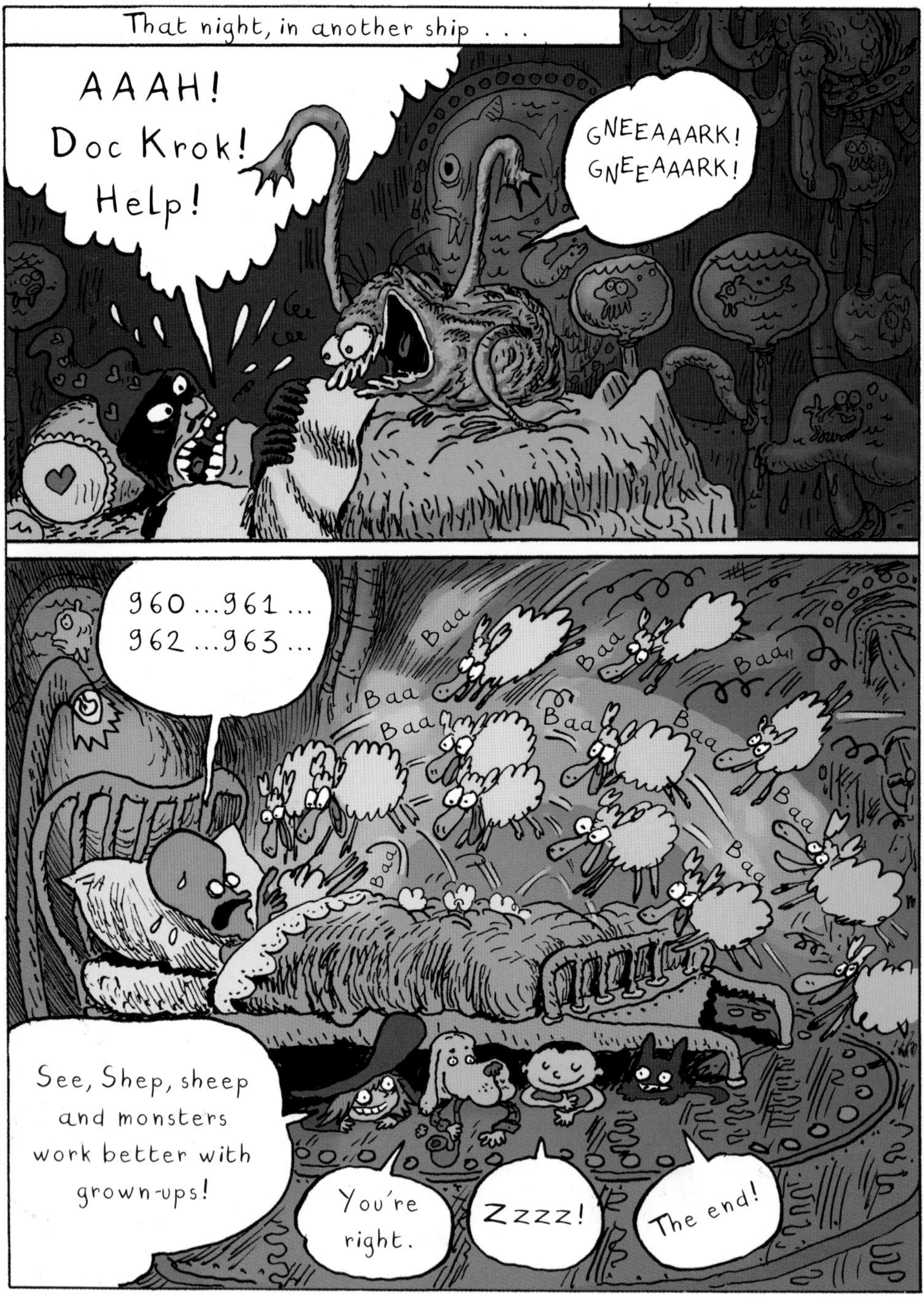
That night, in another ship . . .
AAAH! Doc Krok! Help!
GNEEAAARK! GNEEAAARK!
960 ... 961 ... 962 ... 963 ...
Baa
See, Shep, sheep and monsters work better with grown-ups!
You're right.
Zzzz!
The end!

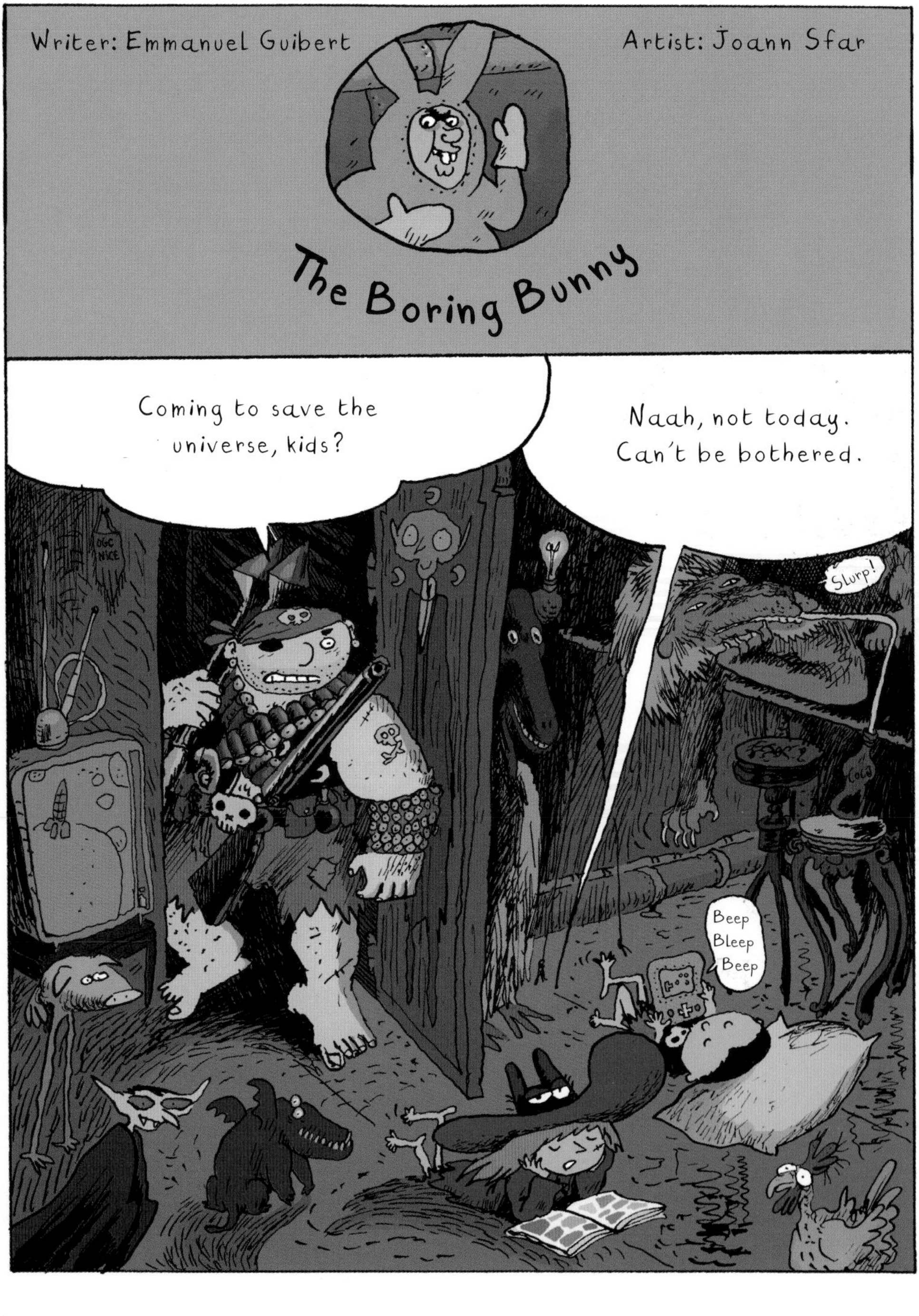
Writer: Emmanuel Guibert
Artist: Joann Sfar
The Boring Bunny
Coming to save the universe, kids?
Naah, not today. Can't be bothered.
Slurp!
Beep Bleep Beep

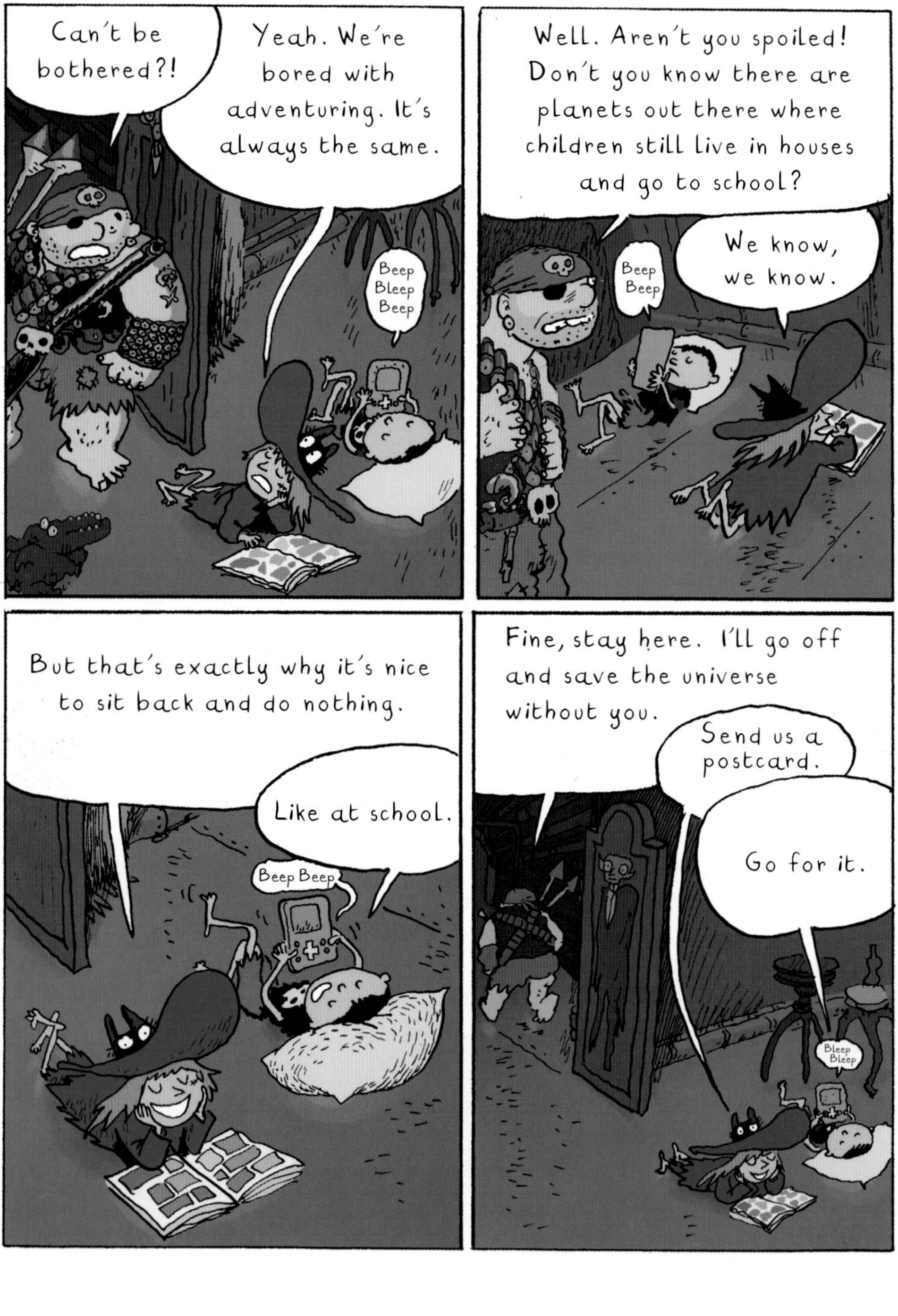
Can't be bothered?!
Yeah. We're bored with adventuring. It's always the same.
Beep Bleep Beep
Well. Aren't you spoiled! Don't you know there are planets out there where children still live in houses and go to school?
Beep Beep
We know, we know.
But that's exactly why it's nice to sit back and do nothing.
Like at school.
Beep Beep
Fine, stay here. I'll go off and save the universe without you.
Send us a postcard.
Go for it.
Bleep Bleep

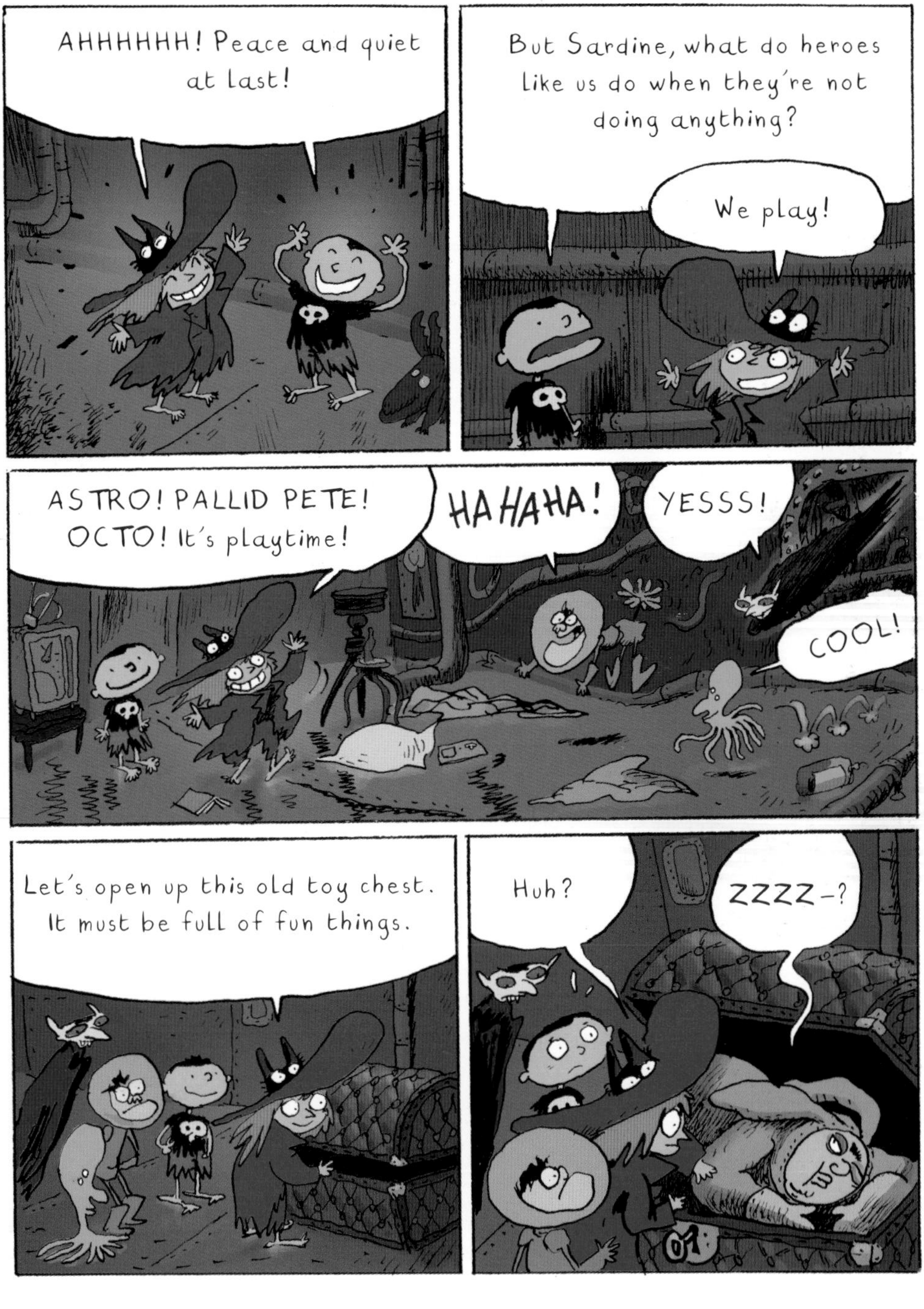
AHHHHHH! Peace and quiet at last!
But Sardine, what do heroes like us do when they're not doing anything?
We play!
ASTRO! PALLID PETE! OCTO! It's playtime!
HAHAHA!
YESSS!
COOL!
Let's open up this old toy chest. It must be full of fun things.
Huh?
ZZZZ-?

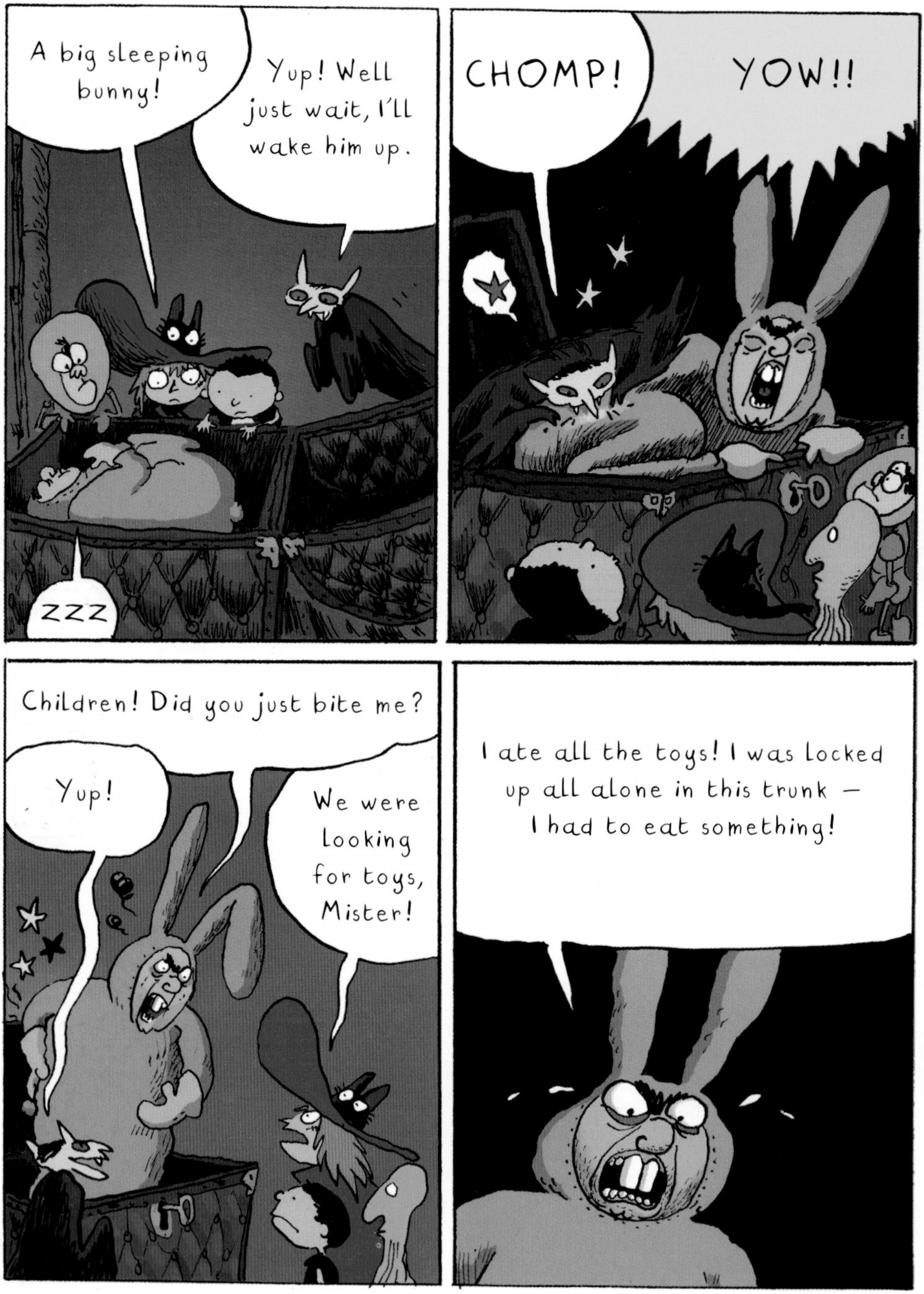
A big sleeping bunny!
Yup! Well just wait, I'll wake him up.
ZZZ
CHOMP!
YOW!!
Children! Did you just bite me?
Yup!
We were looking for toys, Mister!
I ate all the toys! I was locked up all alone in this trunk — I had to eat something!

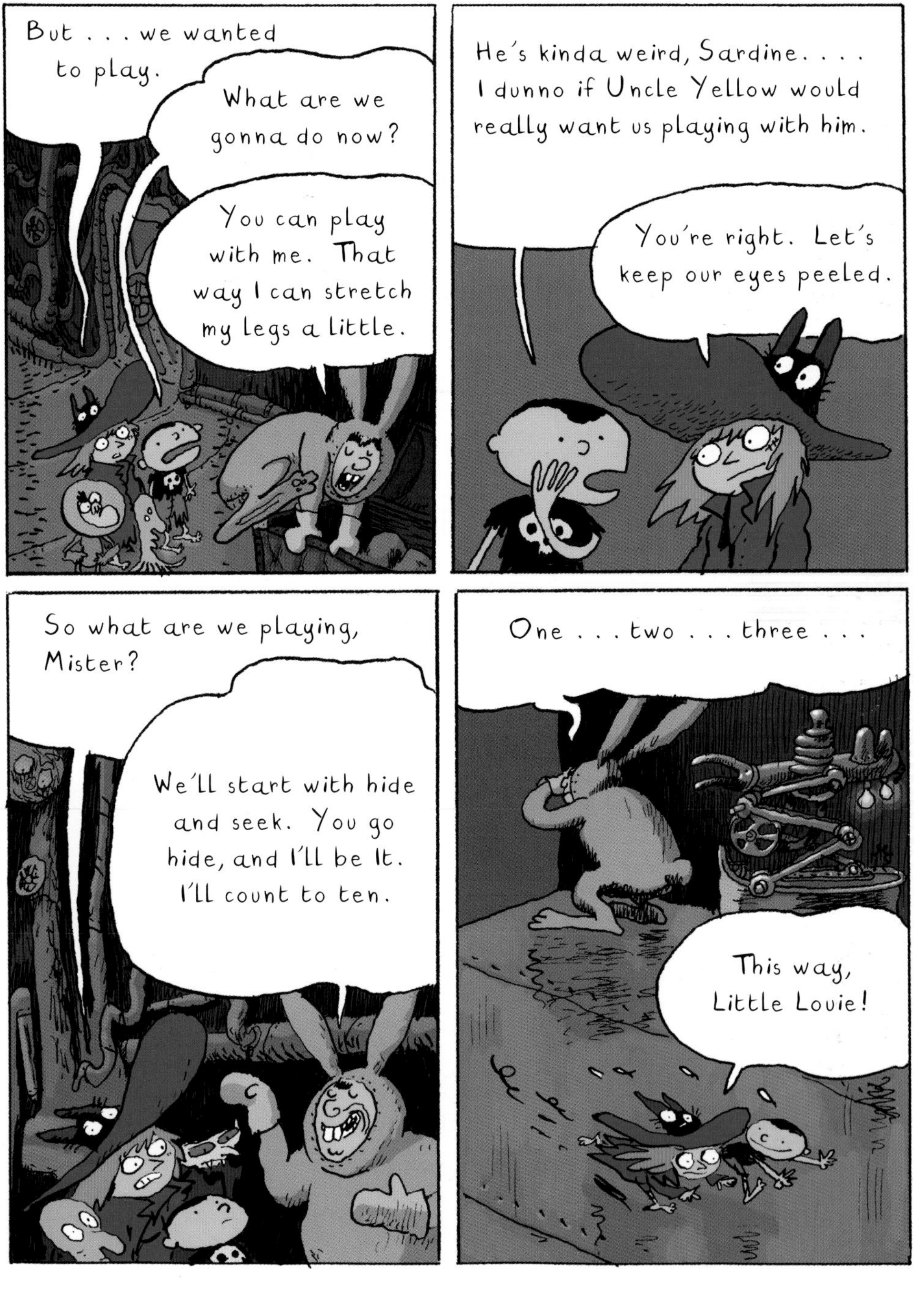
But . . . we wanted to play.
What are we gonna do now?
You can play with me. That way I can stretch my legs a little.
He's kinda weird, Sardine. . . . I dunno if Uncle Yellow would really want us playing with him.
You're right. Let's keep our eyes peeled.
So what are we playing, Mister?
We'll start with hide and seek. You go hide, and I'll be It. I'll count to ten.
One . . . two . . . three . . .
This way, Little Louie!

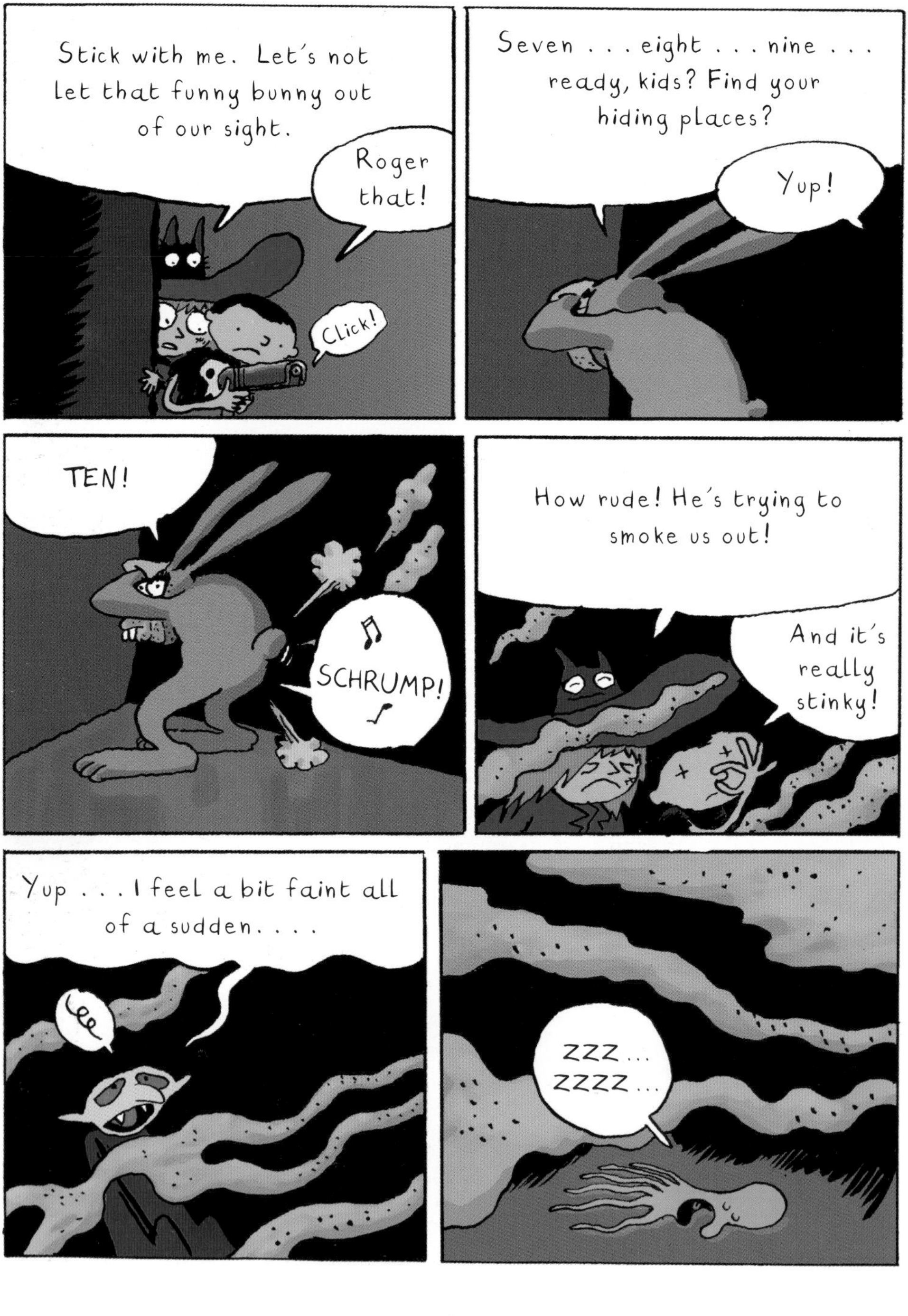
Stick with me. Let's not let that funny bunny out of our sight.
Roger that!
Click!
Seven . . . eight . . . nine . . . ready, kids? Find your hiding places?
Yup!
TEN!
SCHRUMP!
How rude! He's trying to smoke us out!
And it's really stinky!
Yup . . . I feel a bit faint all of a sudden. . . .
ZZZ...
ZZZZ...

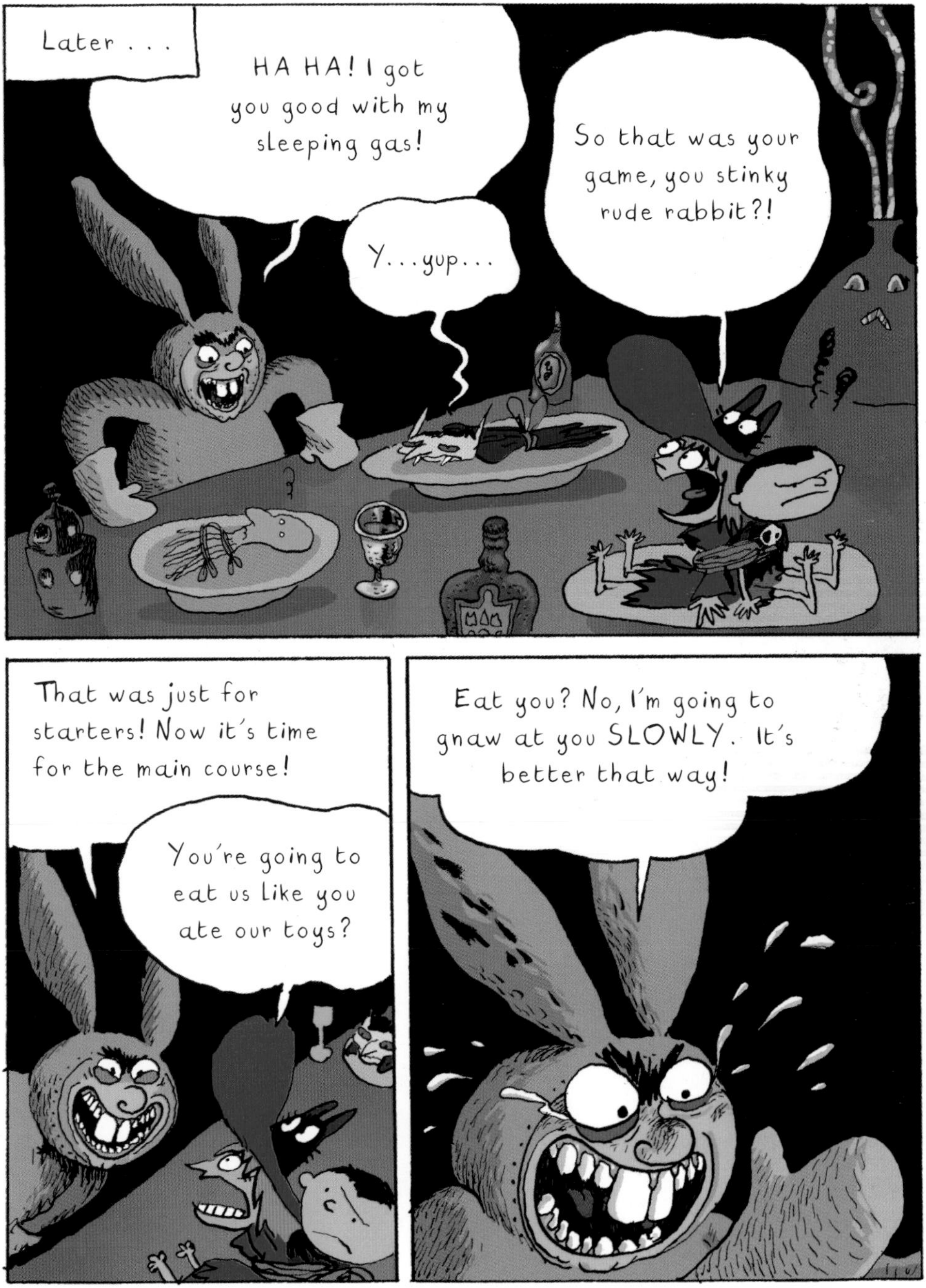
Later . . .
HA HA! I got you good with my sleeping gas!
Y . . . yup . . .
So that was your game, you stinky rude rabbit?!
That was just for starters! Now it's time for the main course!
You're going to eat us like you ate our toys?
Eat you? No, I'm going to gnaw at you SLOWLY. It's better that way!

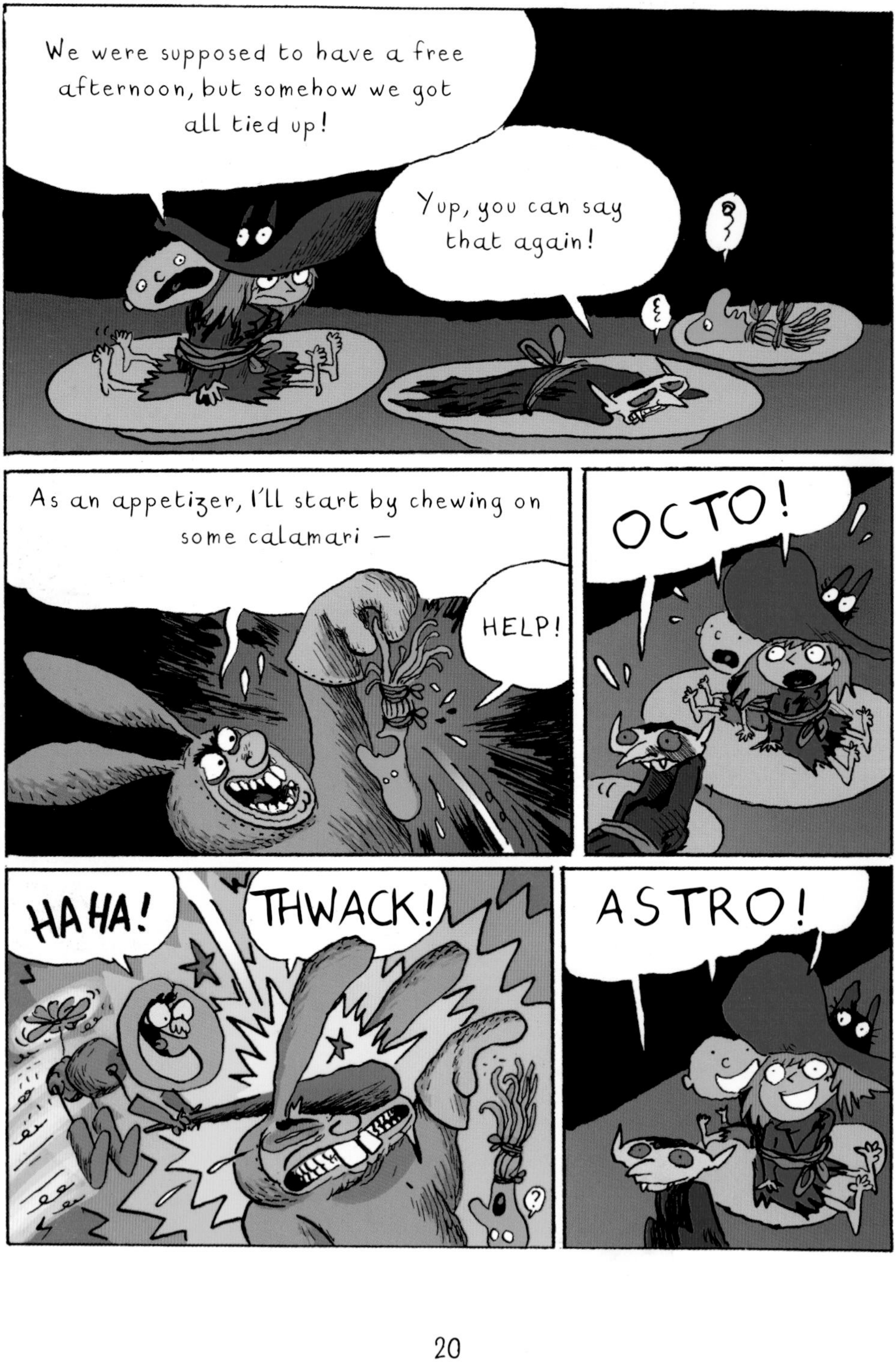
We were supposed to have a free afternoon, but somehow we got all tied up!
Yup, you can say that again!
?
As an appetizer, I'll start by chewing on some calamari –
HELP!
OCTO!
HAHA!
THWACK!
?
ASTRO!

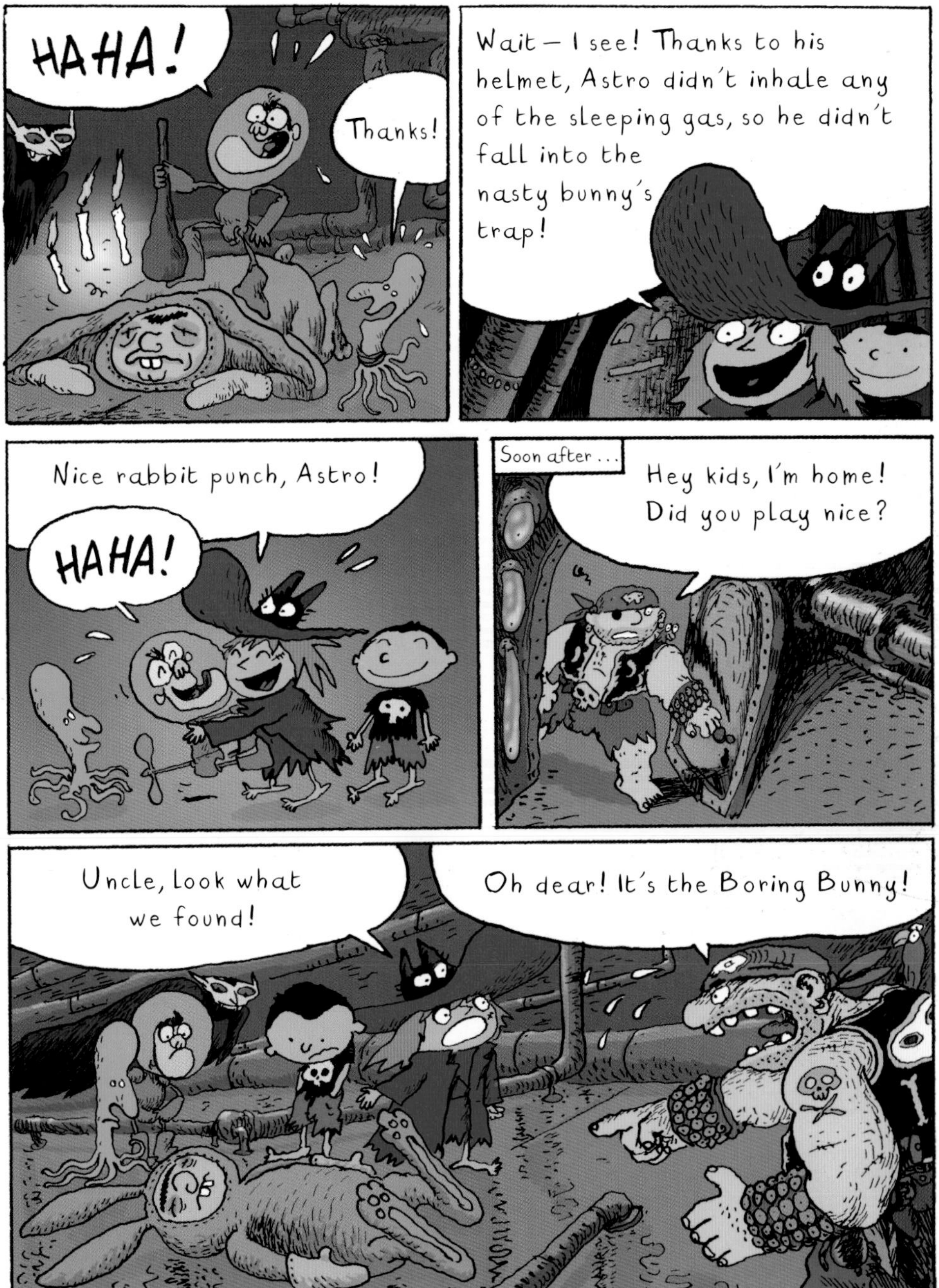
HAHA!
Thanks!
Wait — I see! Thanks to his helmet, Astro didn't inhale any of the sleeping gas, so he didn't fall into the nasty bunny's trap!
Nice rabbit punch, Astro!
HAHA!
Soon after...
Hey kids, I'm home! Did you play nice?
Uncle, look what we found!
Oh dear! It's the Boring Bunny!

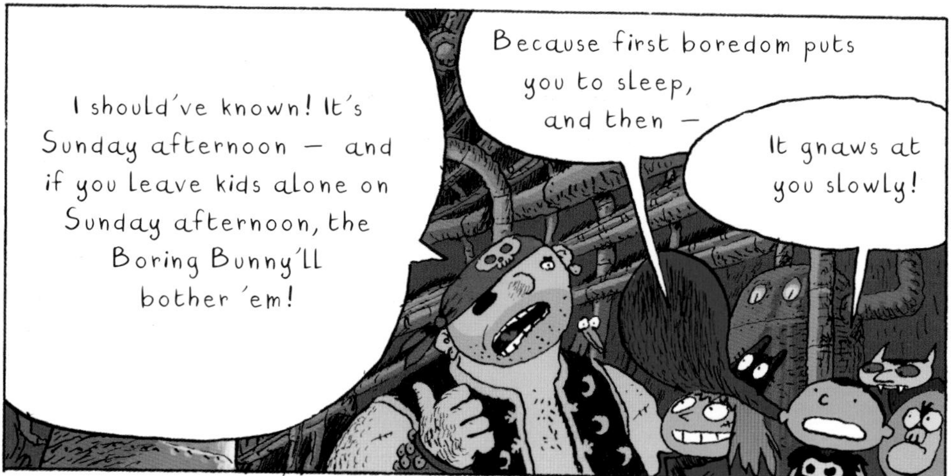
I should've known! It's Sunday afternoon — and if you leave kids alone on Sunday afternoon, the Boring Bunny'll bother 'em!
Because first boredom puts you to sleep, and then —
It gnaws at you slowly!

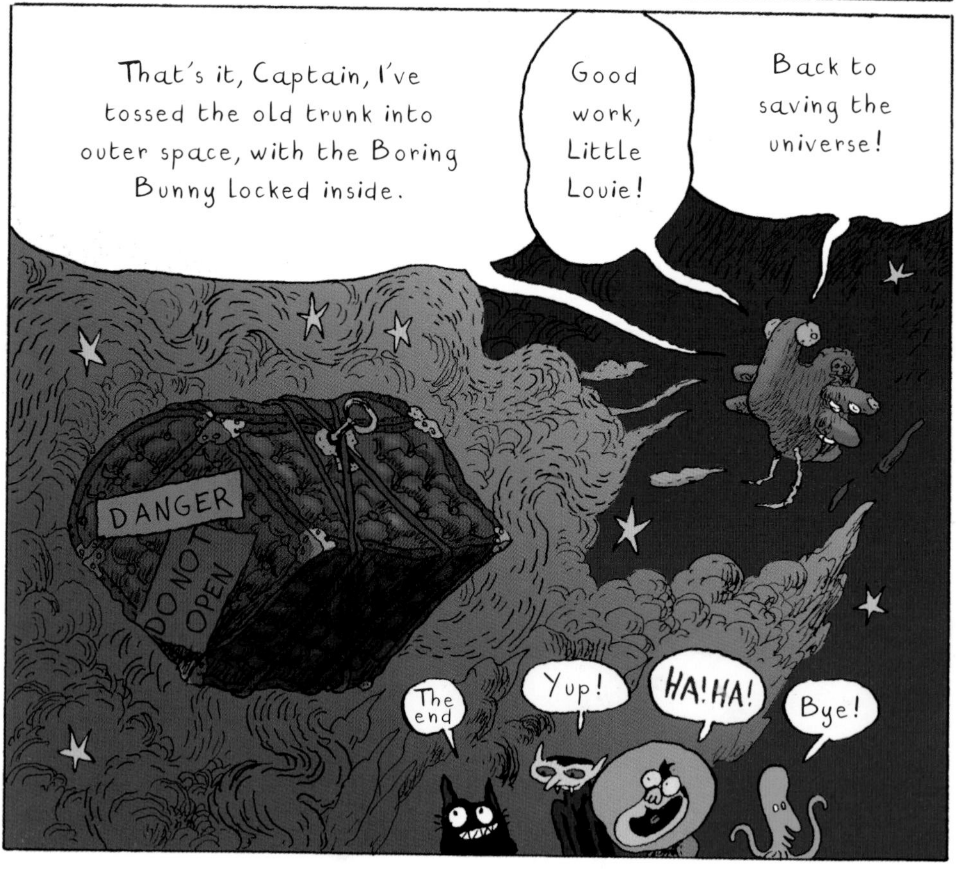
That's it, Captain, I've tossed the old trunk into outer space, with the Boring Bunny locked inside.
Good work, Little Louie!
Back to saving the universe!
DANGER
DO NOT OPEN
The end
Yup!
HA!HA!
Bye!

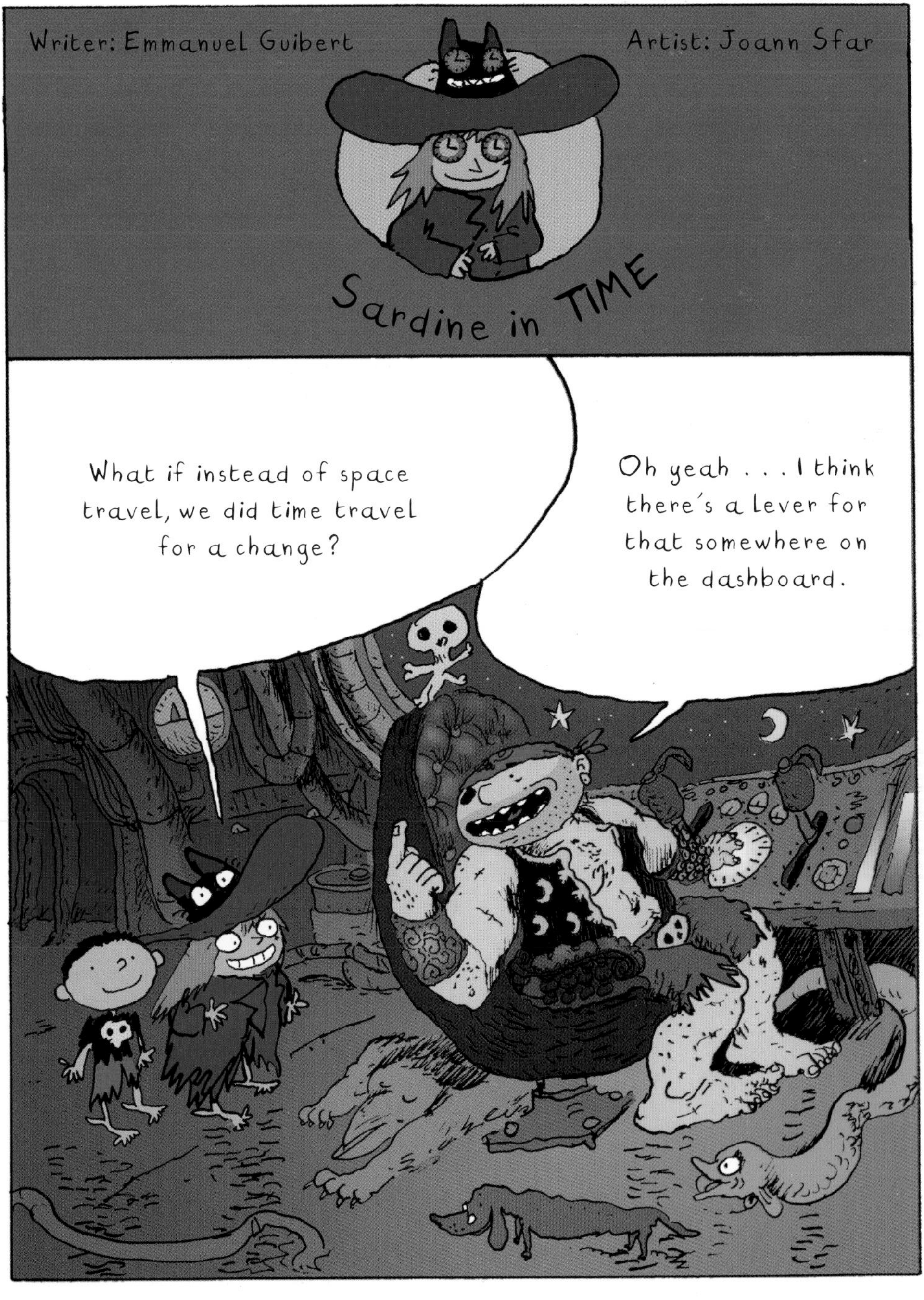
Writer: Emmanuel Guibert
Artist: Joann Sfar
Sardine in TIME
What if instead of space travel, we did time travel for a change?
Oh yeah . . . I think there's a lever for that somewhere on the dashboard.

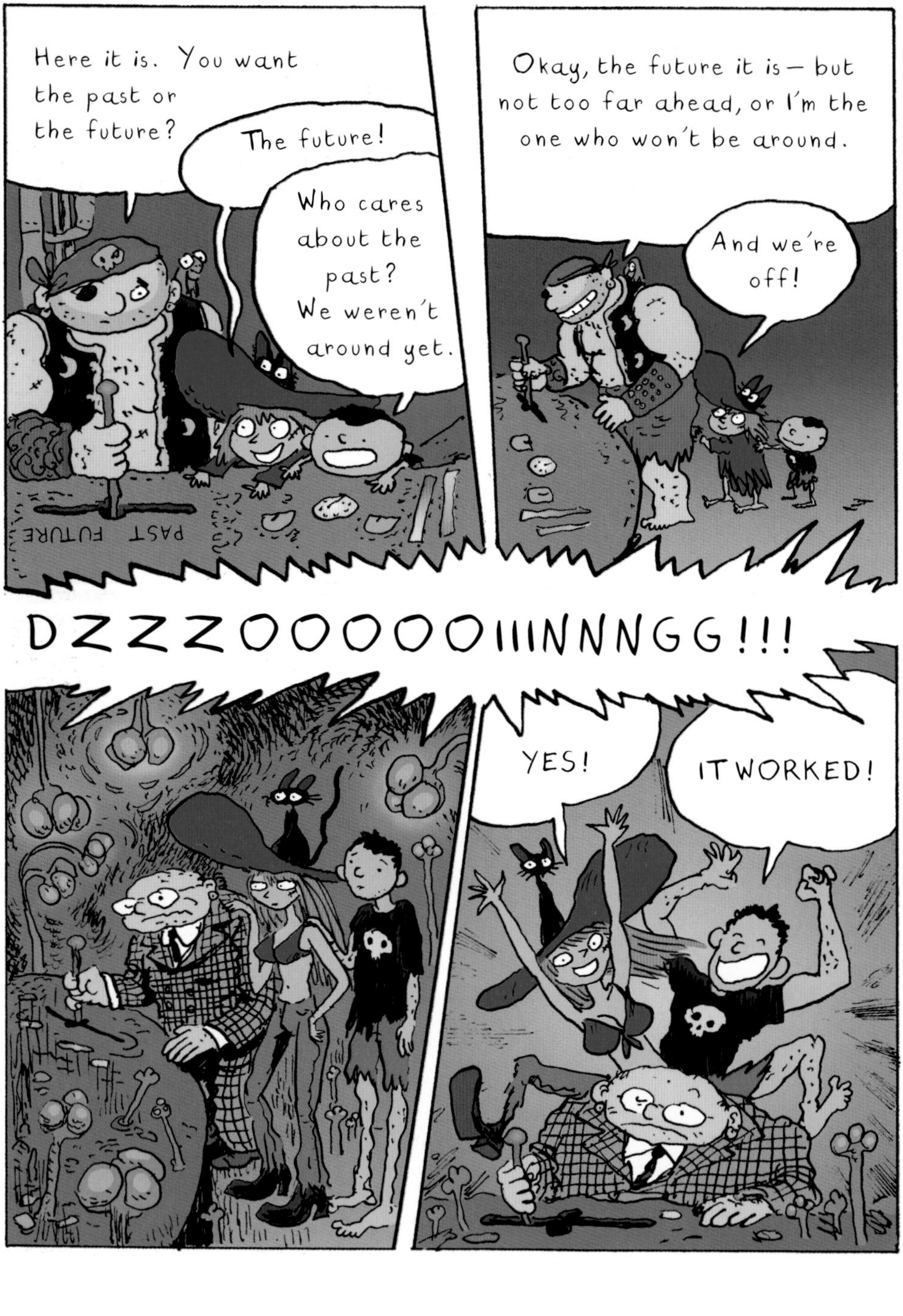
Here it is. You want the past or the future?
The future!
Who cares about the past? We weren't around yet.
PAST FUTURE
Okay, the future it is — but not too far ahead, or I'm the one who won't be around.
And we're off!
DZZZOOOOOIIINNNGG!!!
YES!
IT WORKED!

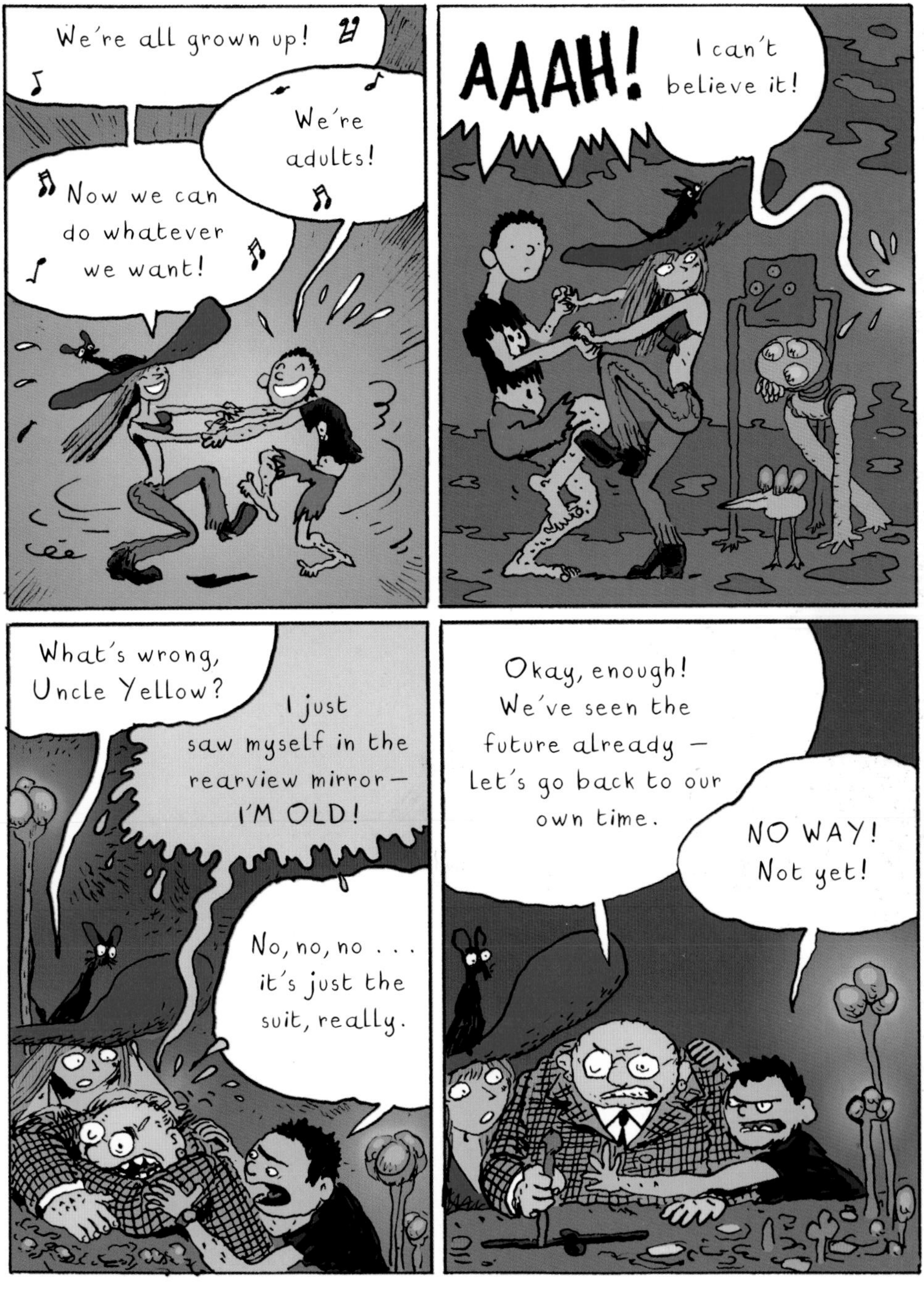
We're all grown up!
We're adults!
Now we can do whatever we want!
AAAH!
I can't believe it!
What's wrong, Uncle Yellow?
I just saw myself in the rearview mirror — I'M OLD!
No, no, no . . . it's just the suit, really.
Okay, enough! We've seen the future already — let's go back to our own time.
NO WAY! Not yet!

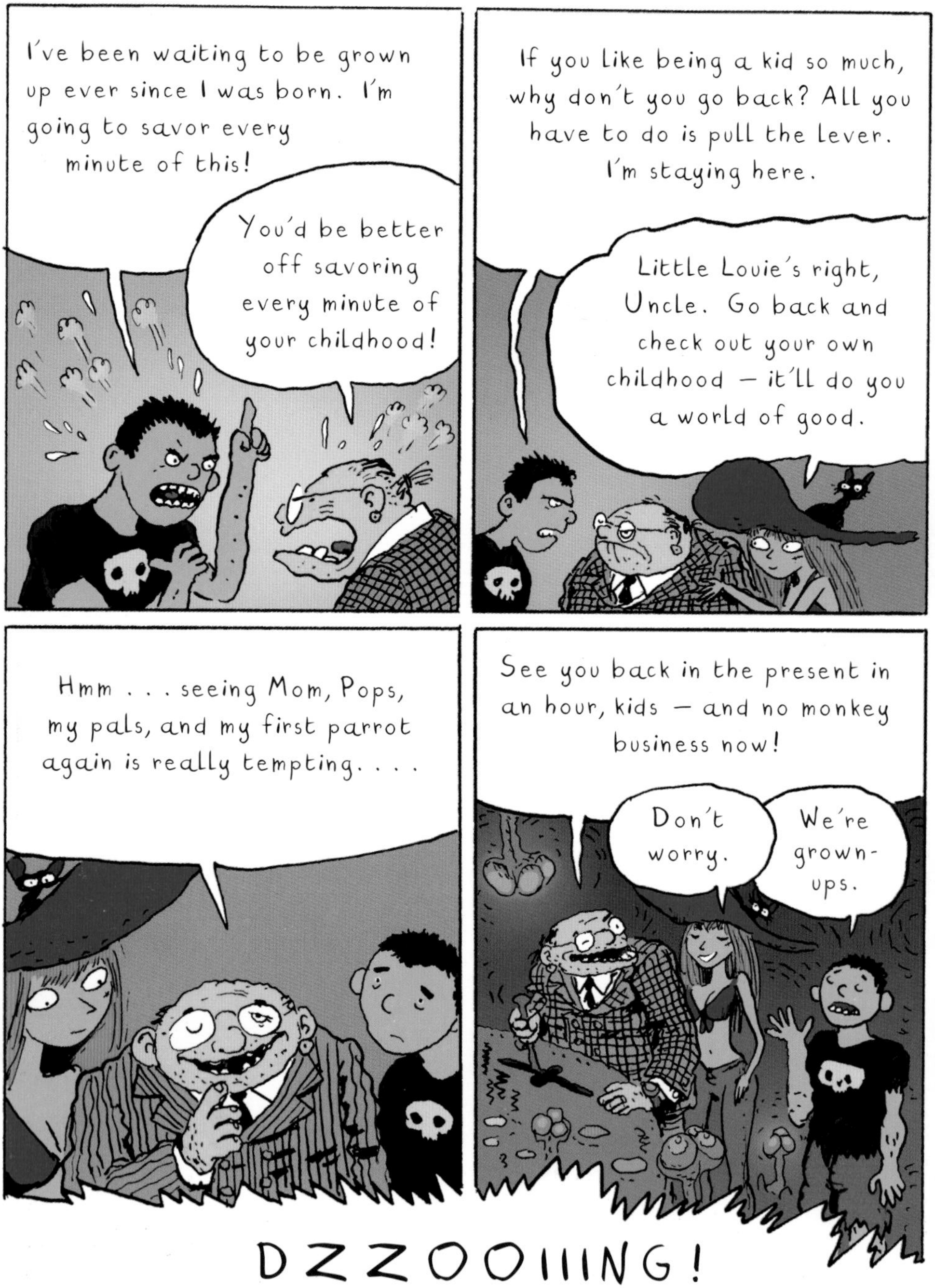

I've been waiting to be grown up ever since I was born. I'm going to savor every minute of this!
You'd be better off savoring every minute of your childhood!
If you like being a kid so much, why don't you go back? All you have to do is pull the lever. I'm staying here.
Little Louie's right, Uncle. Go back and check out your own childhood — it'll do you a world of good.
Hmm . . . seeing Mom, Pops, my pals, and my first parrot again is really tempting. . . .
See you back in the present in an hour, kids — and no monkey business now!
Don't worry.
We're grown-ups.
DZZOOIIING!

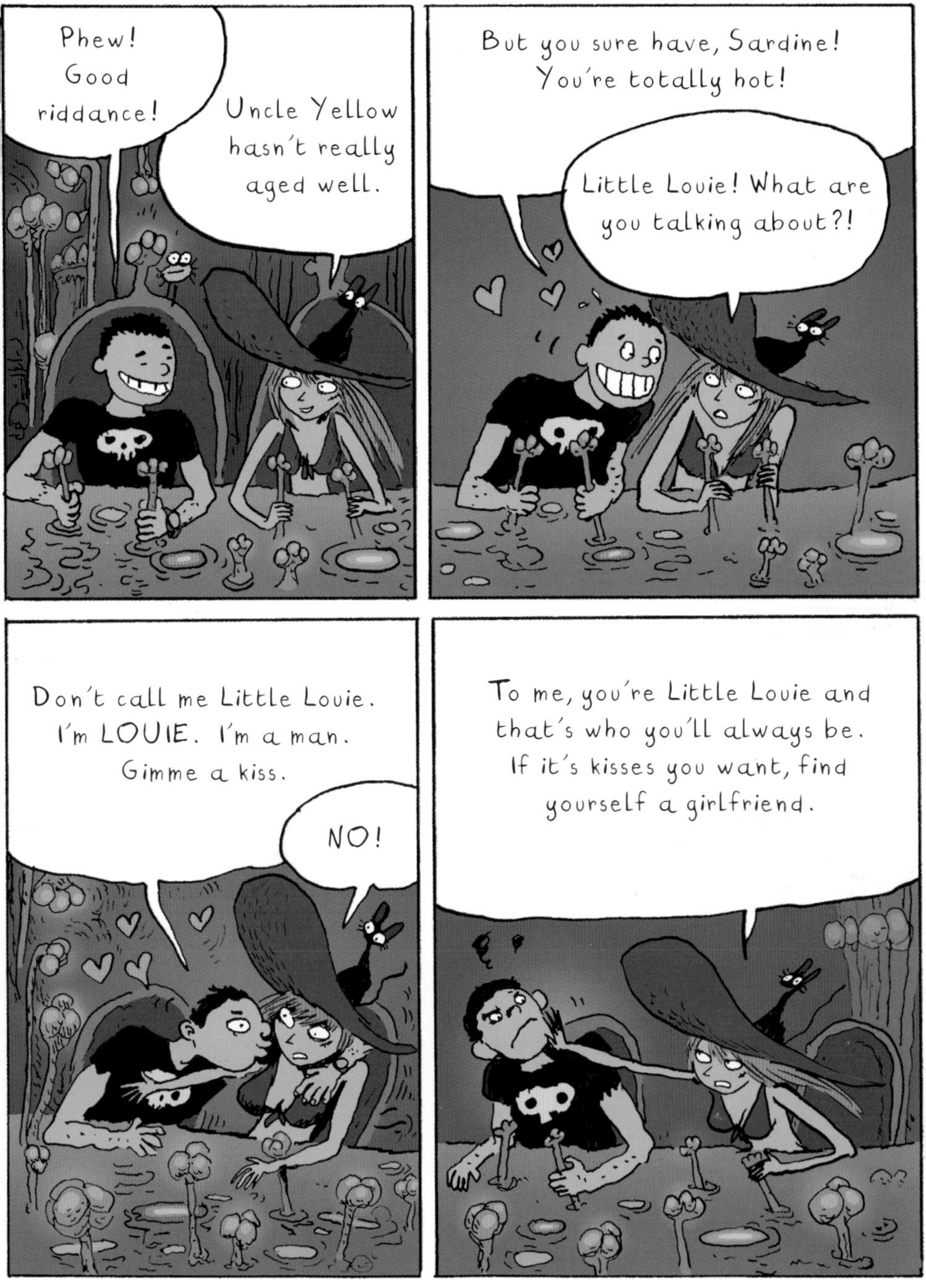
Phew! Good riddance!
Uncle Yellow hasn't really aged well.
But you sure have, Sardine! You're totally hot!
Little Louie! What are you talking about?!
Don't call me Little Louie. I'm LOUIE. I'm a man. Gimme a kiss.
NO!
To me, you're Little Louie and that's who you'll always be. If it's kisses you want, find yourself a girlfriend.

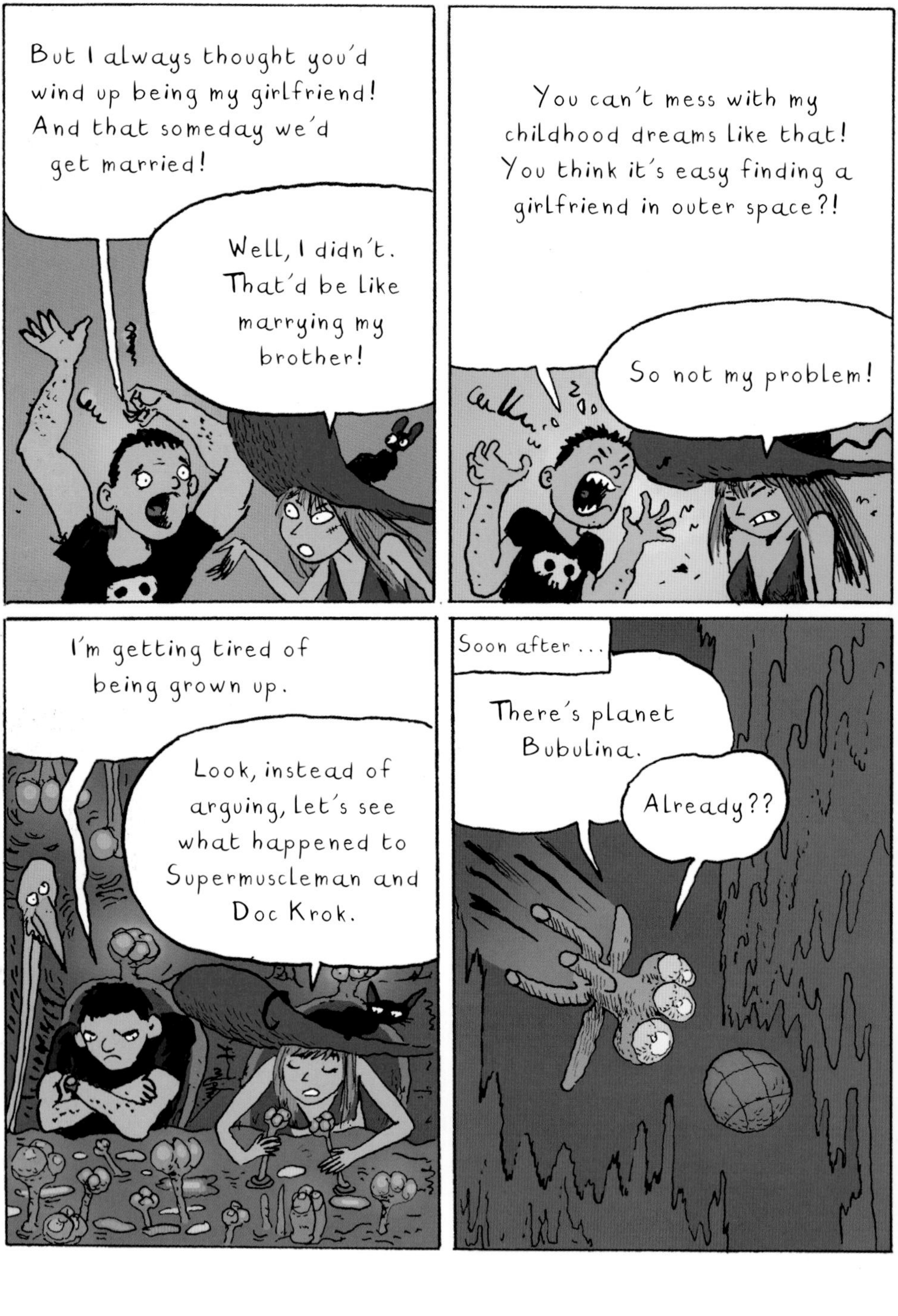
But I always thought you'd wind up being my girlfriend! And that someday we'd get married!
Well, I didn't. That'd be like marrying my brother!
You can't mess with my childhood dreams like that! You think it's easy finding a girlfriend in outer space?!
So not my problem!
I'm getting tired of being grown up.
Look, instead of arguing, let's see what happened to Supermuscleman and Doc Krok.
Soon after ...
There's planet Bubulina.
Already??

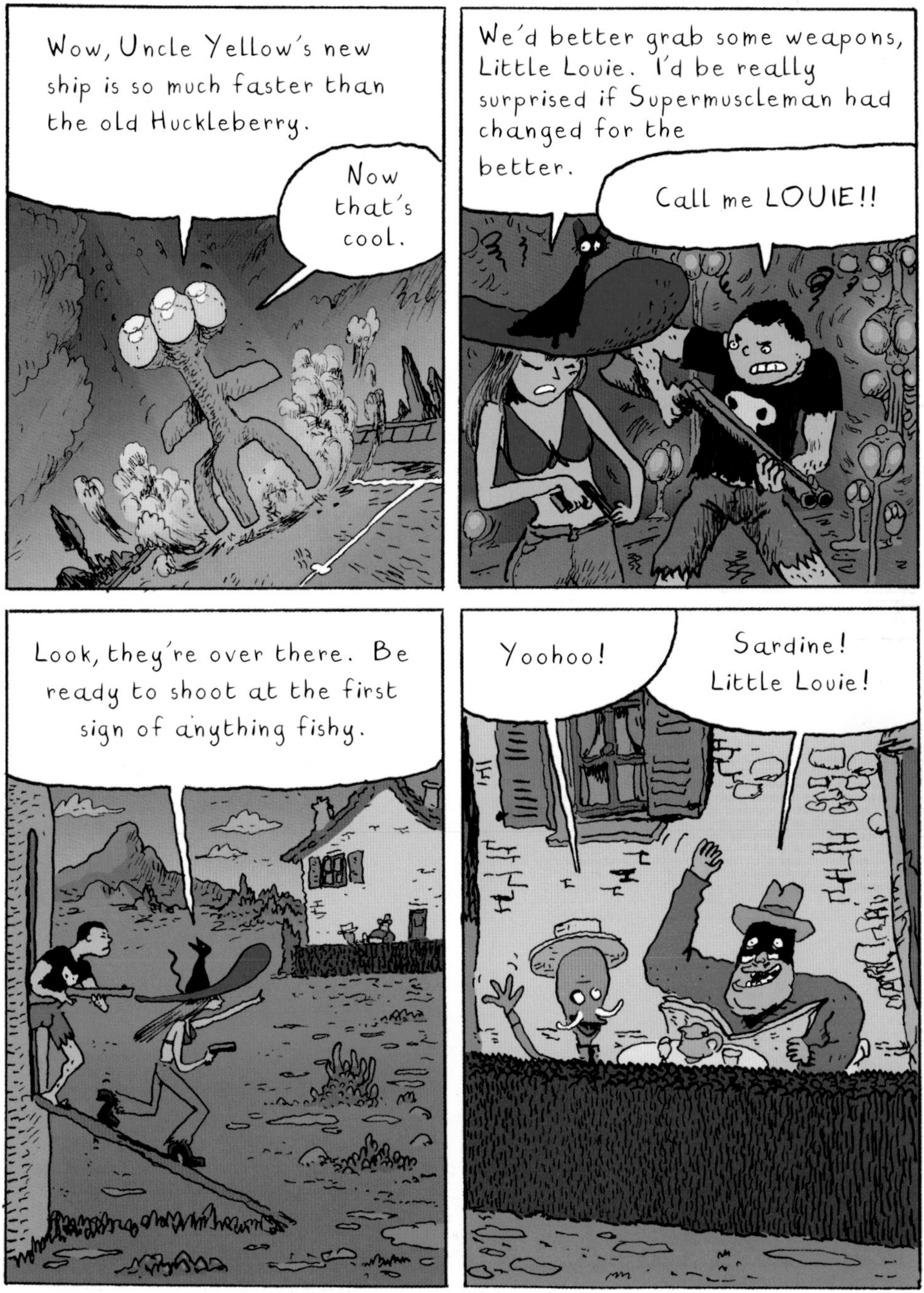
Wow, Uncle Yellow's new ship is so much faster than the old Huckleberry.
Now that's cool.
We'd better grab some weapons, Little Louie. I'd be really surprised if Supermuscleman had changed for the better.
Call me LOUIE!!
Look, they're over there. Be ready to shoot at the first sign of anything fishy.
Yoohoo!
Sardine! Little Louie!

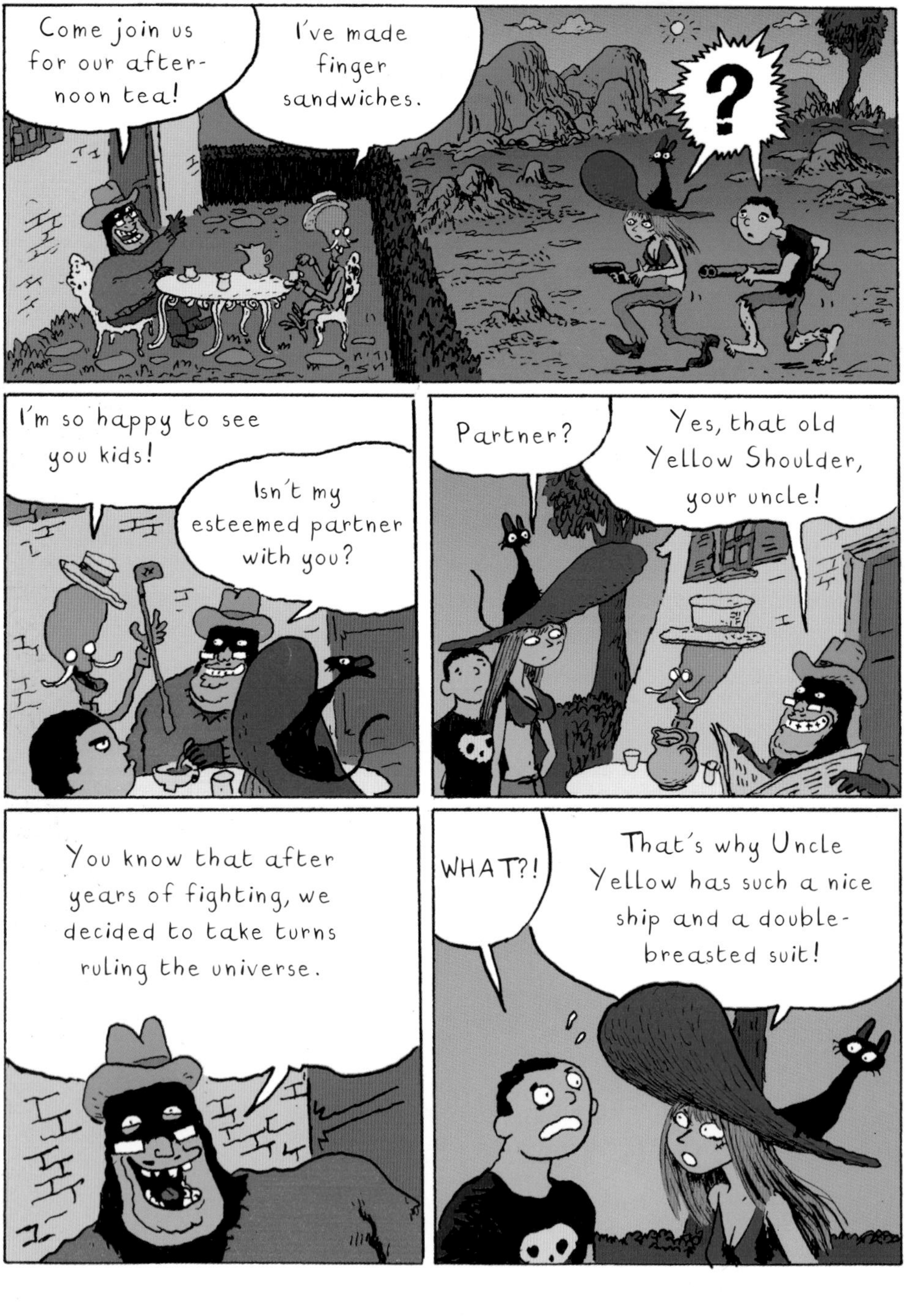
Come join us for our after-noon tea!
I've made finger sandwiches.
?
I'm so happy to see you kids!
Isn't my esteemed partner with you?
Partner?
Yes, that old Yellow Shoulder, your uncle!
You know that after years of fighting, we decided to take turns ruling the universe.
WHAT?!
That's why Uncle Yellow has such a nice ship and a double-breasted suit!

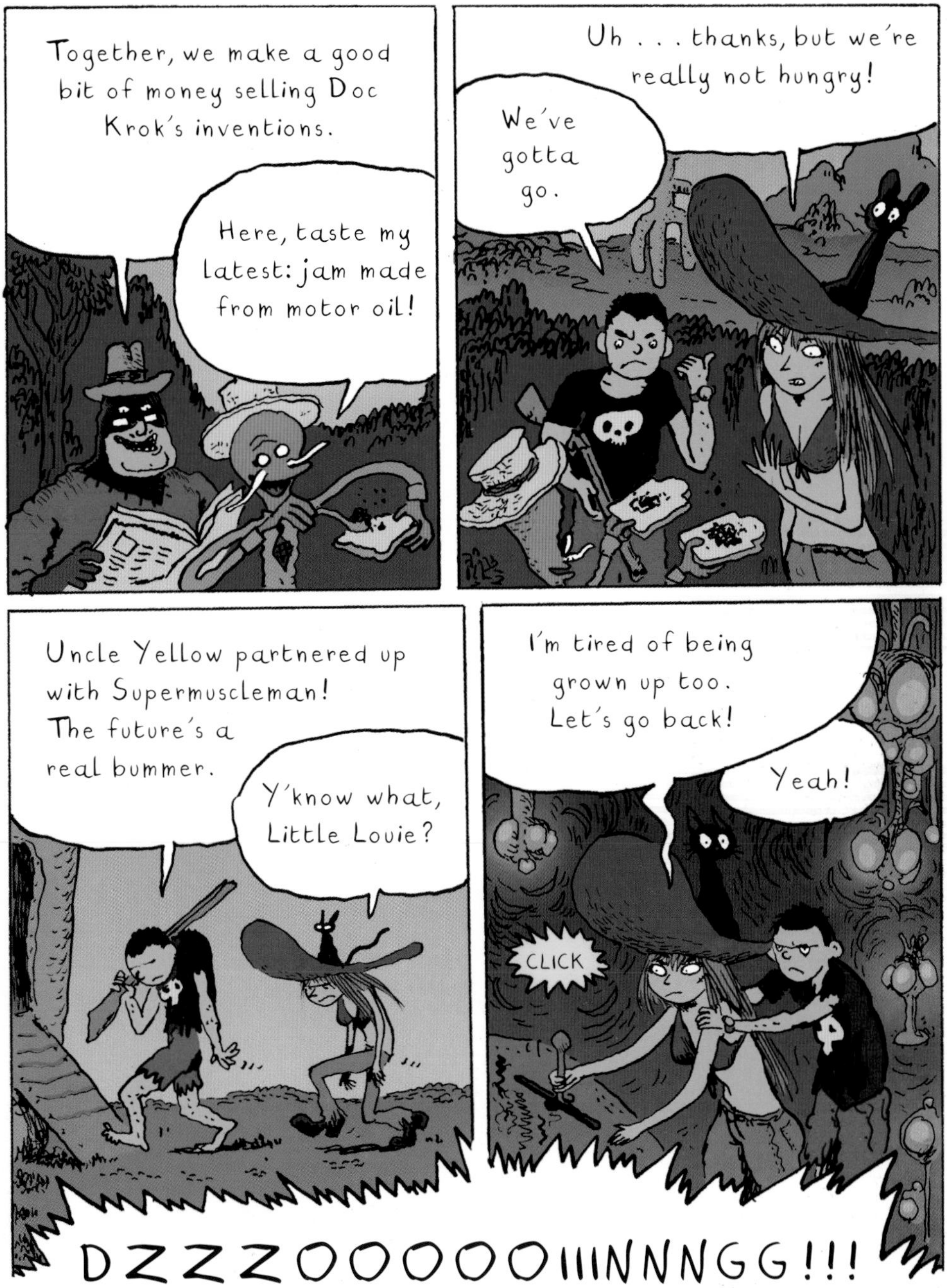
Together, we make a good bit of money selling Doc Krok's inventions.
Here, taste my latest: jam made from motor oil!
Uh . . . thanks, but we're really not hungry!
We've gotta go.
Uncle Yellow partnered up with Supermuscleman! The future's a real bummer.
Y'know what, Little Louie?
I'm tired of being grown up too. Let's go back!
Yeah!
CLICK
DZZZOOOOOIIINNNGG!!!

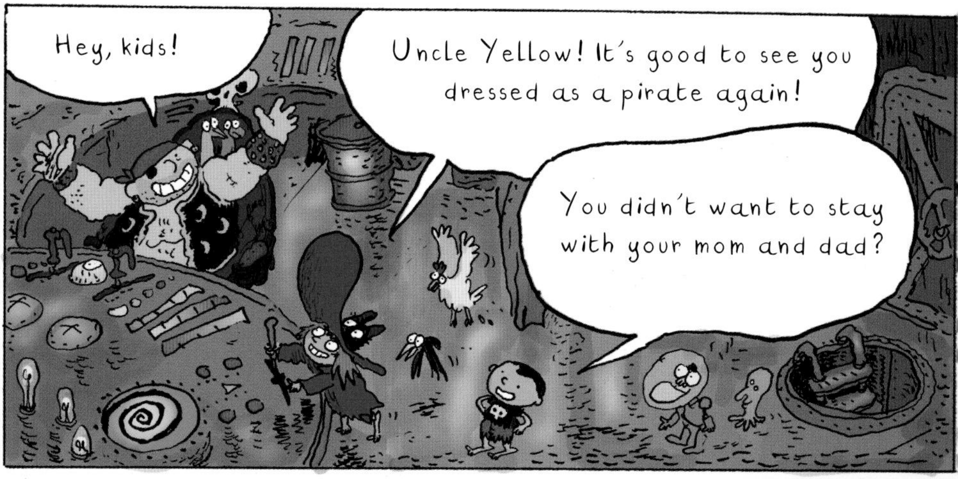
Hey, kids!
Uncle Yellow! It's good to see you dressed as a pirate again!
You didn't want to stay with your mom and dad?

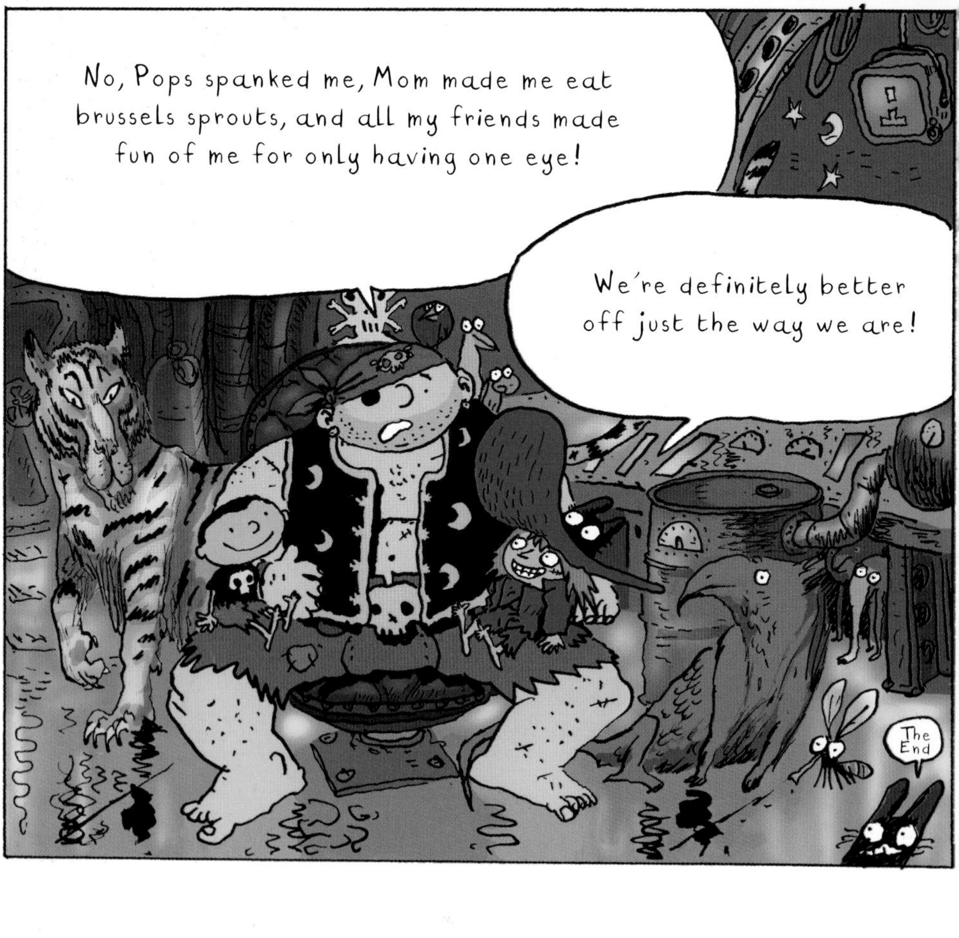
No, Pops spanked me, Mom made me eat brussels sprouts, and all my friends made fun of me for only having one eye!
We're definitely better off just the way we are!
The End

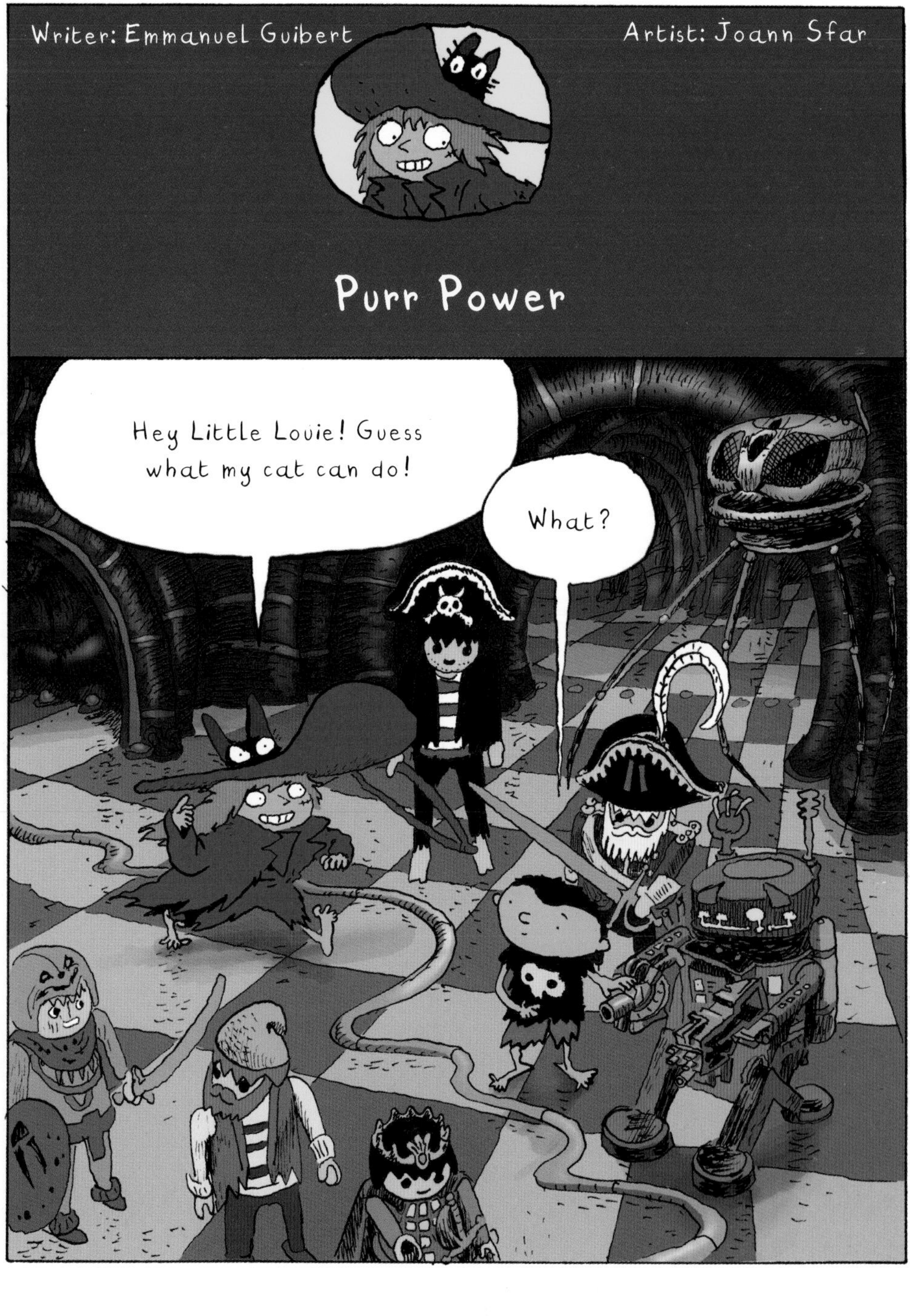
Writer: Emmanuel Guibert
Artist: Joann Sfar
Purr Power
Hey Little Louie! Guess what my cat can do!
What?

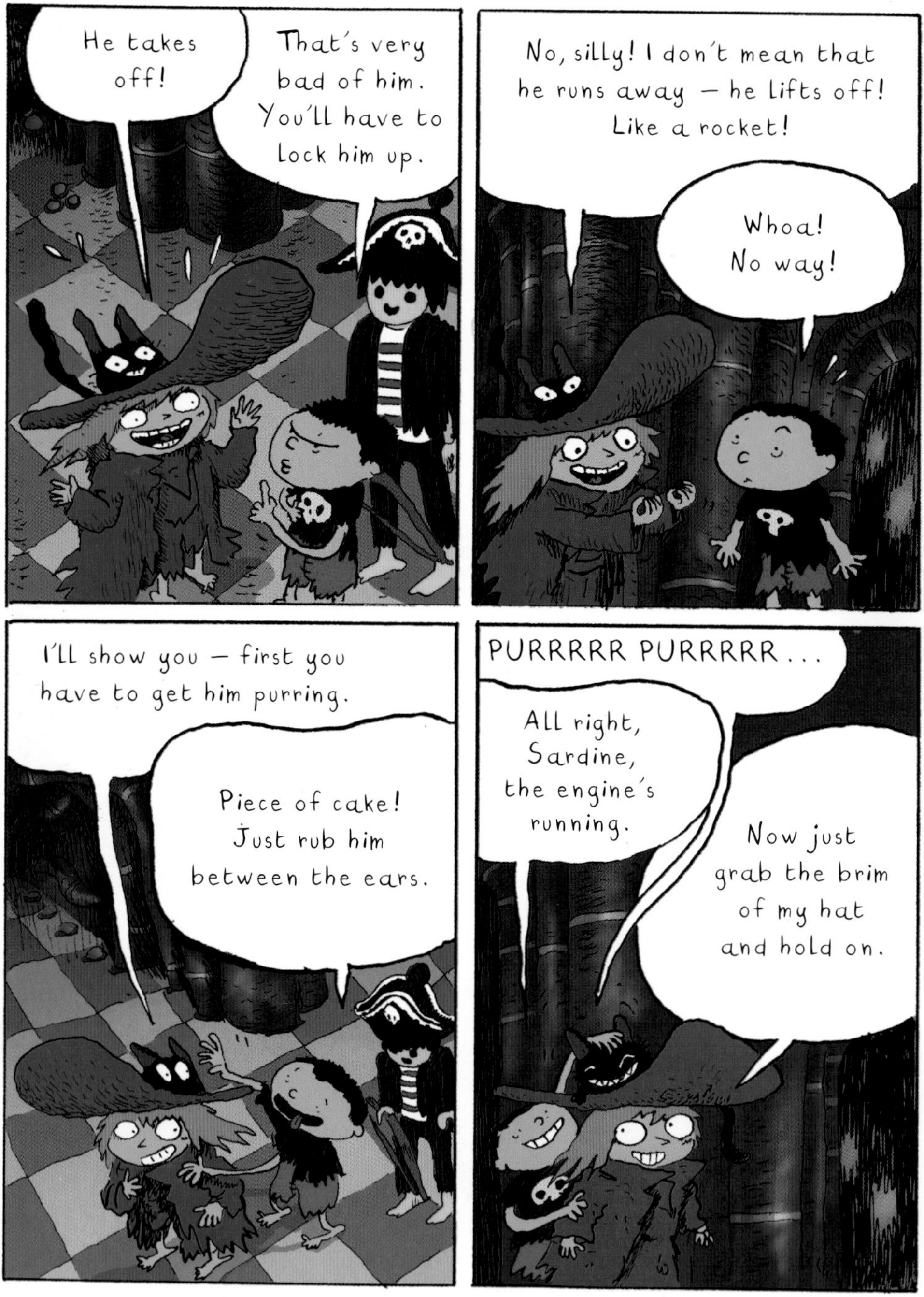
He takes off!
That's very bad of him. You'll have to lock him up.
No, silly! I don't mean that he runs away — he lifts off! Like a rocket!
Whoa! No way!
I'll show you — first you have to get him purring.
Piece of cake! Just rub him between the ears.
PURRRRR PURRRRR . . .
All right, Sardine, the engine's running.
Now just grab the brim of my hat and hold on.

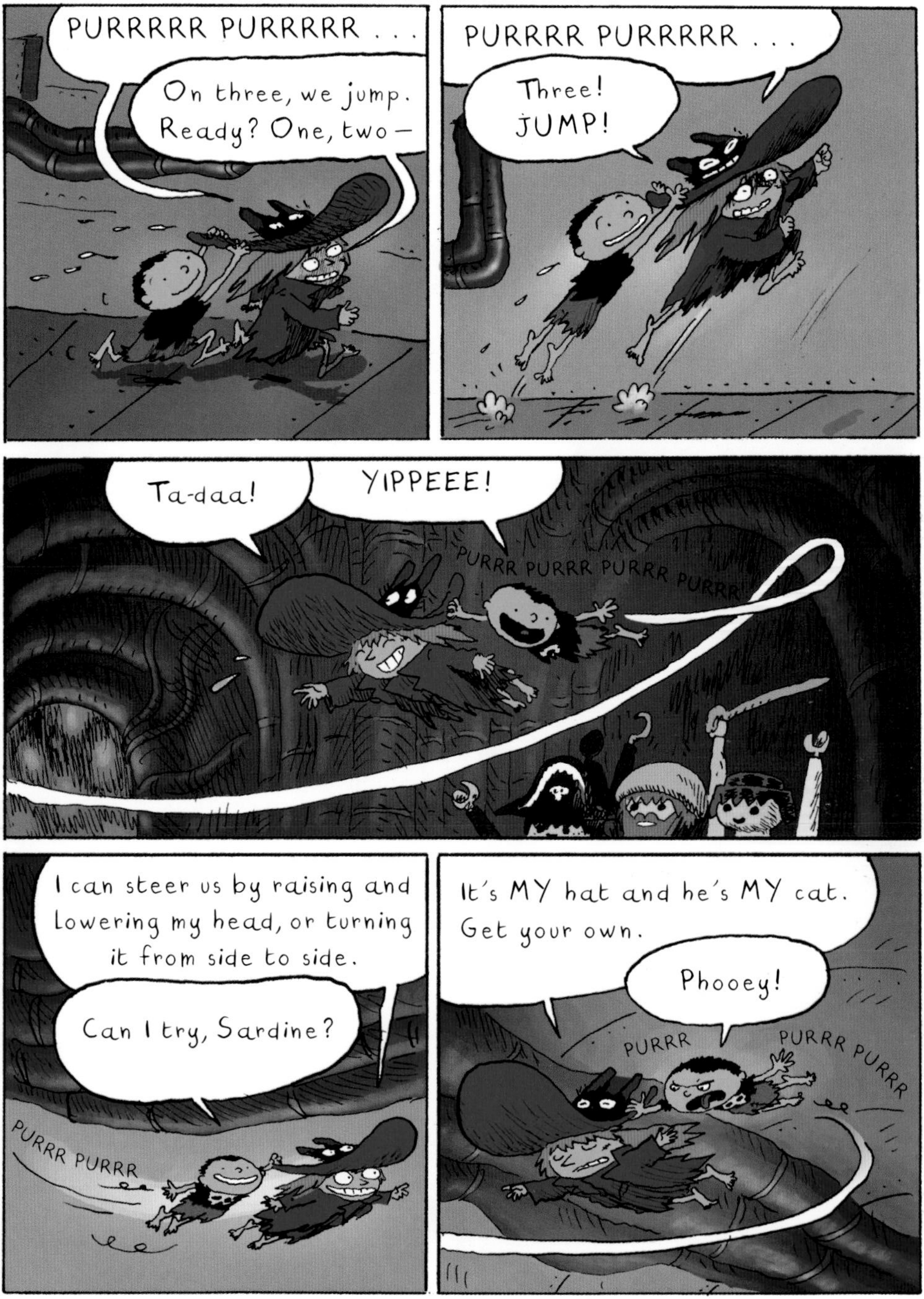
PURRRRR PURRRRR . . .
On three, we jump. Ready? One, two—
PURRRR PURRRRR . . .
Three! JUMP!
Ta-daa!
YIPPEEE!
PURRR PURRR PURRR PURRR
I can steer us by raising and lowering my head, or turning it from side to side.
Can I try, Sardine?
PURRR PURRR
It's MY hat and he's MY cat. Get your own.
Phooey!
PURRR
PURRR PURRR

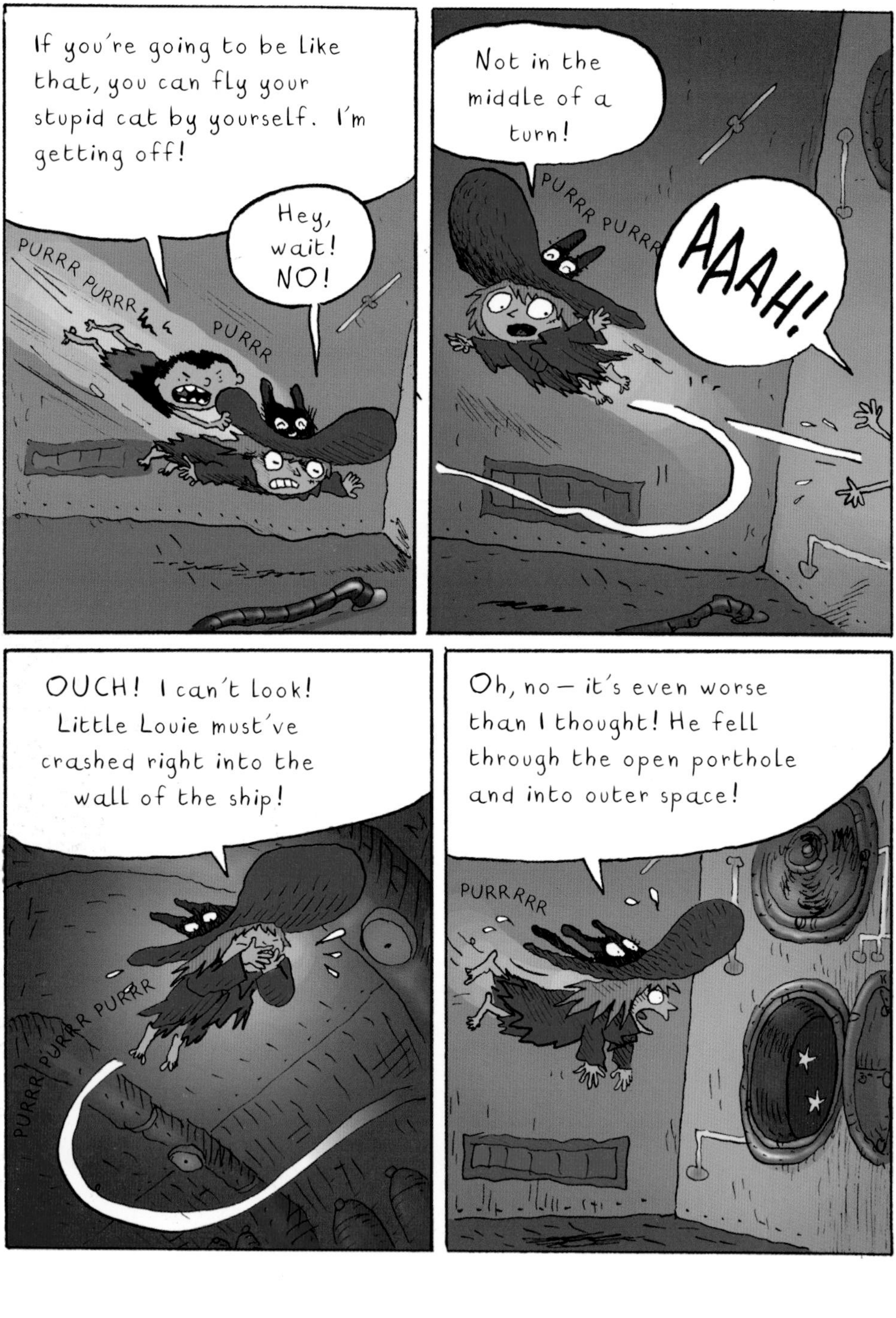
If you're going to be like that, you can fly your stupid cat by yourself. I'm getting off!
Hey, wait! NO!
PURRR PURRR
PURRR
Not in the middle of a turn!
PURRR PURRR
AAAH!
OUCH! I can't look! Little Louie must've crashed right into the wall of the ship!
PURRR PURRR PURRR PURRR
Oh, no — it's even worse than I thought! He fell through the open porthole and into outer space!
PURRRRR

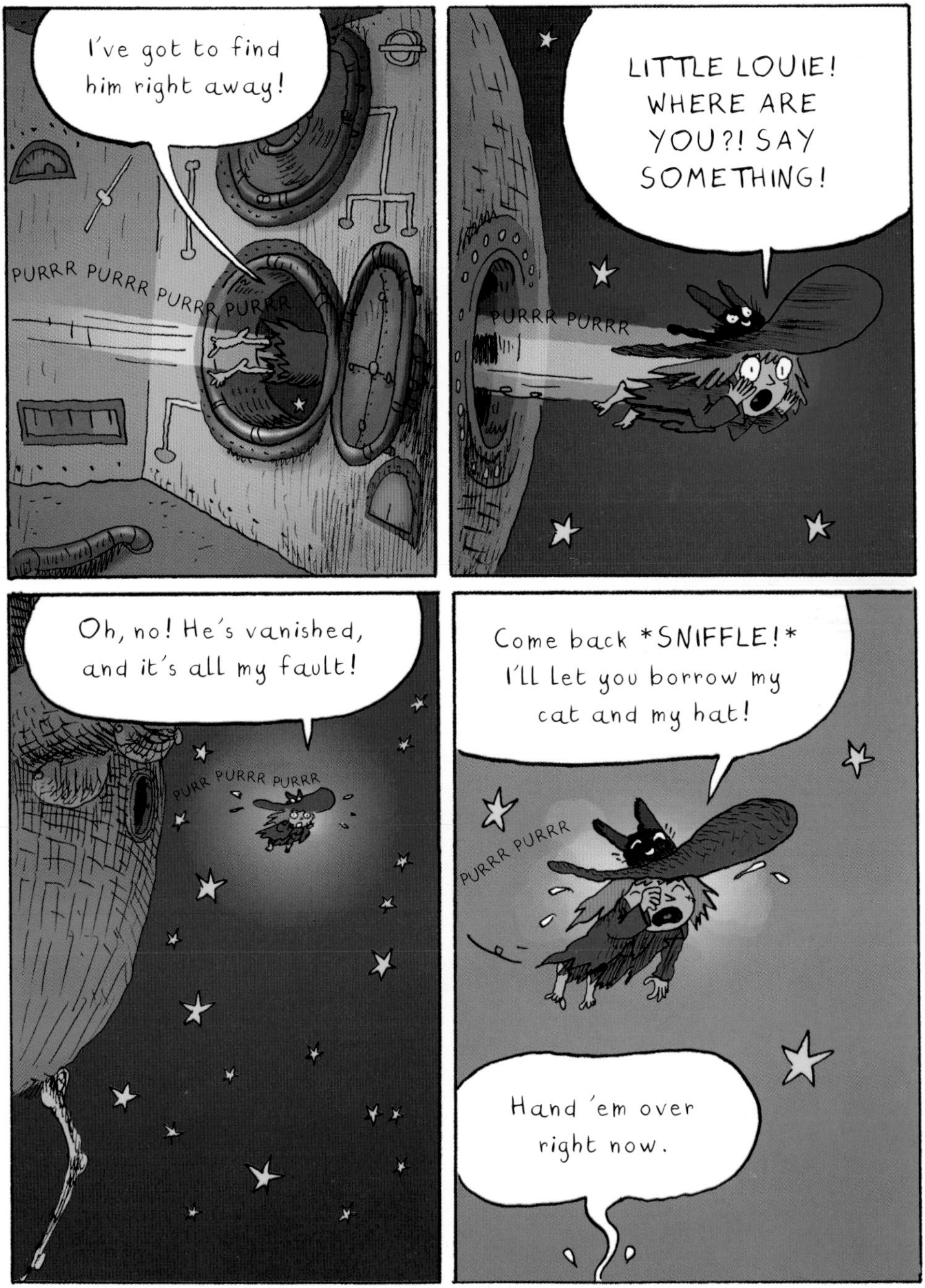
I've got to find him right away!
PURRR PURRR PURRR PURRR
LITTLE LOUIE! WHERE ARE YOU?! SAY SOMETHING!
PURRR PURRR
Oh, no! He's vanished, and it's all my fault!
PURR PURRR PURRR
Come back *SNIFFLE!* I'll let you borrow my cat and my hat!
PURRR PURRR
Hand 'em over right now.

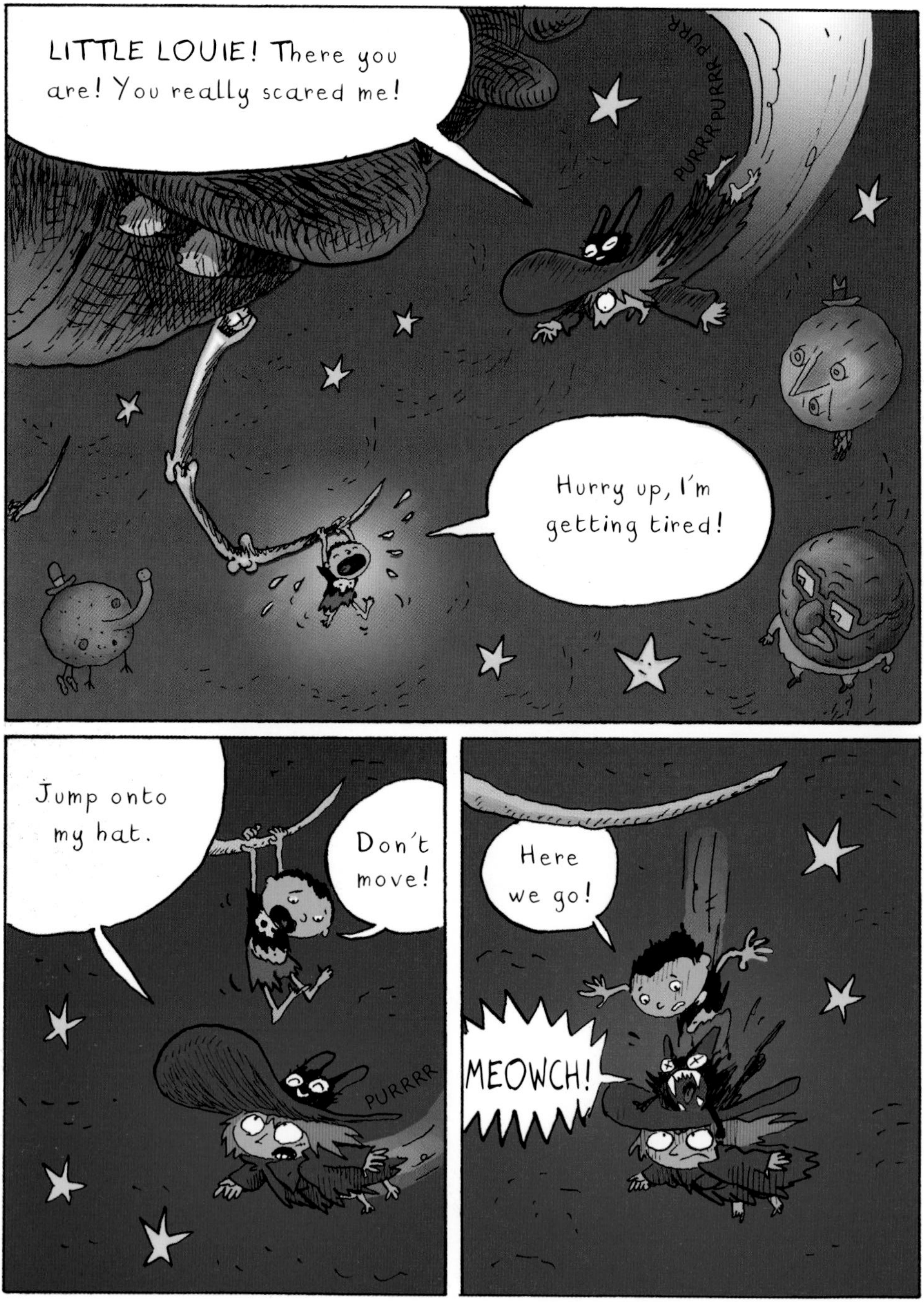
LITTLE LOUIE! There you are! You really scared me!
PURRR PURRR PURR
Hurry up, I'm getting tired!
Jump onto my hat.
Don't move!
PURRRR
Here we go!
MEOWCH!

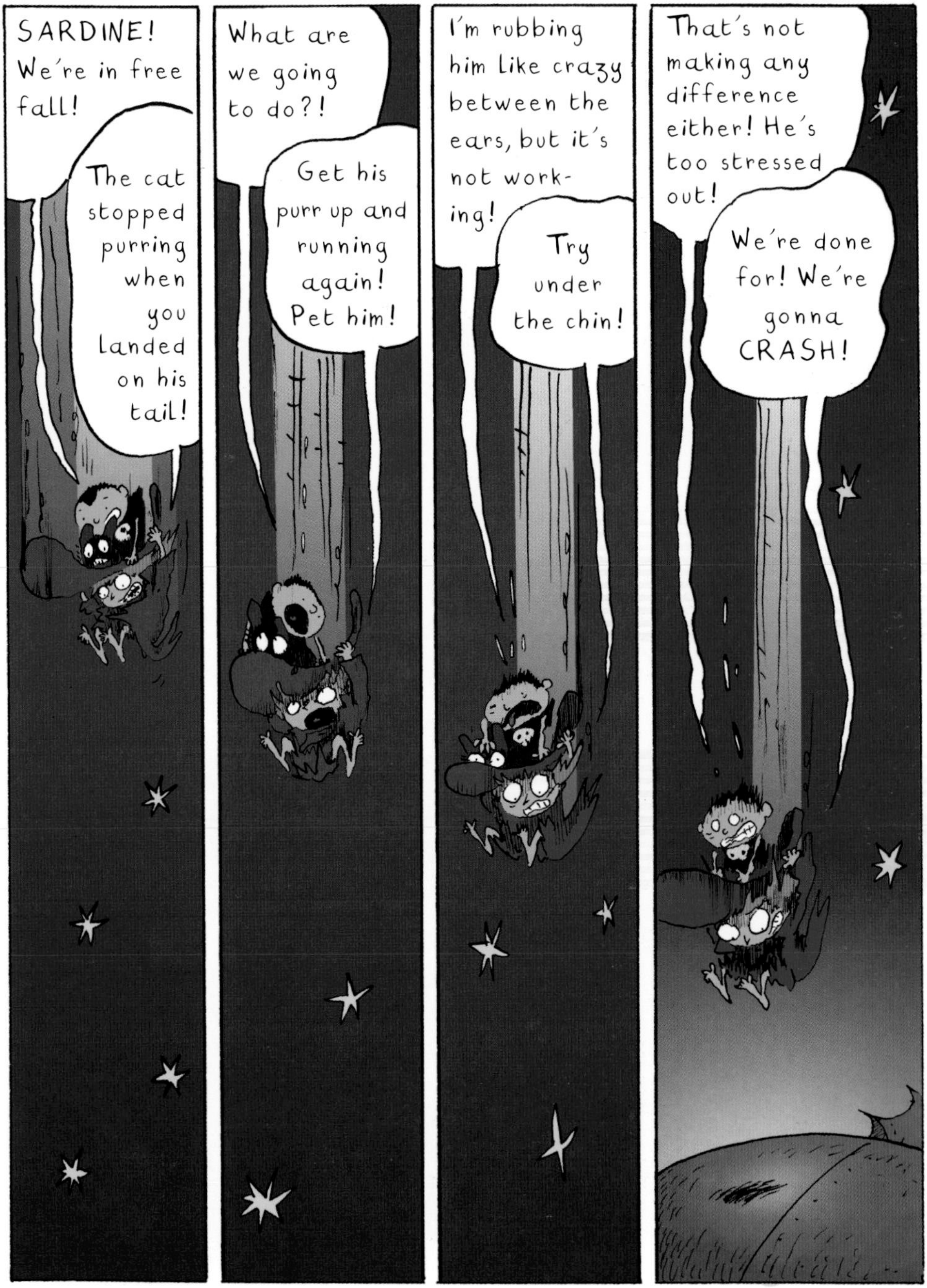
SARDINE! We're in free fall!
The cat stopped purring when you landed on his tail!
What are we going to do?!
Get his purr up and running again! Pet him!
I'm rubbing him like crazy between the ears, but it's not work-ing!
Try under the chin!
That's not making any difference either! He's too stressed out!
We're done for! We're gonna CRASH!

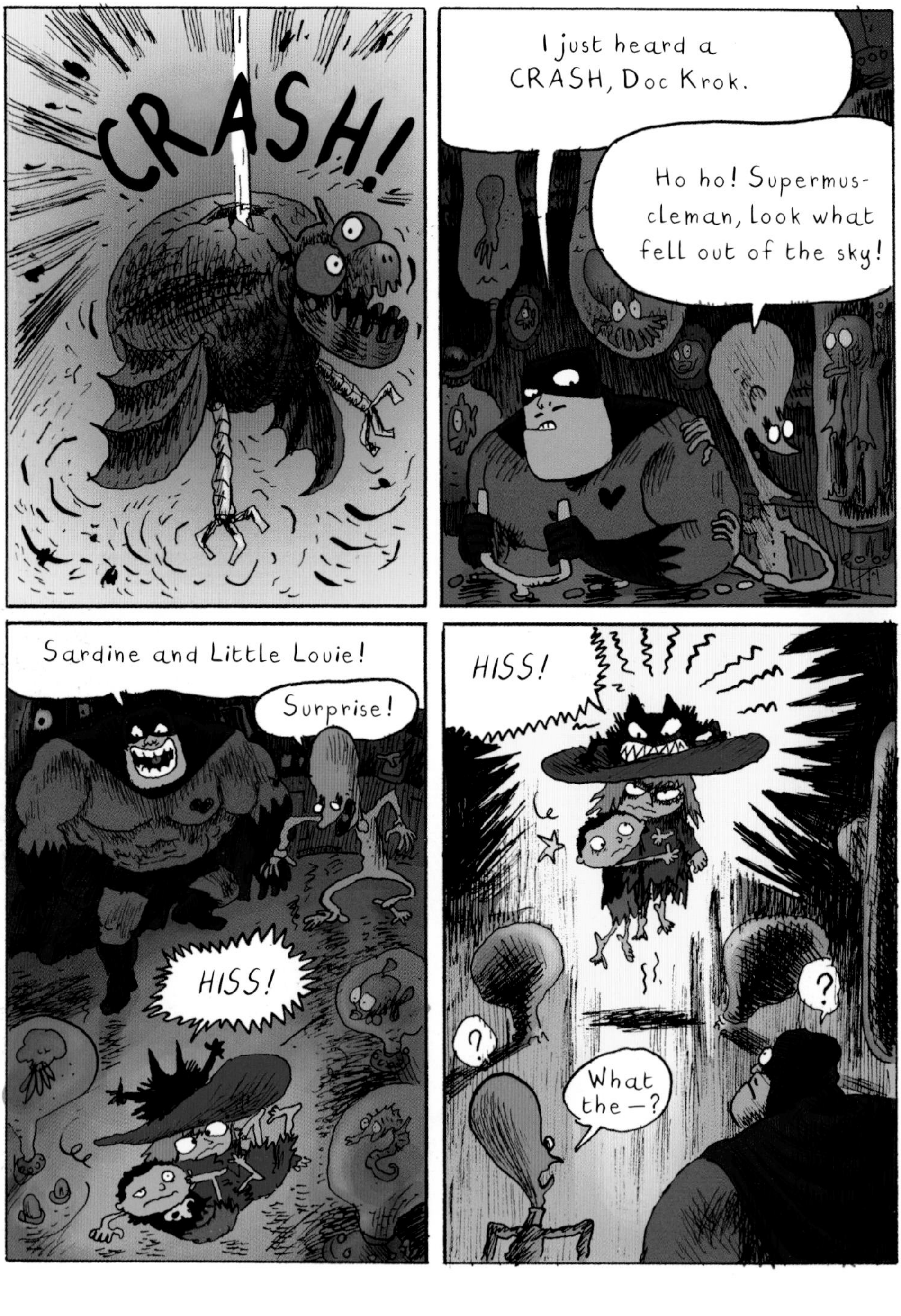
CRASH!
I just heard a CRASH, Doc Krok.
Ho ho! Supermus-cleman, look what fell out of the sky!
Sardine and Little Louie!
Surprise!
HISS!
HISS!
?
?
What the—?

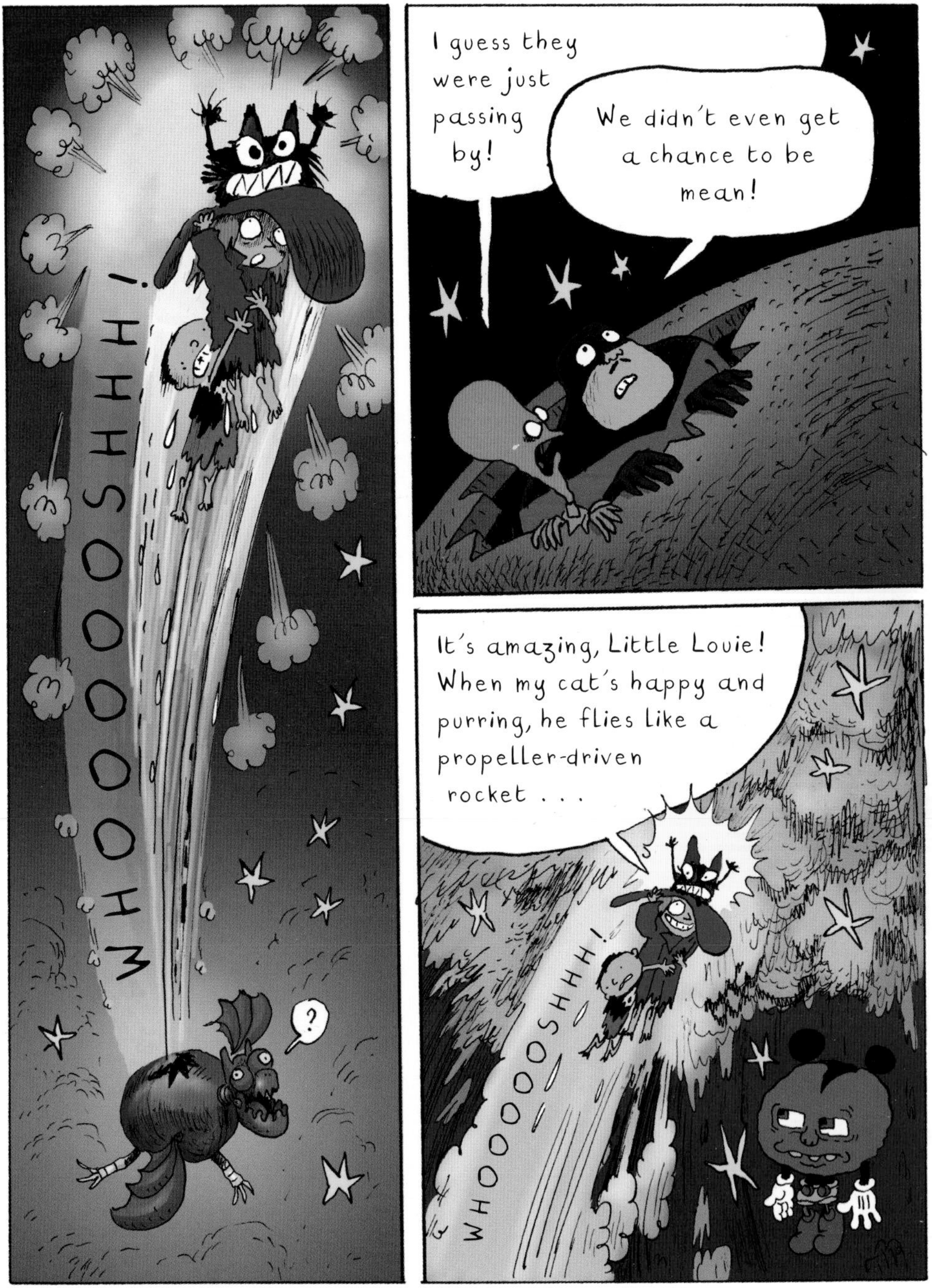
WHOOOOOOSHHH!
?
I guess they were just passing by!
We didn't even get a chance to be mean!
It's amazing, Little Louie! When my cat's happy and purring, he flies like a propeller-driven rocket . . .
WHOOOOOSHHH!

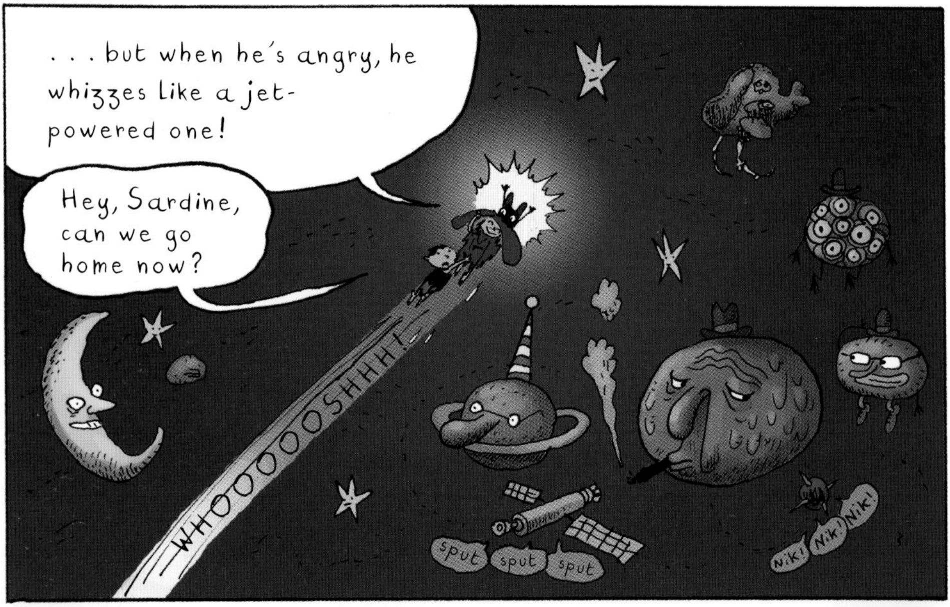
. . . but when he's angry, he whizzes like a jet-powered one!
Hey, Sardine, can we go home now?
WHOOOOOOSHHHH!
sput
sput
sput
Nik!
Nik!
Nik!

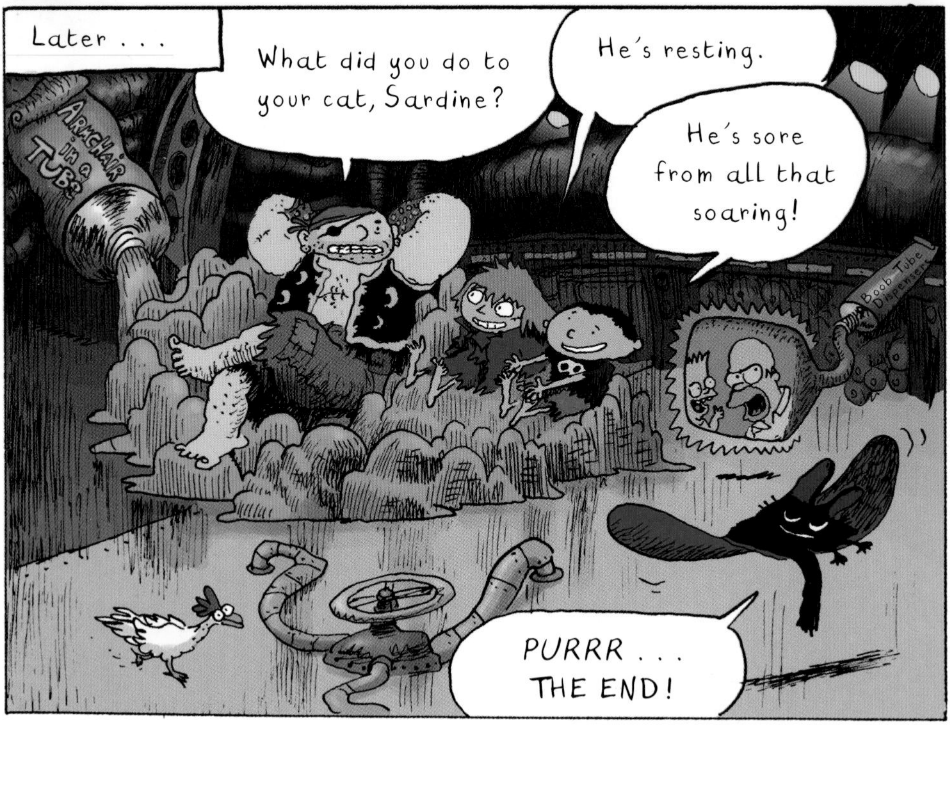
Later . . .
What did you do to your cat, Sardine?
He's resting.
He's sore from all that soaring!
Armchair in a Tube
Boob Tube Dispenser
PURRR . . . THE END!

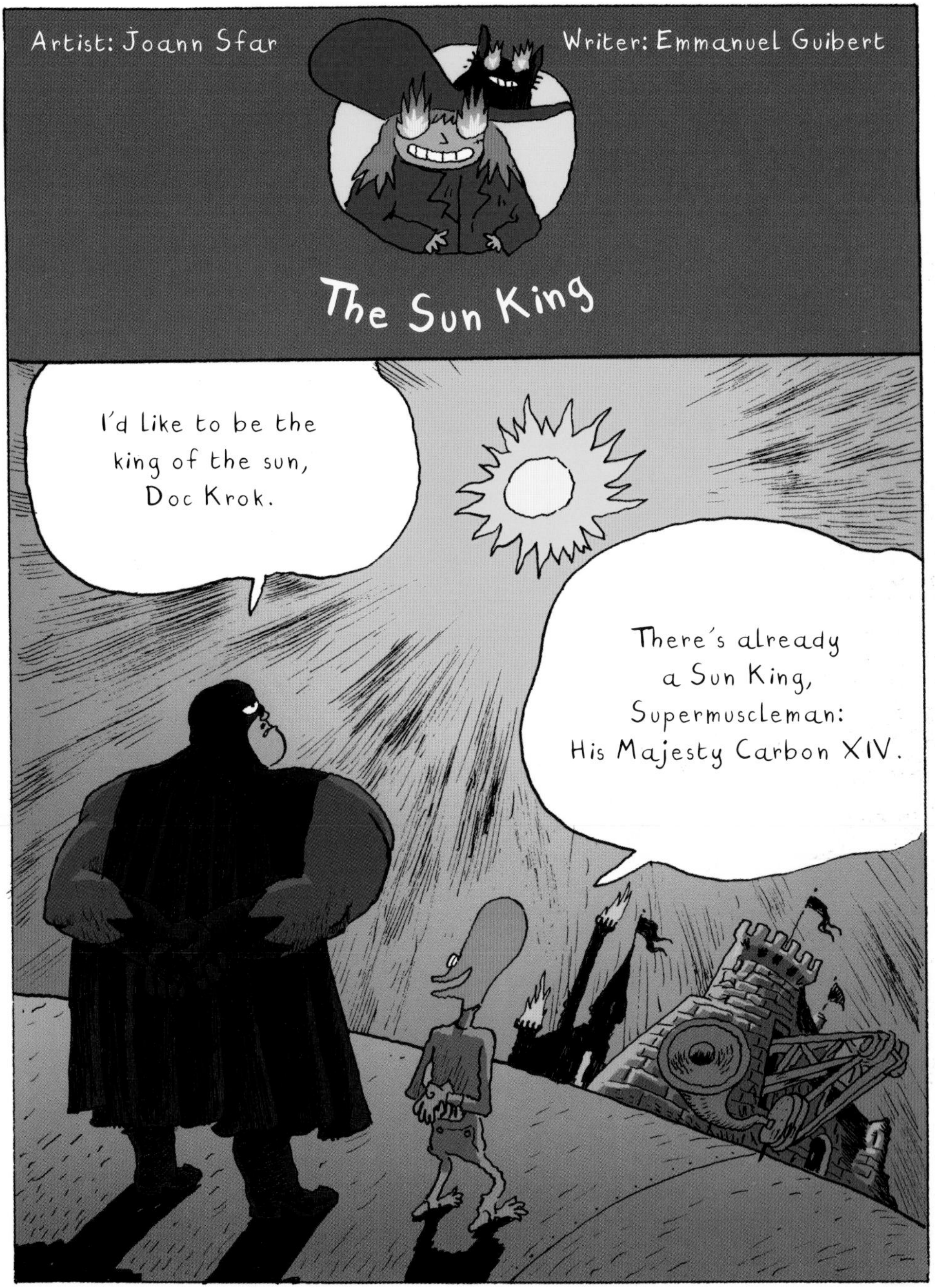
Artist: Joann Sfar
Writer: Emmanuel Guibert
The Sun King
I'd like to be the king of the sun, Doc Krok.
There's already a Sun King, Supermuscleman: His Majesty Carbon XIV.

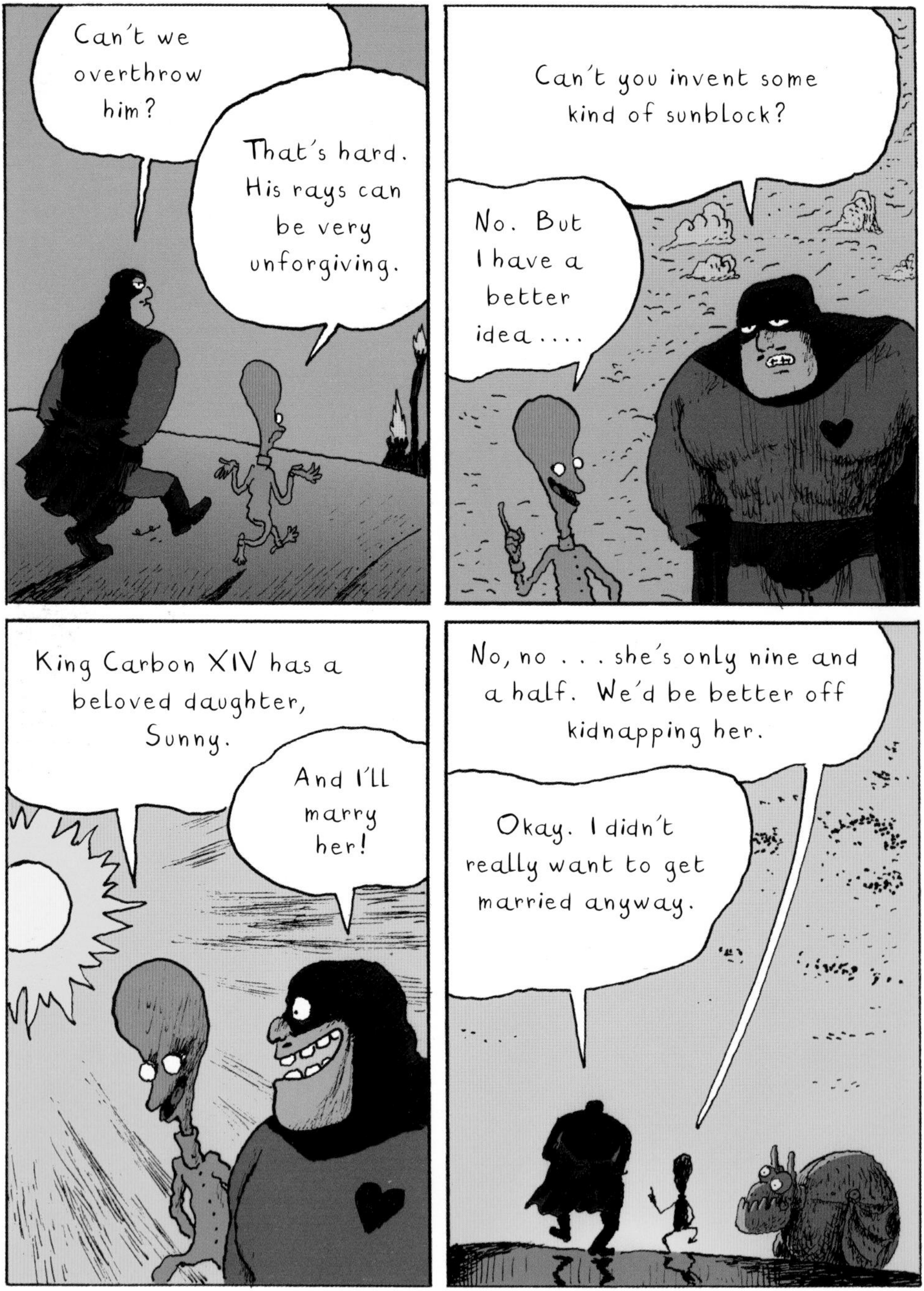
Can't we overthrow him?
That's hard. His rays can be very unforgiving.
Can't you invent some kind of sunblock?
No. But I have a better idea....
King Carbon XIV has a beloved daughter, Sunny.
And I'll marry her!
No, no . . . she's only nine and a half. We'd be better off kidnapping her.
Okay. I didn't really want to get married anyway.

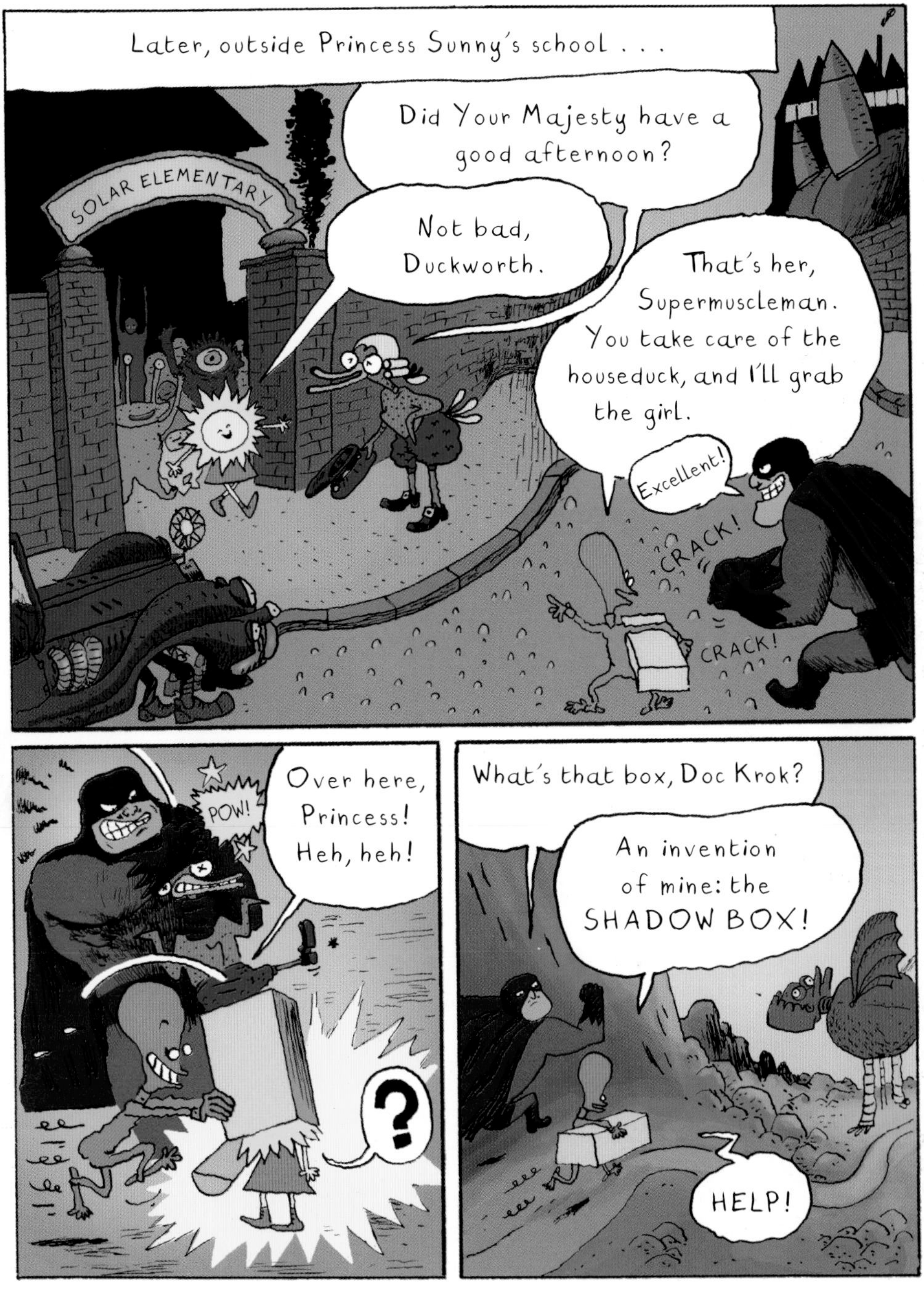
Later, outside Princess Sunny's school . . .
SOLAR ELEMENTARY
Did Your Majesty have a good afternoon?
Not bad, Duckworth.
That's her, Supermuscleman. You take care of the houseduck, and I'll grab the girl.
Excellent!
CRACK!
CRACK!
POW!
Over here, Princess! Heh, heh!
?
What's that box, Doc Krok?
An invention of mine: the SHADOW BOX!
HELP!

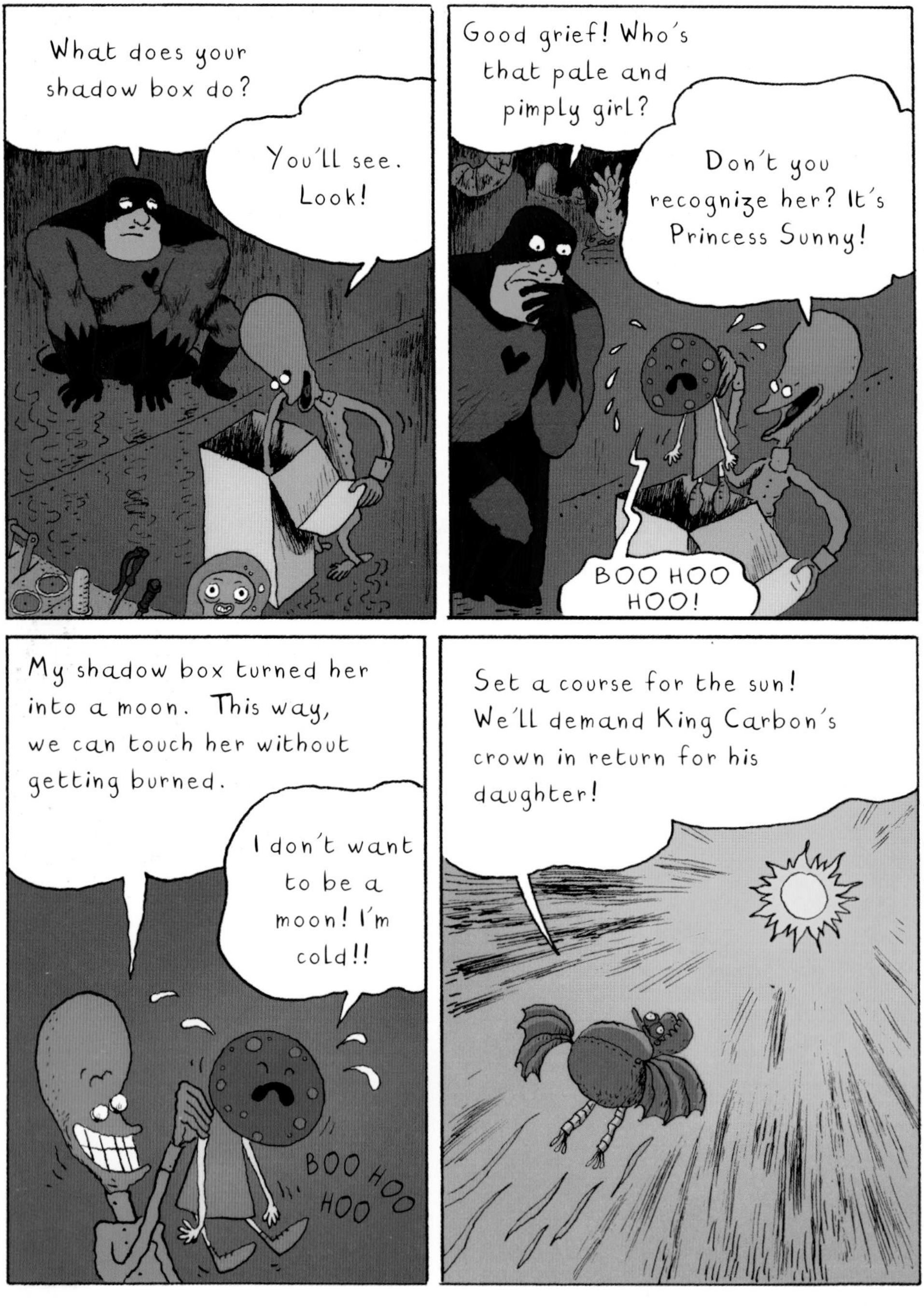
What does your shadow box do?
You'll see. Look!
Good grief! Who's that pale and pimply girl?
Don't you recognize her? It's Princess Sunny!
BOO HOO HOO!
My shadow box turned her into a moon. This way, we can touch her without getting burned.
I don't want to be a moon! I'm cold!!
BOO HOO HOO
Set a course for the sun! We'll demand King Carbon's crown in return for his daughter!

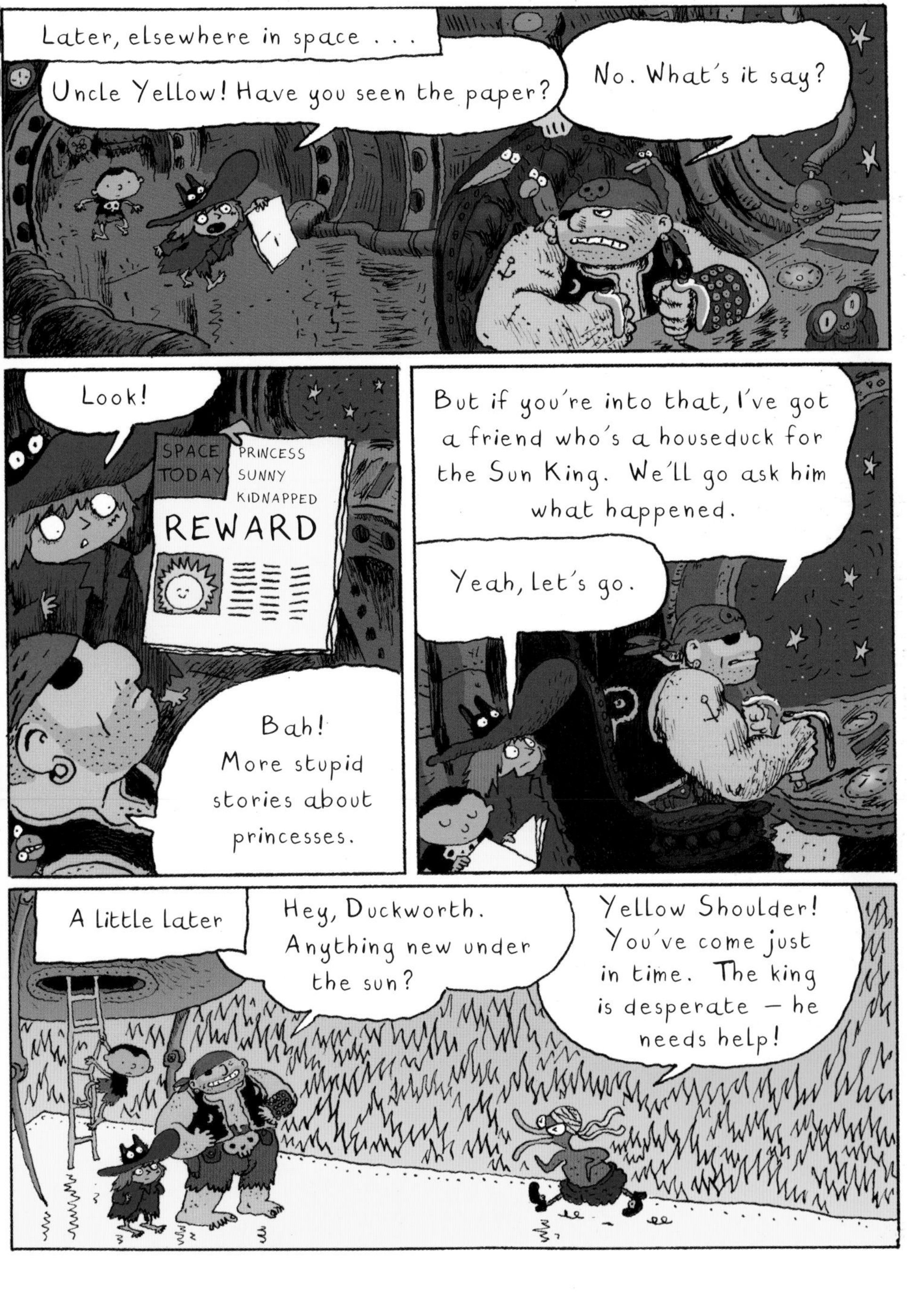
Later, elsewhere in space . . .
Uncle Yellow! Have you seen the paper?
No. What's it say?
Look!
SPACE TODAY
PRINCESS SUNNY KIDNAPPED
REWARD
Bah! More stupid stories about princesses.
But if you're into that, I've got a friend who's a houseduck for the Sun King. We'll go ask him what happened.
Yeah, let's go.
A little later
Hey, Duckworth. Anything new under the sun?
Yellow Shoulder! You've come just in time. The king is desperate — he needs help!

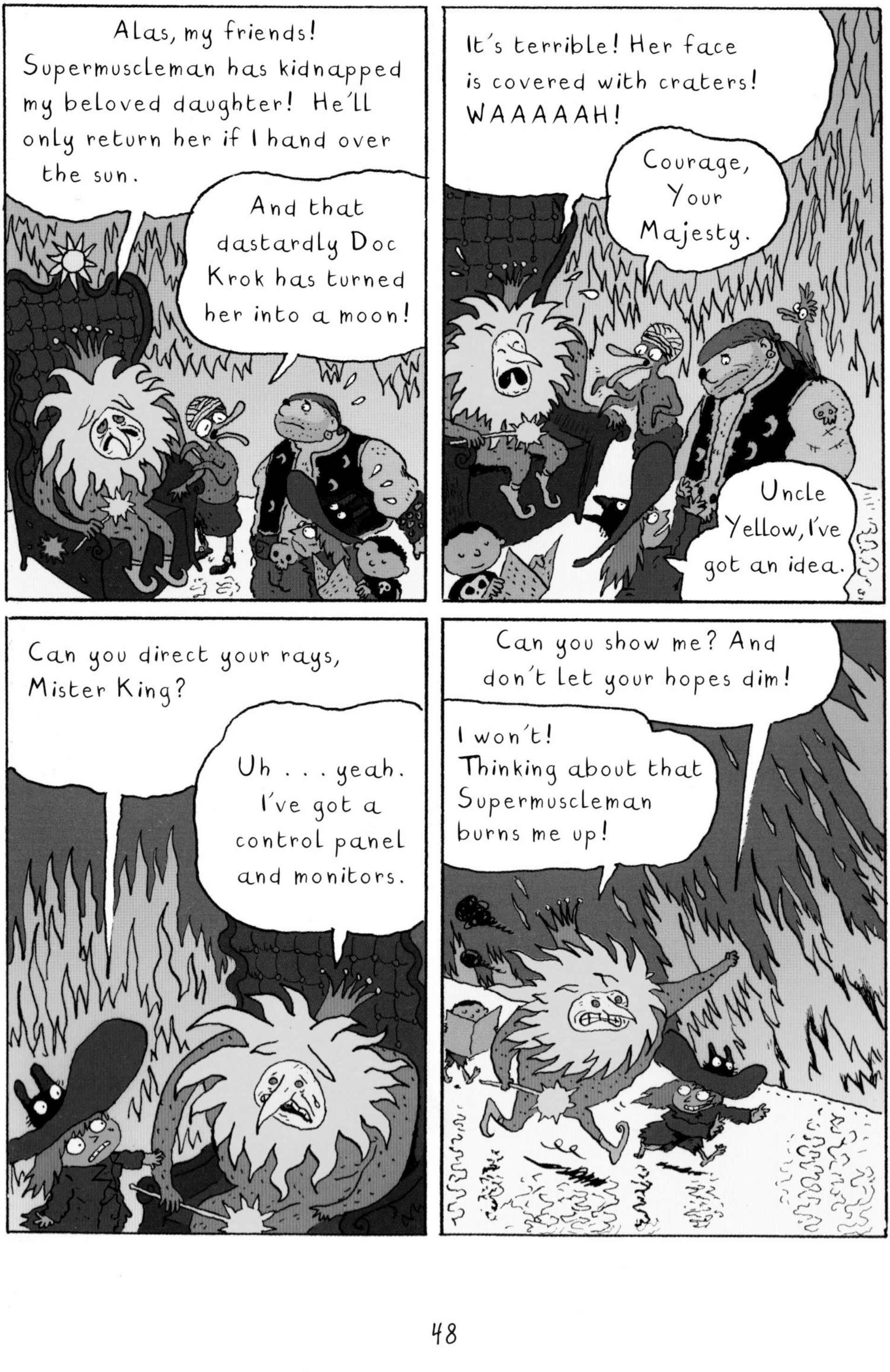
Alas, my friends! Supermuscleman has kidnapped my beloved daughter! He'll only return her if I hand over the sun.
And that dastardly Doc Krok has turned her into a moon!
It's terrible! Her face is covered with craters! WAAAAAH!
Courage, Your Majesty.
Uncle Yellow, I've got an idea.
Can you direct your rays, Mister King?
Uh . . . yeah. I've got a control panel and monitors.
Can you show me? And don't let your hopes dim!
I won't! Thinking about that Supermuscleman burns me up!

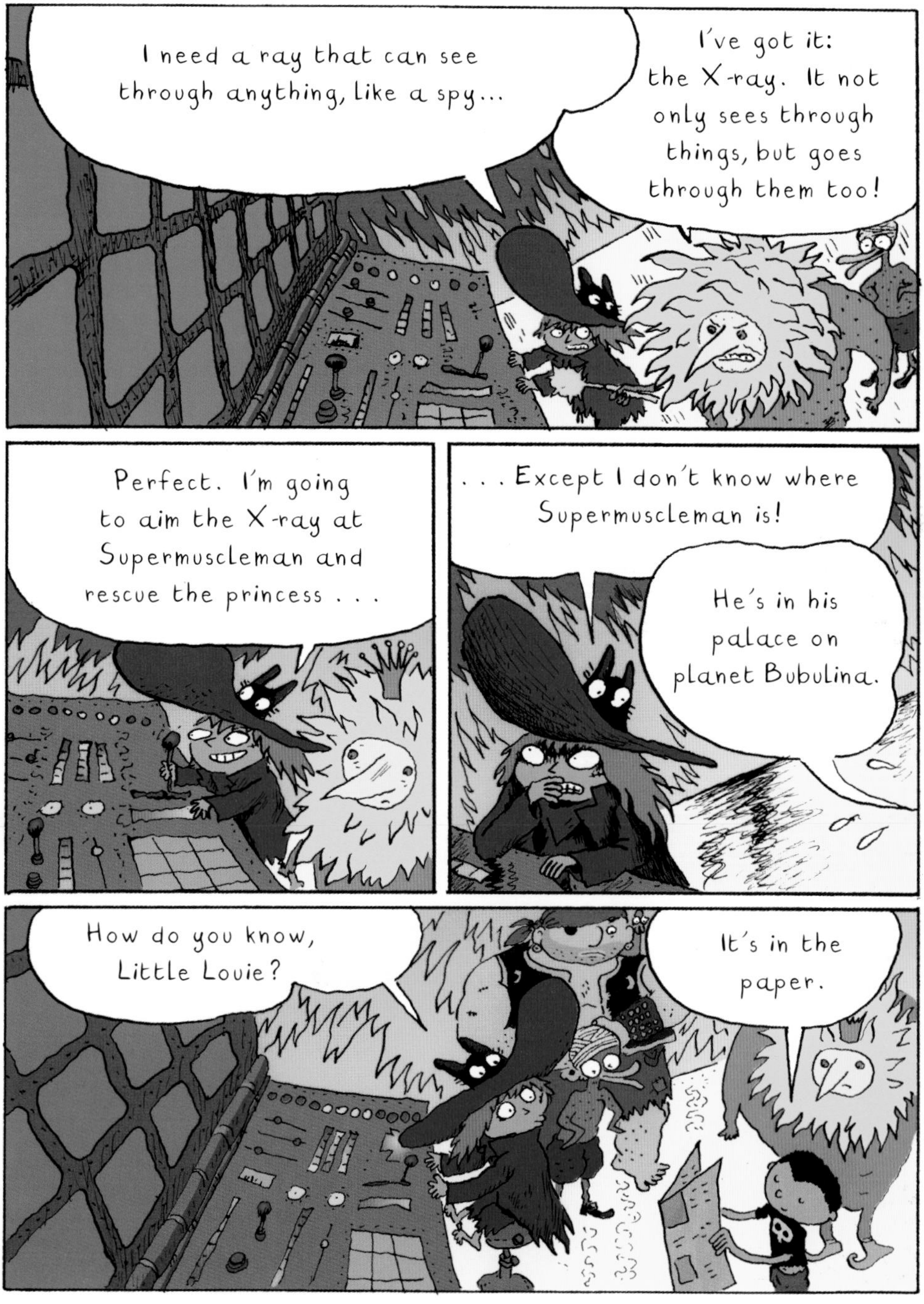
I need a ray that can see through anything, like a spy...
I've got it: the X-ray. It not only sees through things, but goes through them too!
Perfect. I'm going to aim the X-ray at Supermuscleman and rescue the princess . . .
. . . Except I don't know where Supermuscleman is!
He's in his palace on planet Bubulina.
How do you know, Little Louie?
It's in the paper.

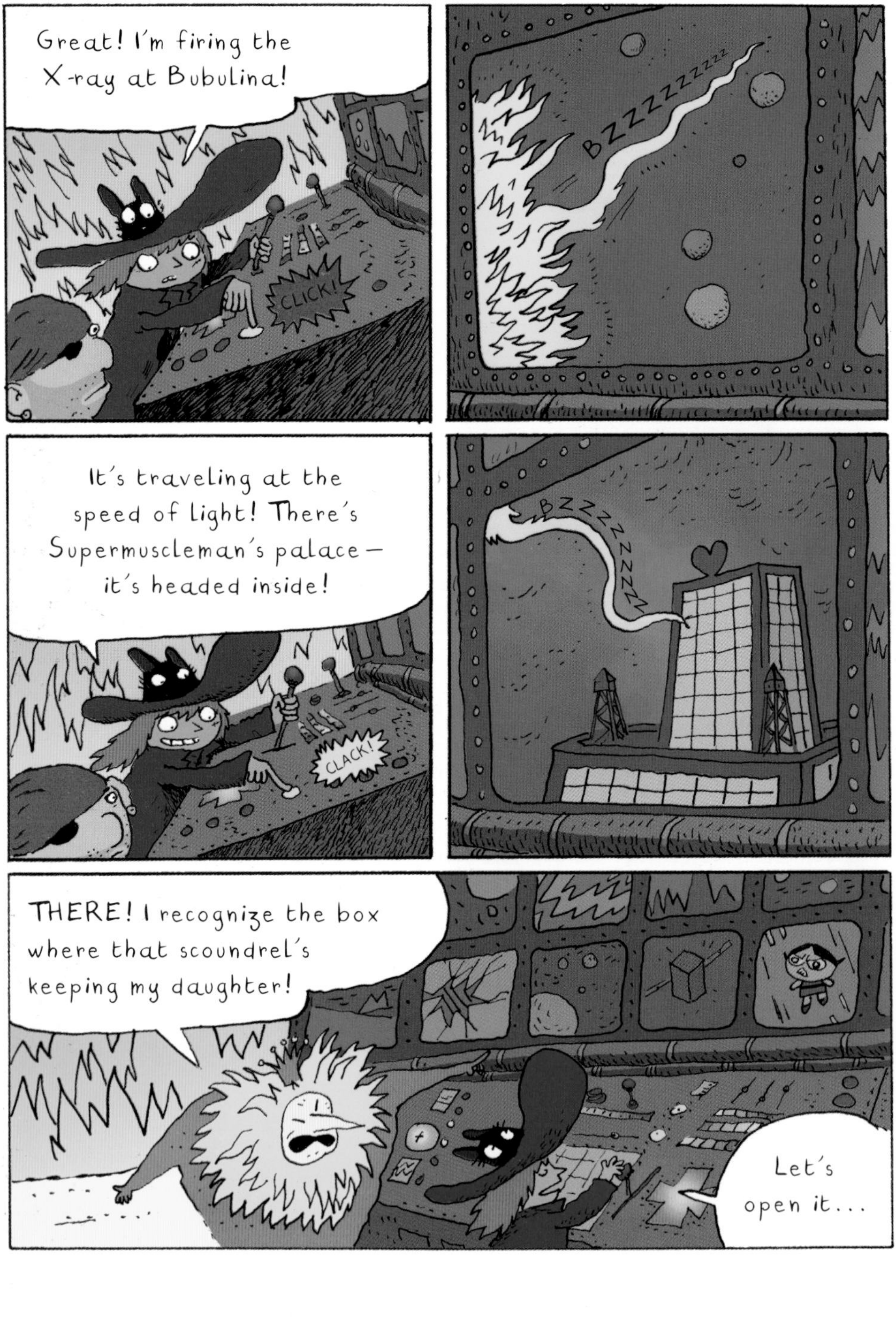
Great! I'm firing the X-ray at Bubulina!
CLICK!
BZZZZZZZZZZ
It's traveling at the speed of light! There's Supermuscleman's palace — it's headed inside!
CLACK!
BZZZZZZZZZ
THERE! I recognize the box where that scoundrel's keeping my daughter!
Let's open it...

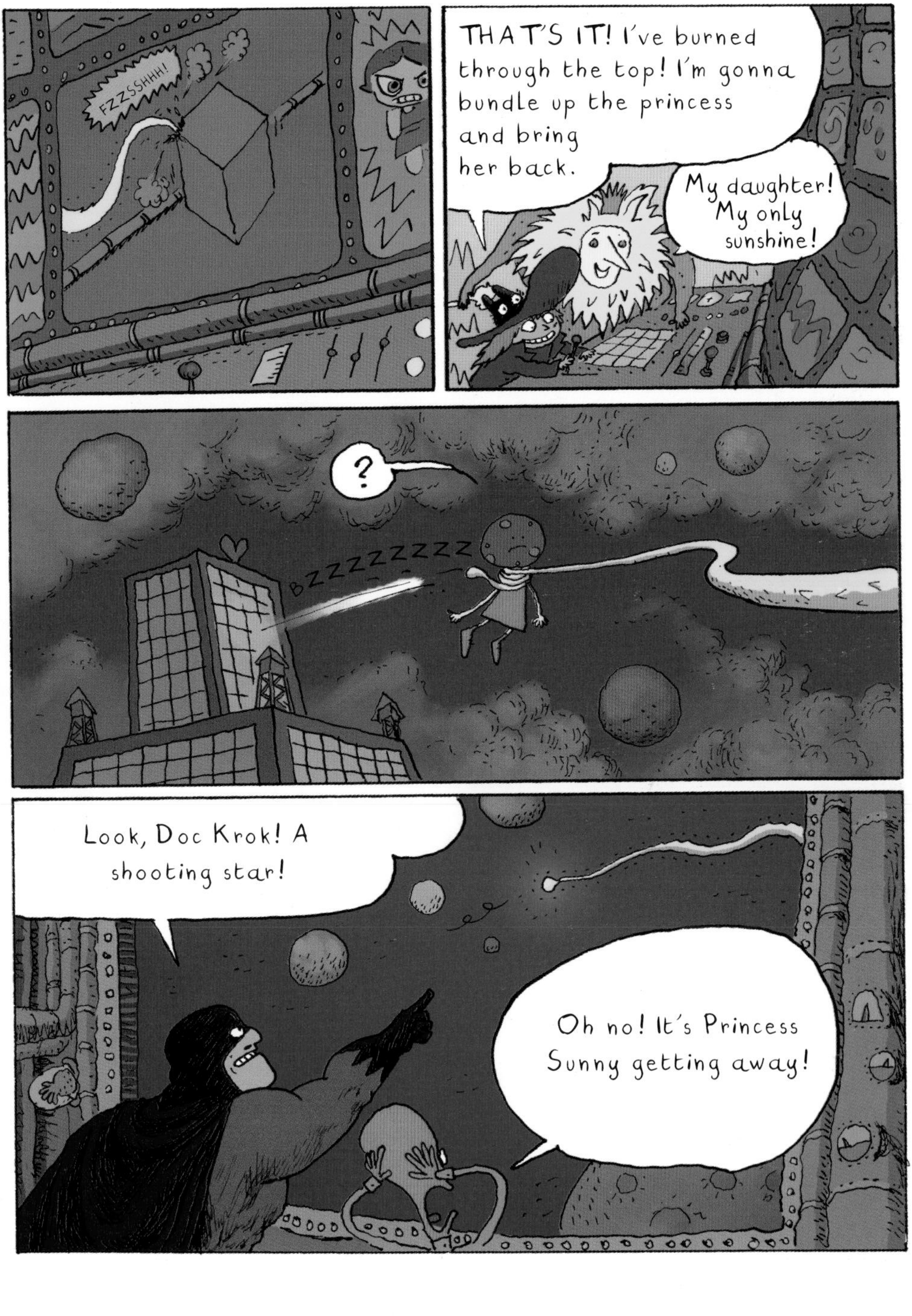
FZZSSHHH!
THAT'S IT! I've burned through the top! I'm gonna bundle up the princess and bring her back.
My daughter! My only sunshine!
?
BZZZZZZZZ
Look, Doc Krok! A shooting star!
Oh no! It's Princess Sunny getting away!

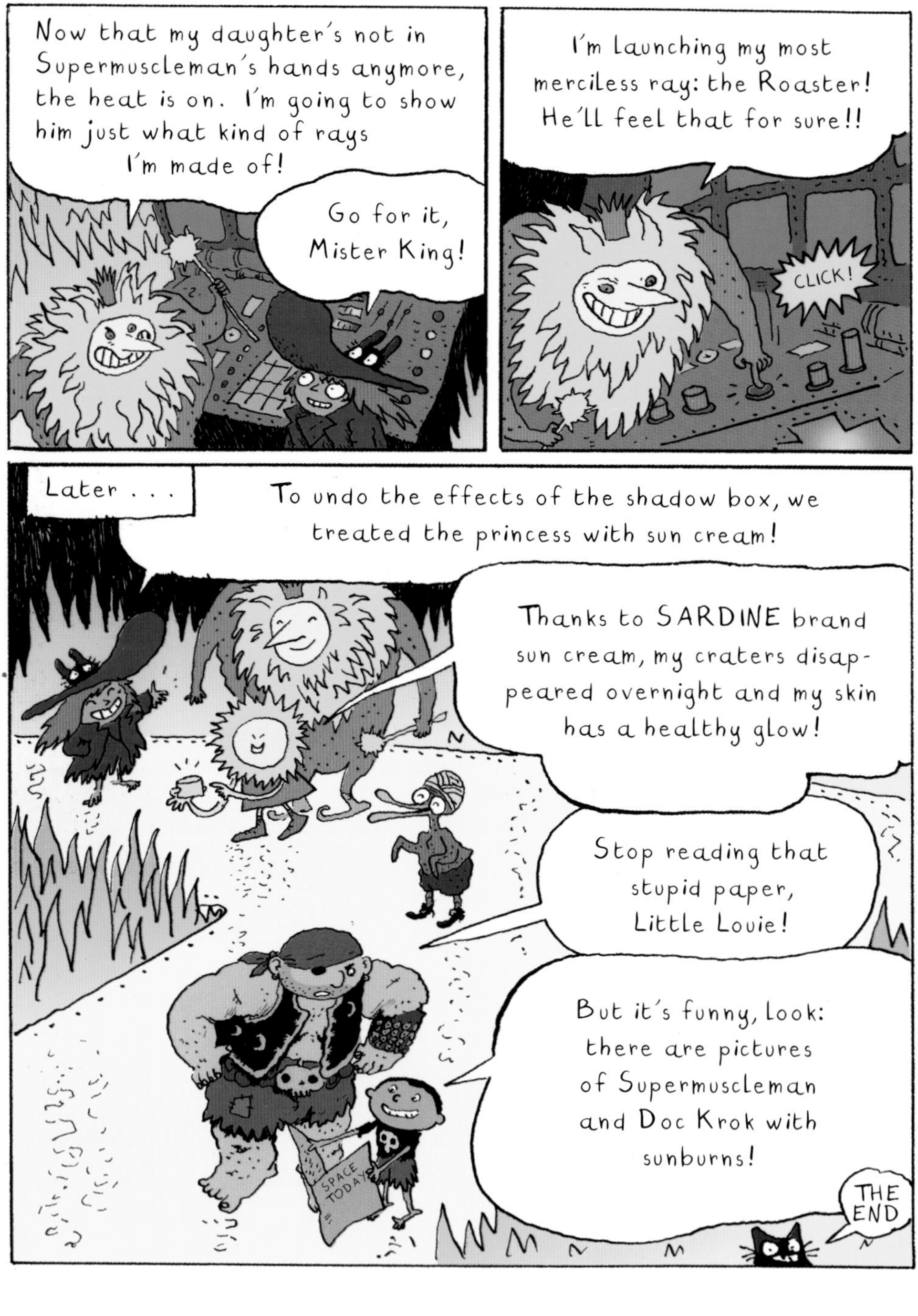
Now that my daughter's not in Supermuscleman's hands anymore, the heat is on. I'm going to show him just what kind of rays I'm made of!
Go for it, Mister King!
I'm launching my most merciless ray: the Roaster! He'll feel that for sure!!
CLICK!
Later . . .
To undo the effects of the shadow box, we treated the princess with sun cream!
Thanks to SARDINE brand sun cream, my craters disappeared overnight and my skin has a healthy glow!
Stop reading that stupid paper, Little Louie!
But it's funny, look: there are pictures of Supermuscleman and Doc Krok with sunburns!
SPACE TODAY
THE END

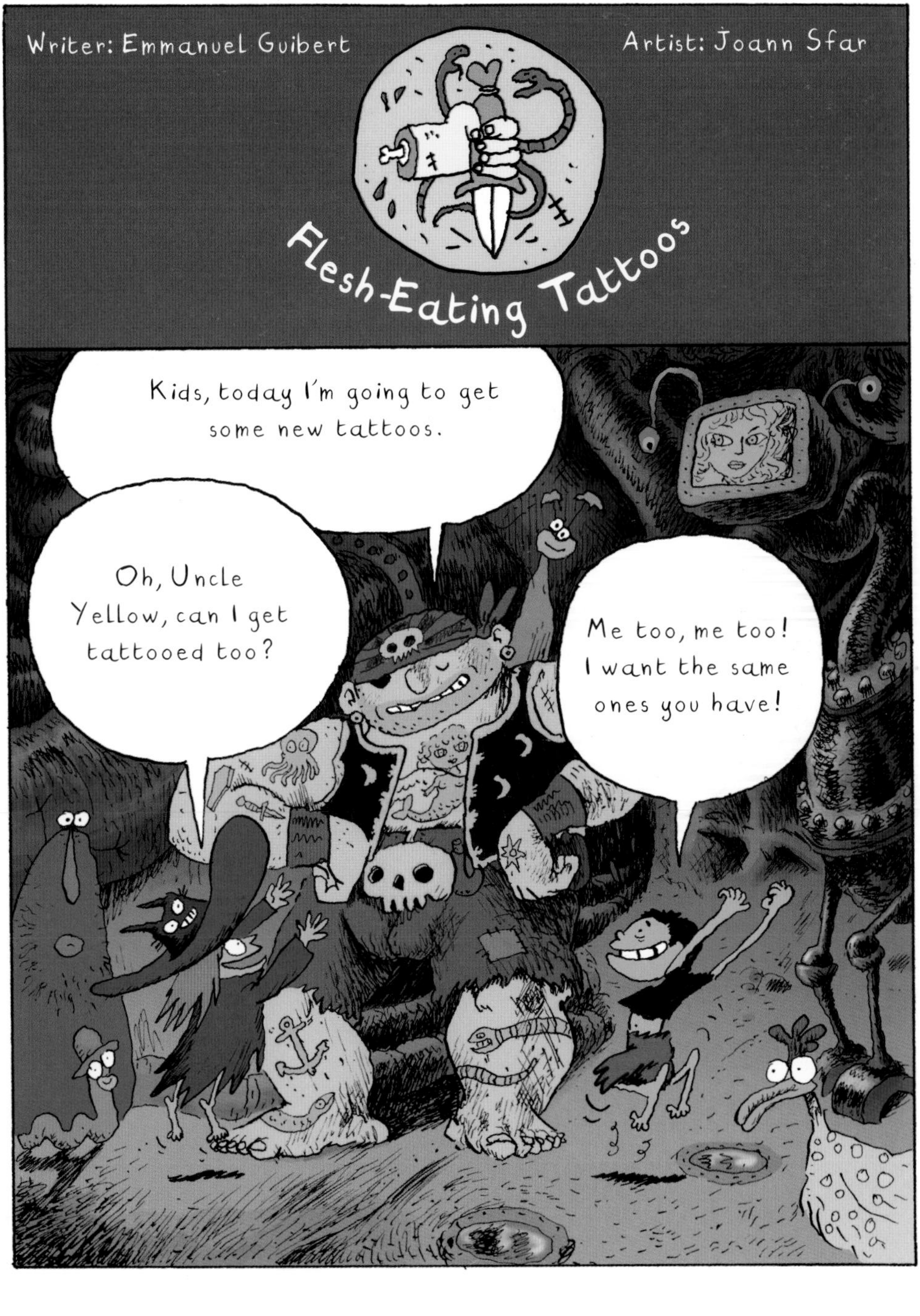
Writer: Emmanuel Guibert
Artist: Joann Sfar
Flesh-Eating Tattoos
Kids, today I'm going to get some new tattoos.
Oh, Uncle Yellow, can I get tattooed too?
Me too, me too! I want the same ones you have!

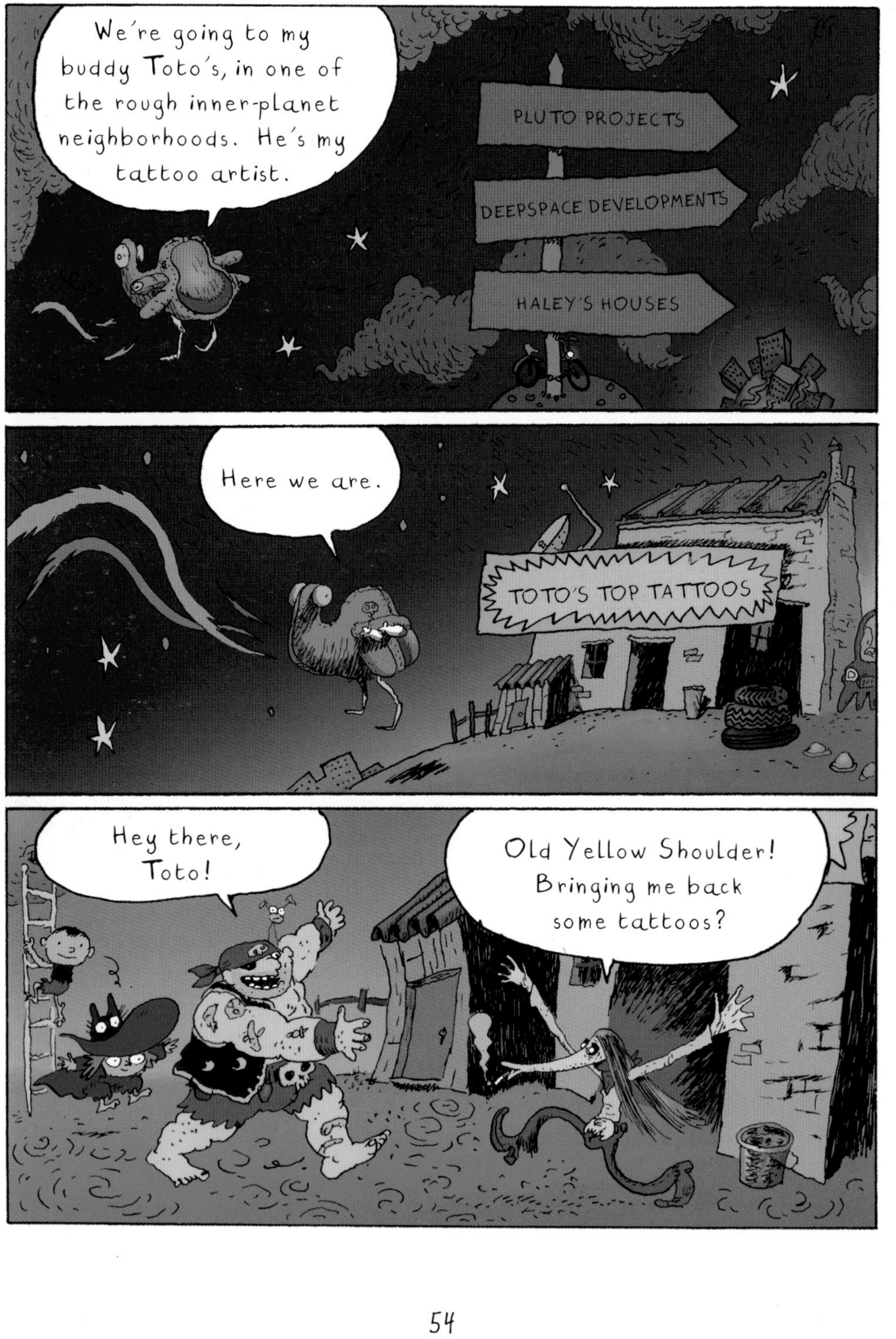
We're going to my buddy Toto's, in one of the rough inner-planet neighborhoods. He's my tattoo artist.
PLUTO PROJECTS
DEEPSPACE DEVELOPMENTS
HALEY'S HOUSES
Here we are.
TOTO'S TOP TATTOOS
Hey there, Toto!
Old Yellow Shoulder! Bringing me back some tattoos?

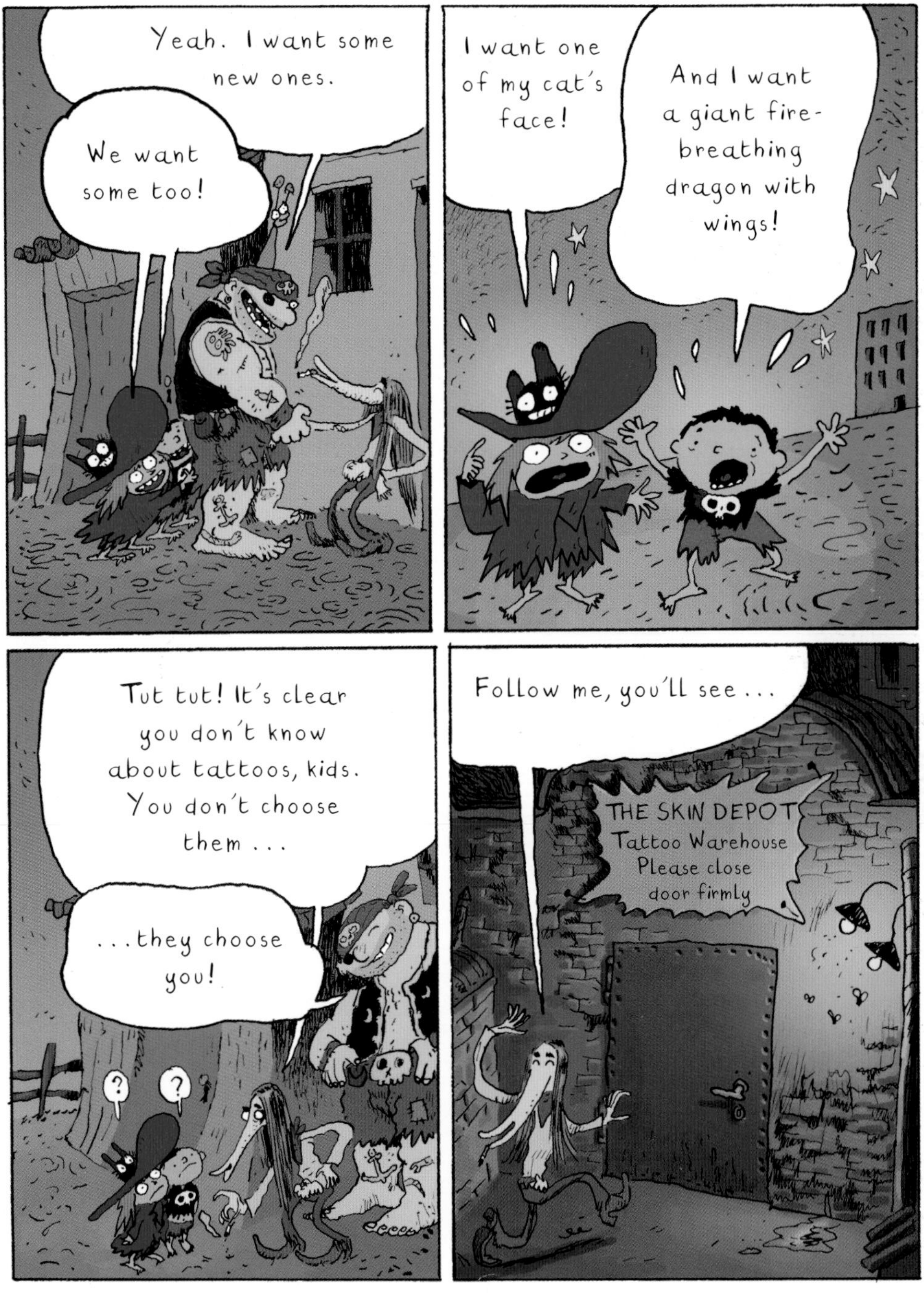
Yeah. I want some new ones.
We want some too!
I want one of my cat's face!
And I want a giant fire-breathing dragon with wings!
Tut tut! It's clear you don't know about tattoos, kids. You don't choose them . . .
. . . they choose you!
?
?
Follow me, you'll see . . .
THE SKIN DEPOT
Tattoo Warehouse
Please close door firmly

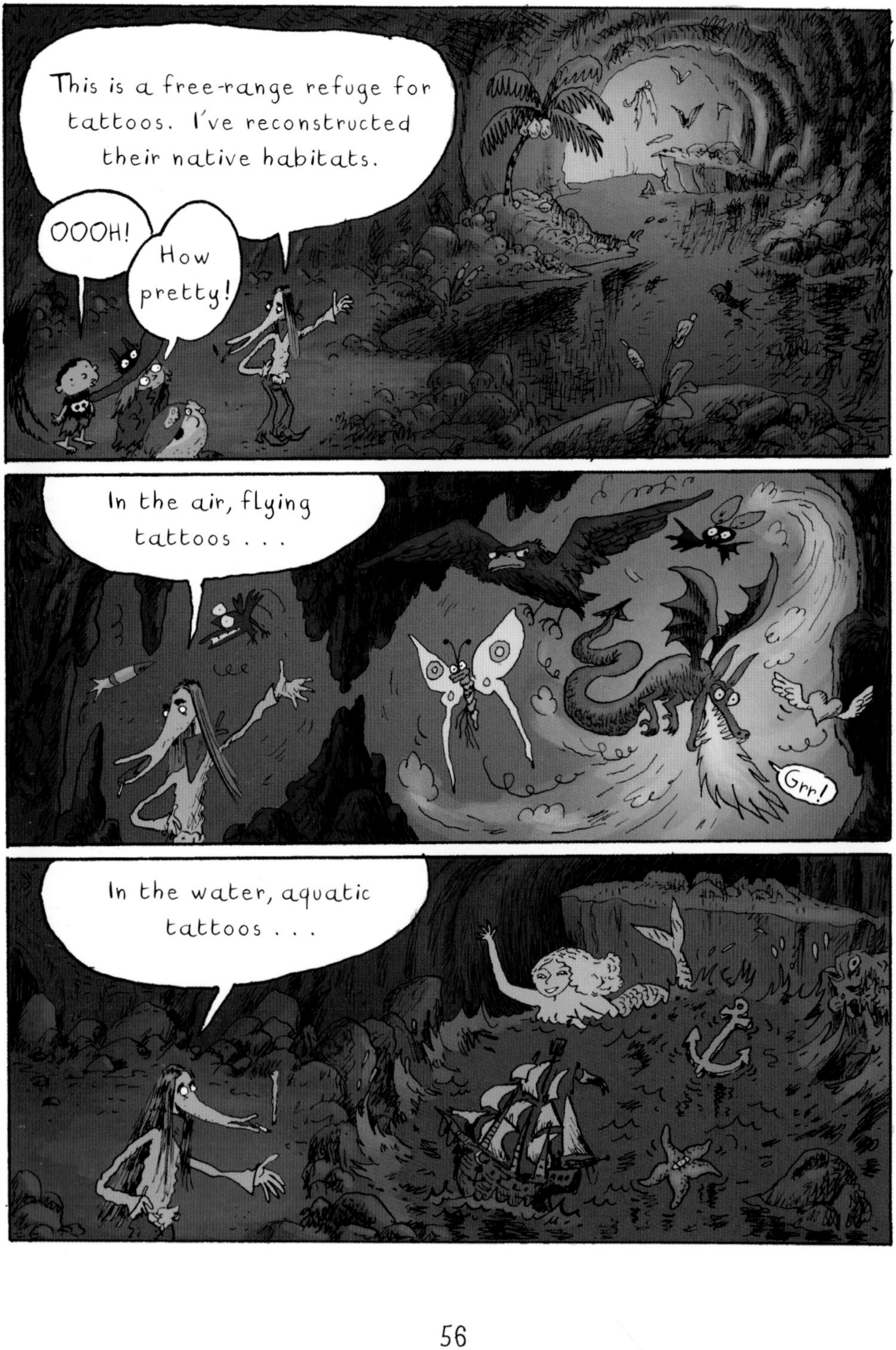
This is a free-range refuge for tattoos. I've reconstructed their native habitats.
OOOH!
How pretty!
In the air, flying tattoos . . .
Grr!
In the water, aquatic tattoos . . .

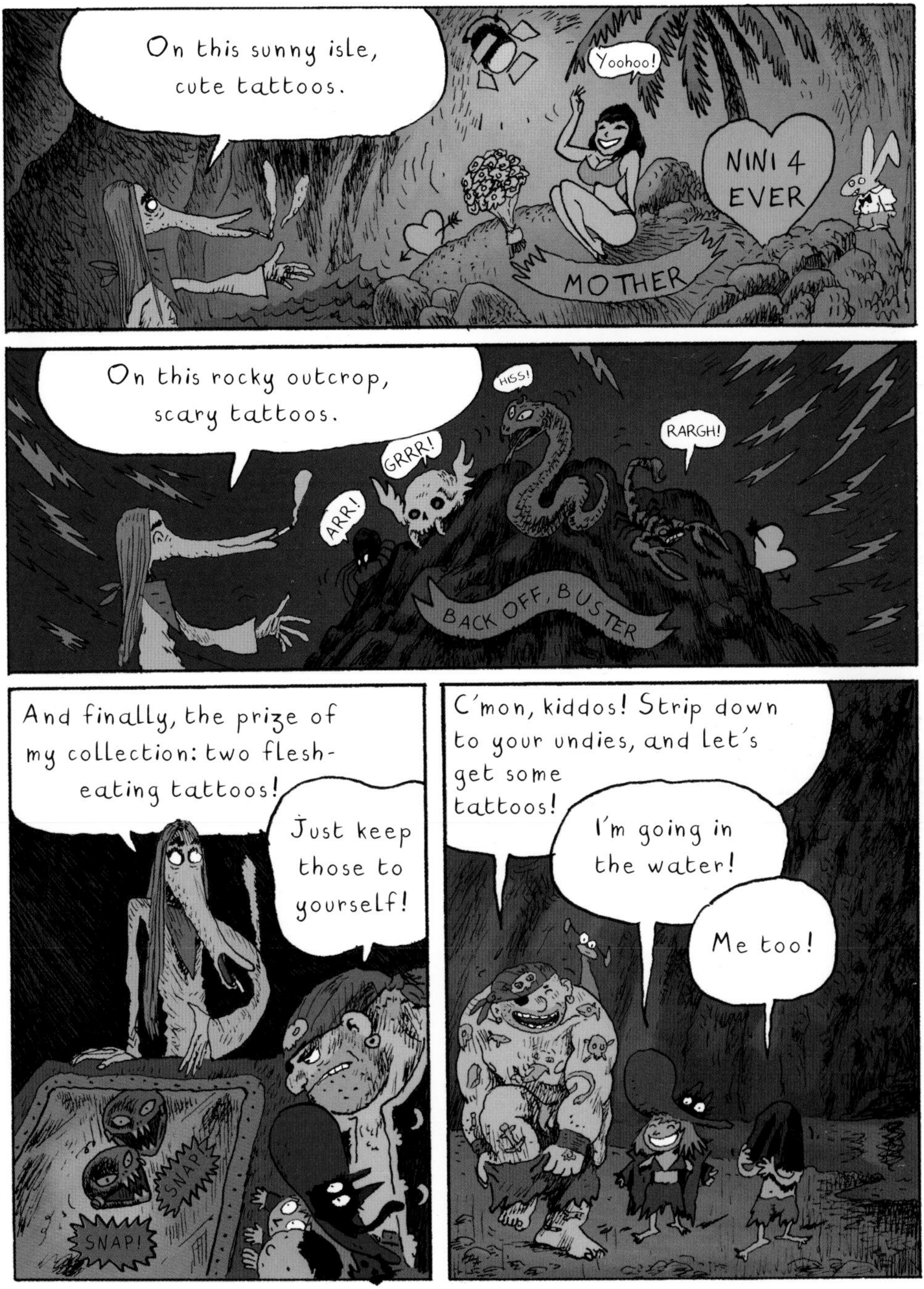
On this sunny isle, cute tattoos.
Yoohoo!
NINI 4 EVER
MOTHER
On this rocky outcrop, scary tattoos.
HISS!
RARGH!
GRRR!
ARR!
BACK OFF, BUSTER
And finally, the prize of my collection: two flesh-eating tattoos!
Just keep those to yourself!
SNAP!
SNAP!
C'mon, kiddos! Strip down to your undies, and let's get some tattoos!
I'm going in the water!
Me too!

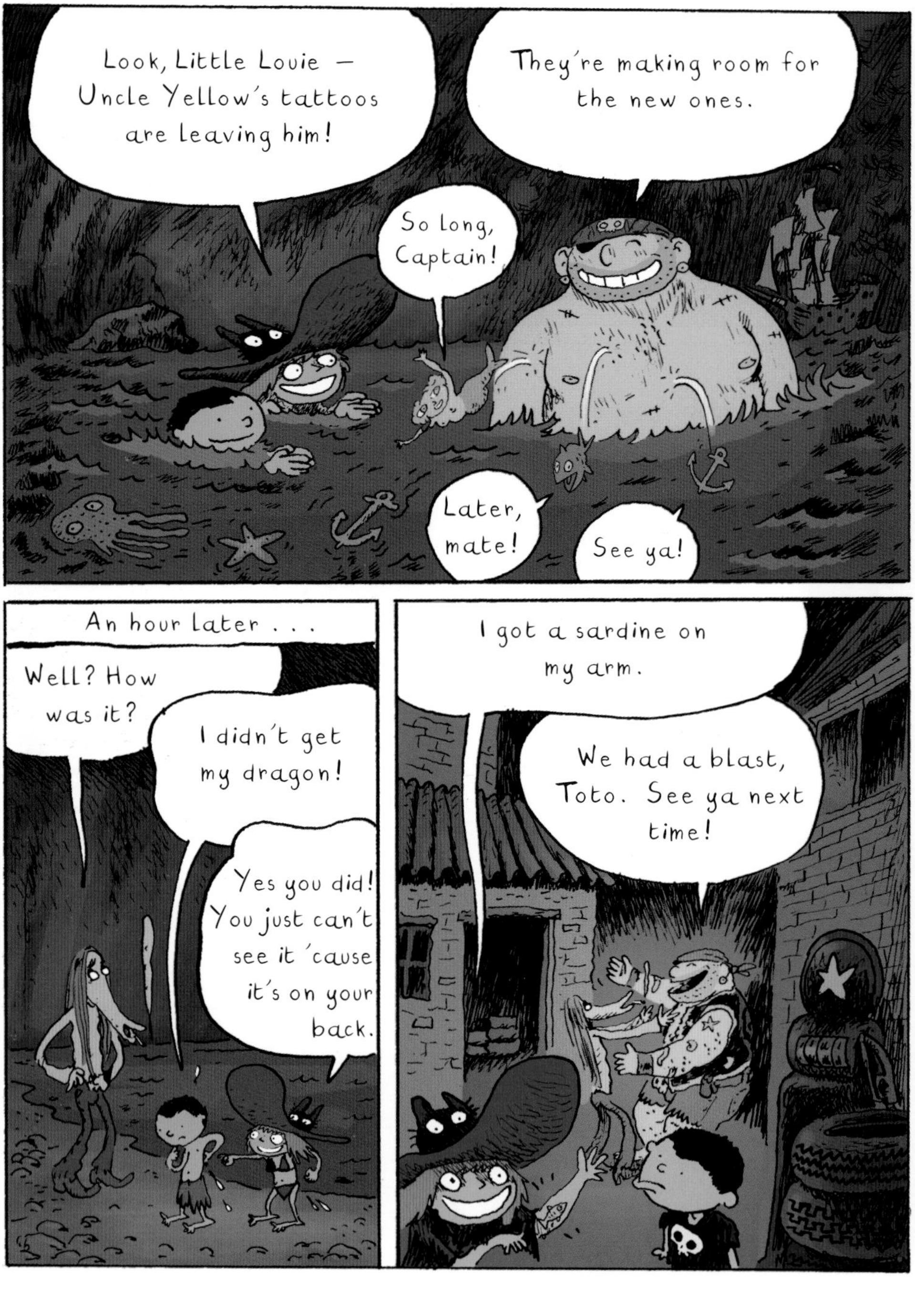
Look, Little Louie — Uncle Yellow's tattoos are leaving him!
They're making room for the new ones.
So long, Captain!
Later, mate!
See ya!
An hour later . . .
Well? How was it?
I didn't get my dragon!
Yes you did! You just can't see it 'cause it's on your back.
I got a sardine on my arm.
We had a blast, Toto. See ya next time!

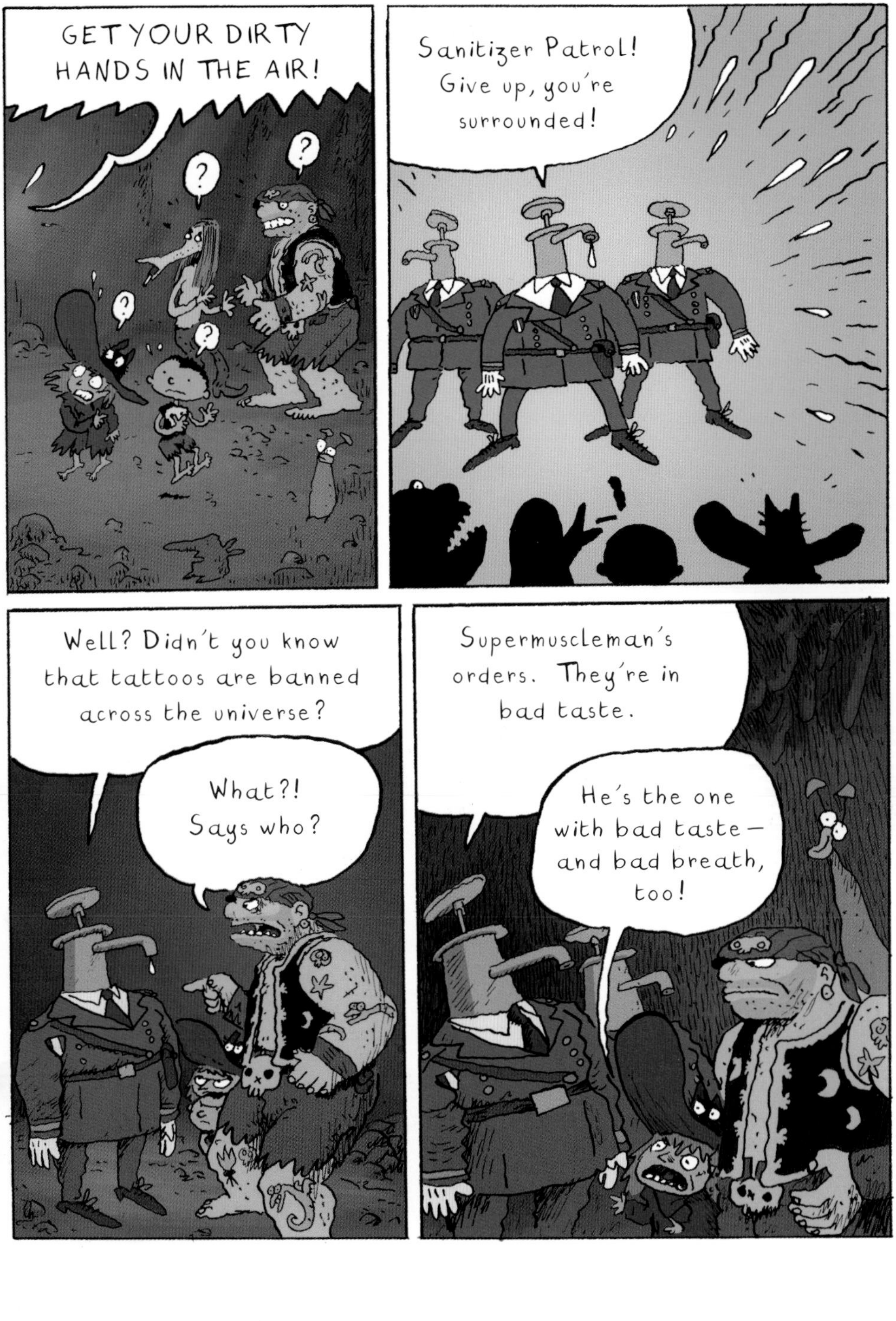
GET YOUR DIRTY HANDS IN THE AIR!
?
?
?
?
Sanitizer Patrol! Give up, you're surrounded!
Well? Didn't you know that tattoos are banned across the universe?
What?! Says who?
Supermuscleman's orders. They're in bad taste.
He's the one with bad taste— and bad breath, too!

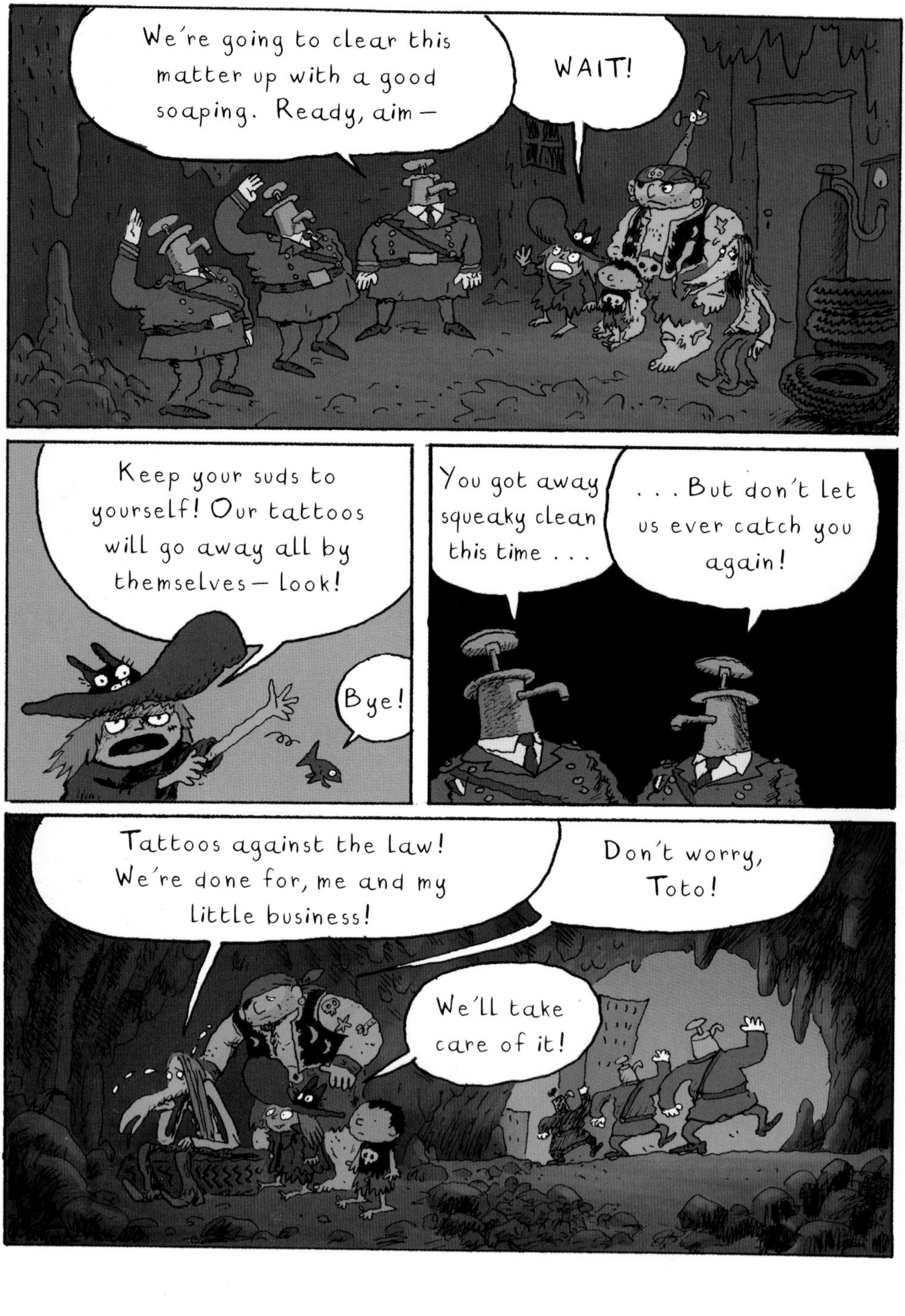
We're going to clear this matter up with a good soaping. Ready, aim—
WAIT!
Keep your suds to yourself! Our tattoos will go away all by themselves—look!
Bye!
You got away squeaky clean this time . . .
. . . But don't let us ever catch you again!
Tattoos against the law! We're done for, me and my little business!
Don't worry, Toto!
We'll take care of it!

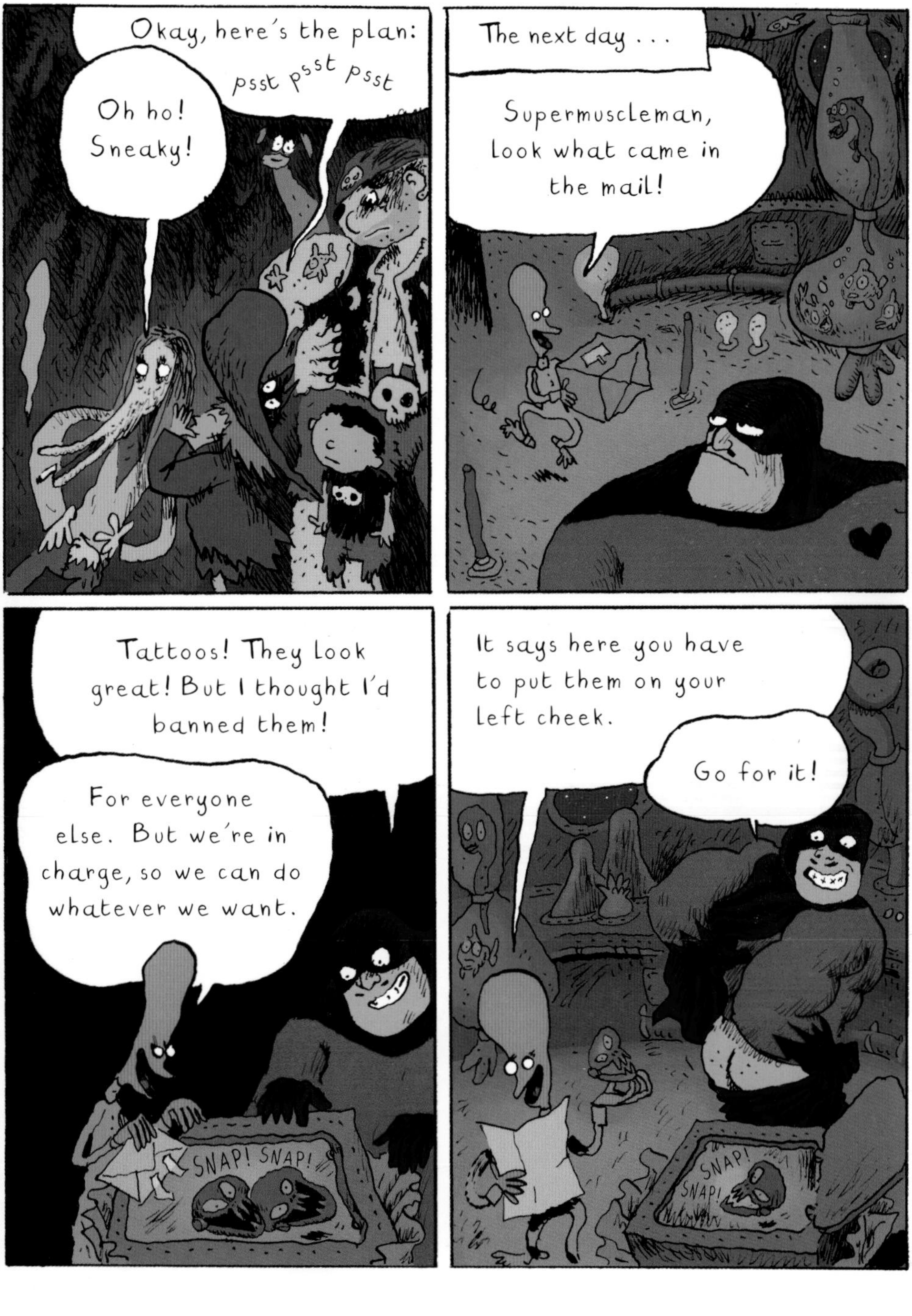
Okay, here's the plan:
psst psst psst
Oh ho! Sneaky!
The next day . . .
Supermuscleman, look what came in the mail!
Tattoos! They look great! But I thought I'd banned them!
For everyone else. But we're in charge, so we can do whatever we want.
SNAP! SNAP!
It says here you have to put them on your left cheek.
Go for it!
SNAP! SNAP!

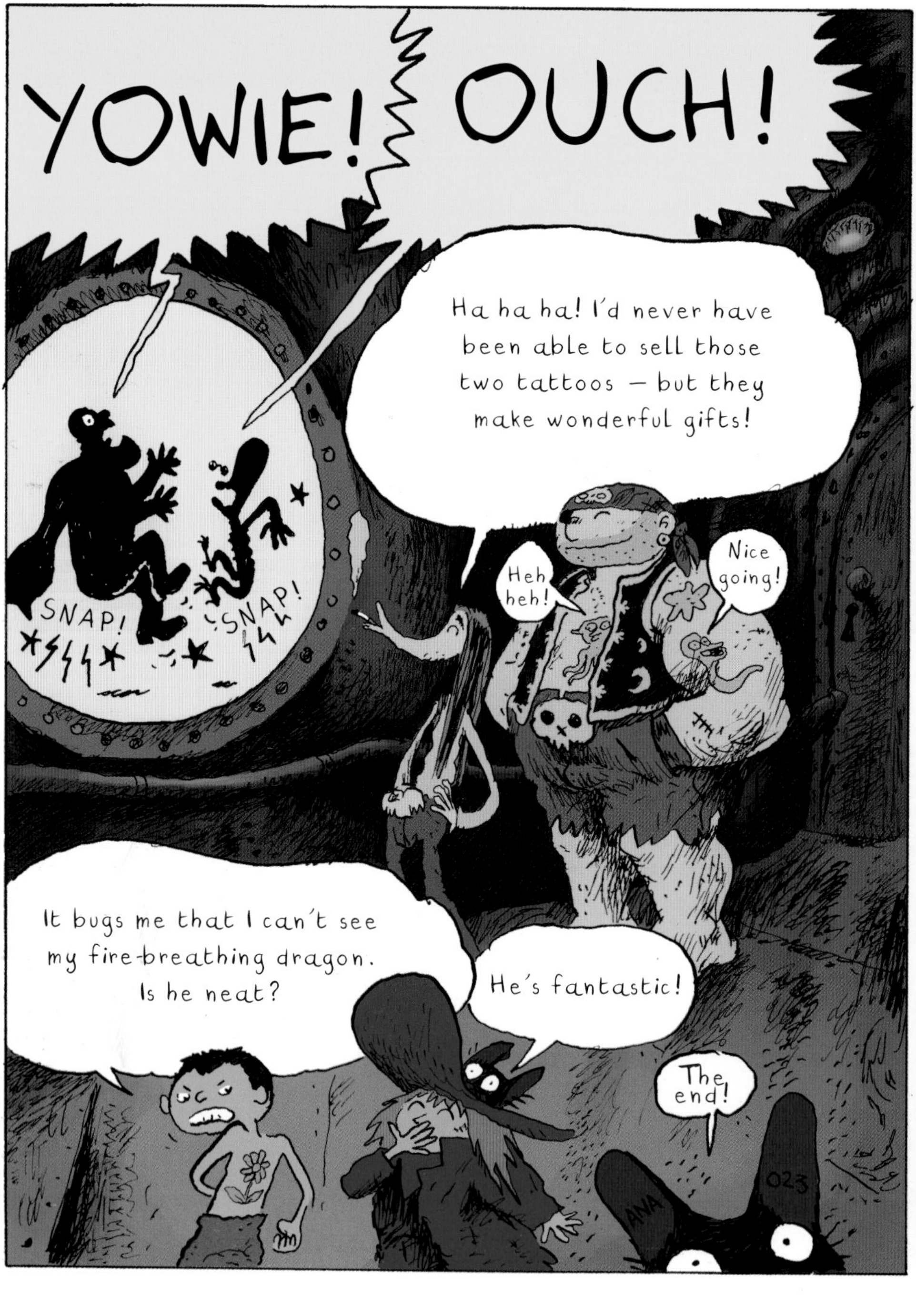
YOWIE!
OUCH!
SNAP!
SNAP!
Ha ha ha! I'd never have been able to sell those two tattoos — but they make wonderful gifts!
Heh heh!
Nice going!
It bugs me that I can't see my fire-breathing dragon. Is he neat?
He's fantastic!
The end!

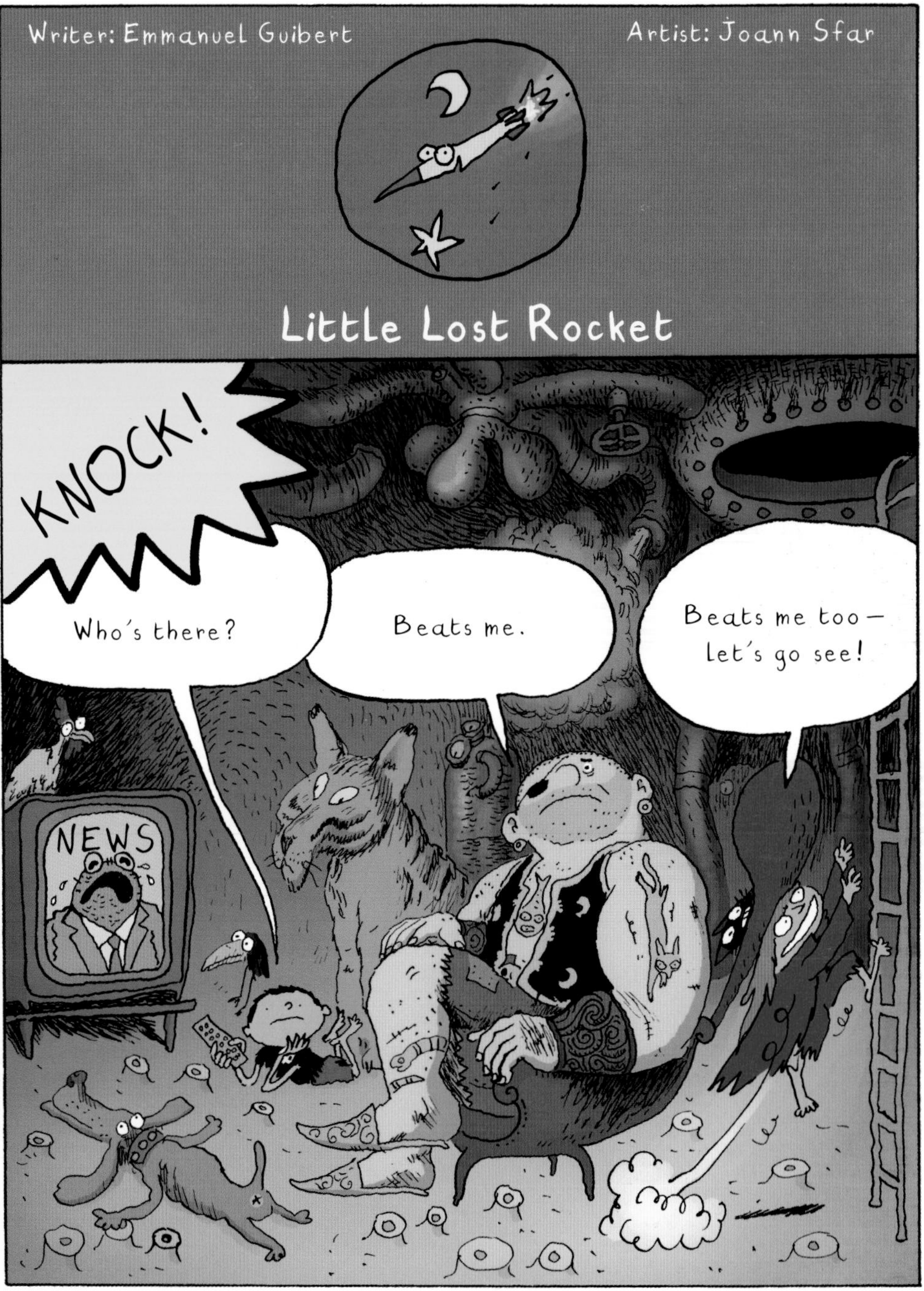
Writer: Emmanuel Guibert
Artist: Joann Sfar
Little Lost Rocket
KNOCK!
Who's there?
Beats me.
Beats me too—
let's go see!
NEWS

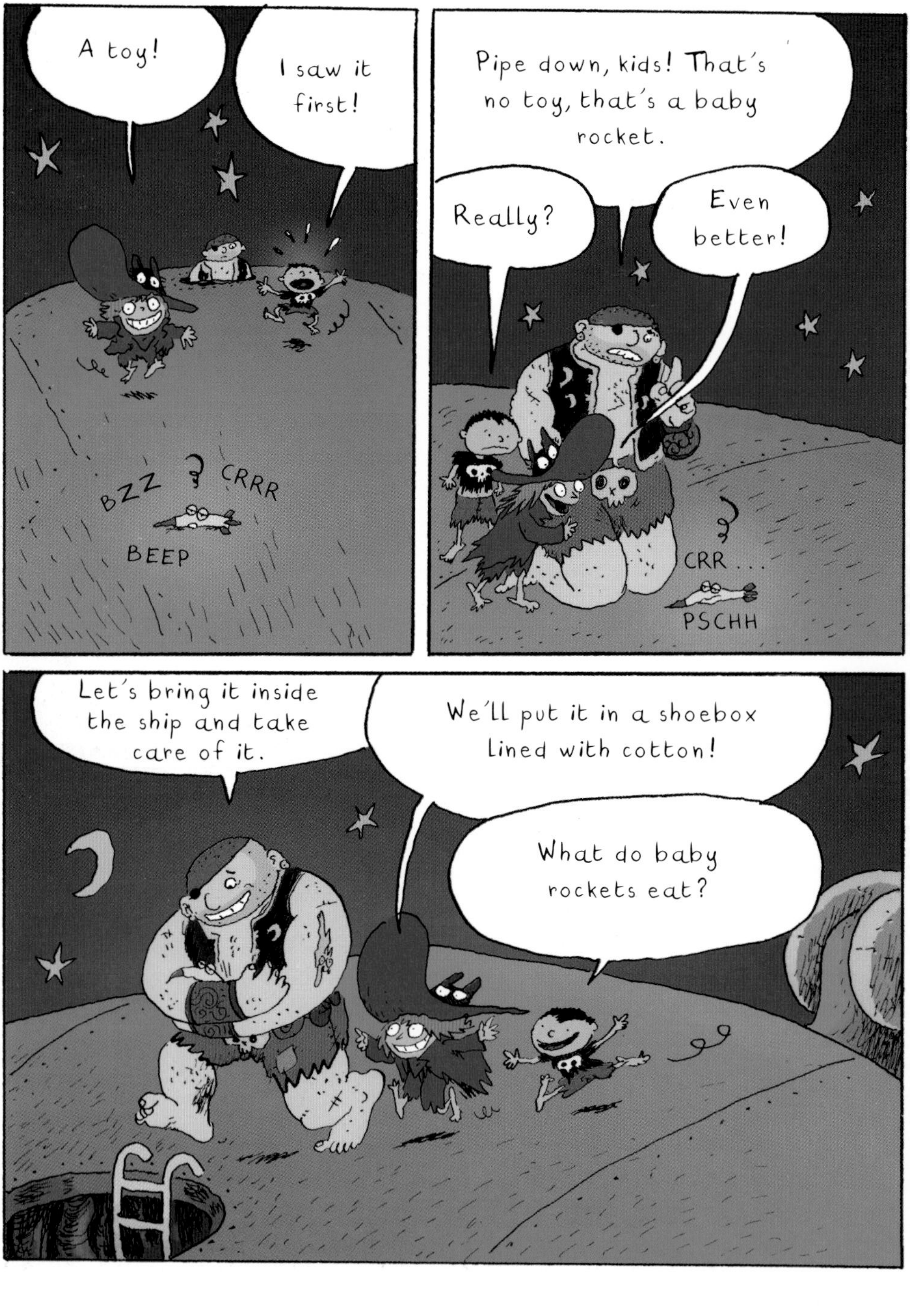
A toy!
I saw it first!
BZZ
CRRR
BEEP
Pipe down, kids! That's no toy, that's a baby rocket.
Really?
Even better!
CRR...
PSCHH
Let's bring it inside the ship and take care of it.
We'll put it in a shoebox lined with cotton!
What do baby rockets eat?

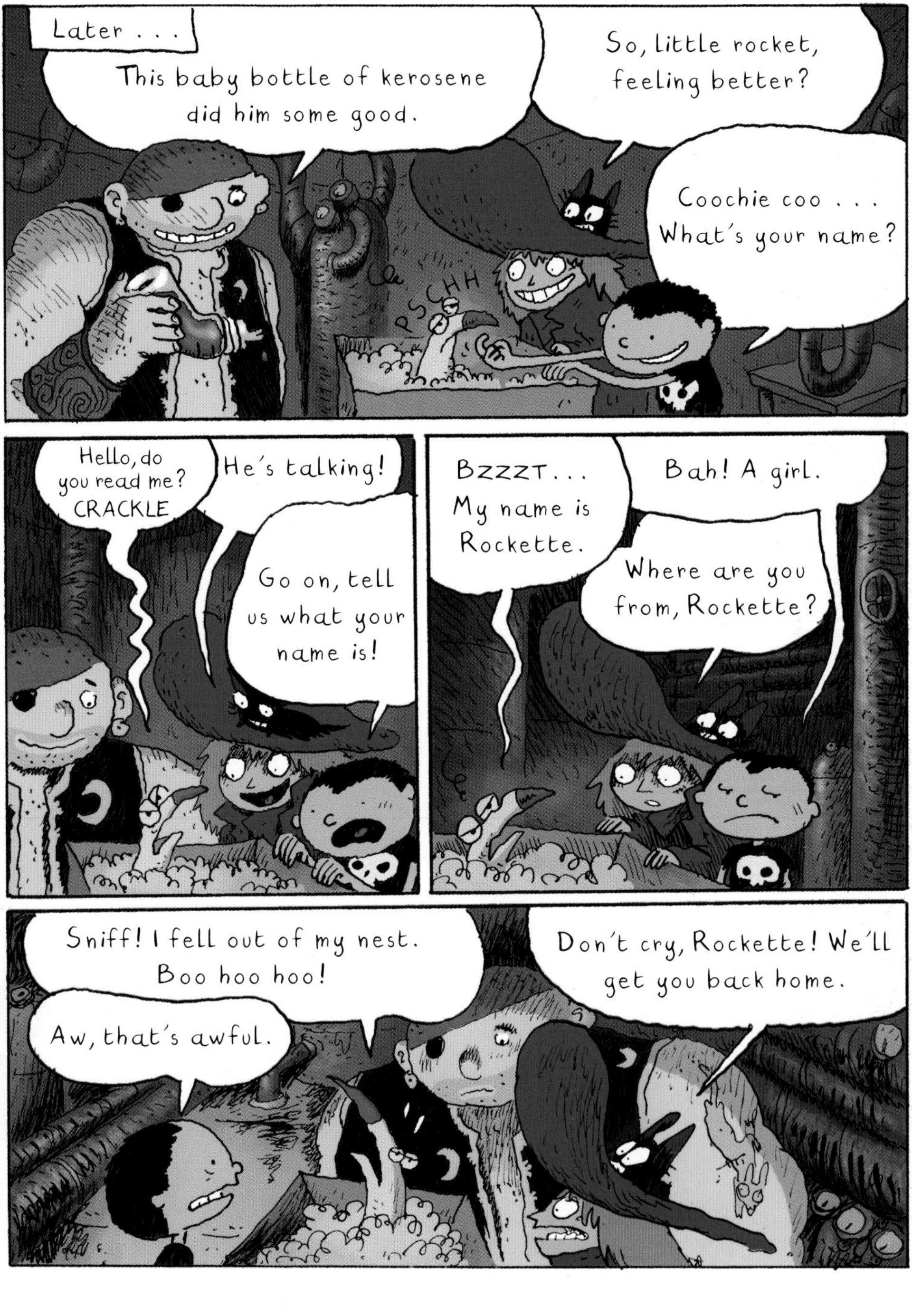
Later . . .
This baby bottle of kerosene did him some good.
So, little rocket, feeling better?
Coochie coo . . . What's your name?
PSCHH
Hello, do you read me? CRACKLE
He's talking!
Go on, tell us what your name is!
BZZZT . . . My name is Rockette.
Bah! A girl.
Where are you from, Rockette?
Sniff! I fell out of my nest. Boo hoo hoo!
Aw, that's awful.
Don't cry, Rockette! We'll get you back home.

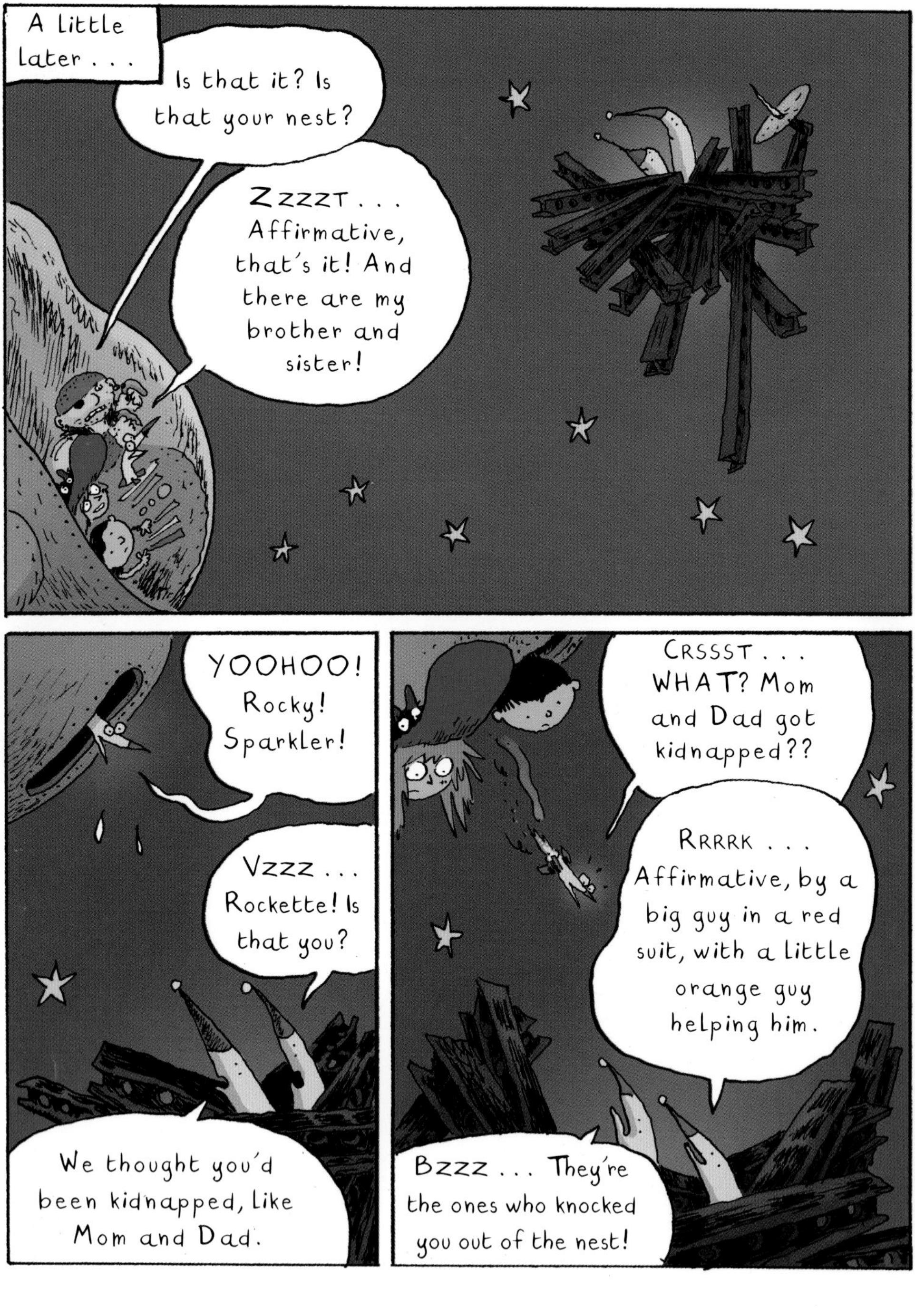
A little later . . .
Is that it? Is that your nest?
ZZZZT . . . Affirmative, that's it! And there are my brother and sister!
YOOHOO! Rocky! Sparkler!
Vzzz . . . Rockette! Is that you?
We thought you'd been kidnapped, like Mom and Dad.
CRSSST . . . WHAT? Mom and Dad got kidnapped??
RRRRK . . . Affirmative, by a big guy in a red suit, with a little orange guy helping him.
Bzzz . . . They're the ones who knocked you out of the nest!

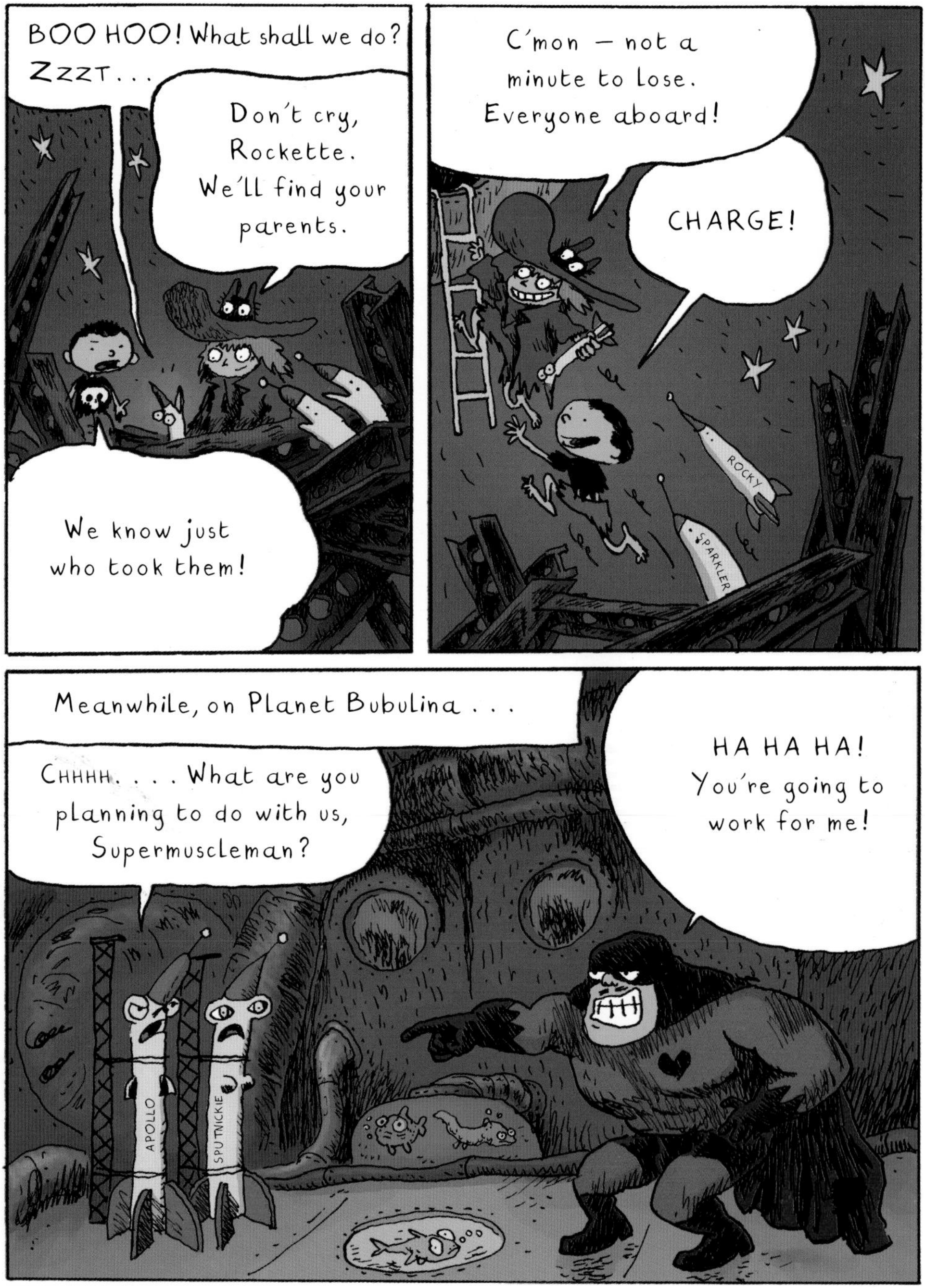
BOO HOO! What shall we do? ZZZT . . .
Don't cry, Rockette. We'll find your parents.
We know just who took them!
C'mon — not a minute to lose. Everyone aboard!
CHARGE!
ROCKY
SPARKLER
Meanwhile, on Planet Bubulina . . .
CHHHH. . . . What are you planning to do with us, Supermuscleman?
HA HA HA! You're going to work for me!
APOLLO
SPUTNICKIE

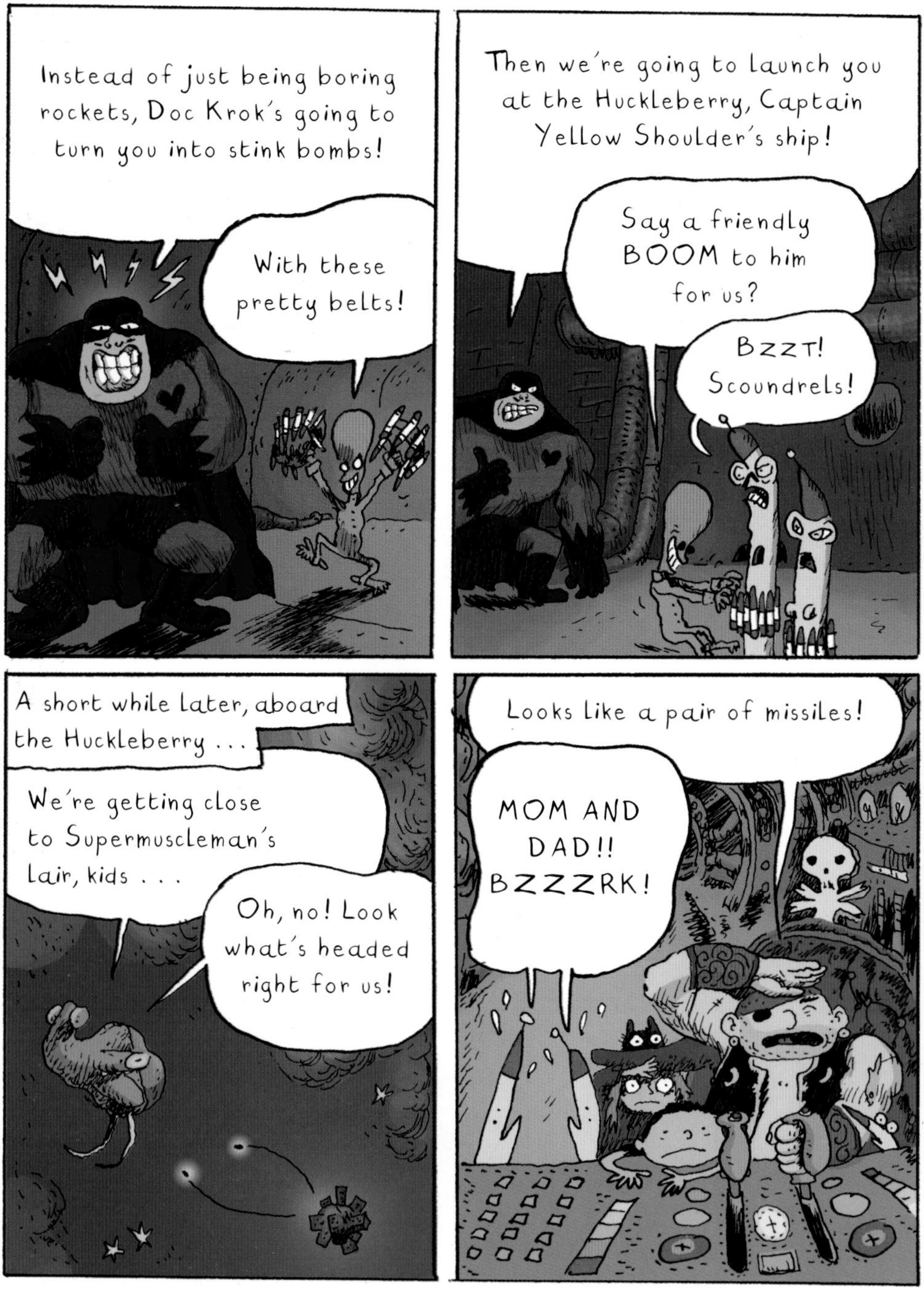
Instead of just being boring rockets, Doc Krok's going to turn you into stink bombs!
With these pretty belts!
Then we're going to launch you at the Huckleberry, Captain Yellow Shoulder's ship!
Say a friendly BOOM to him for us?
BZZT! Scoundrels!
A short while later, aboard the Huckleberry . . .
We're getting close to Supermuscleman's lair, kids . . .
Oh, no! Look what's headed right for us!
Looks like a pair of missiles!
MOM AND DAD!! BZZZRK!

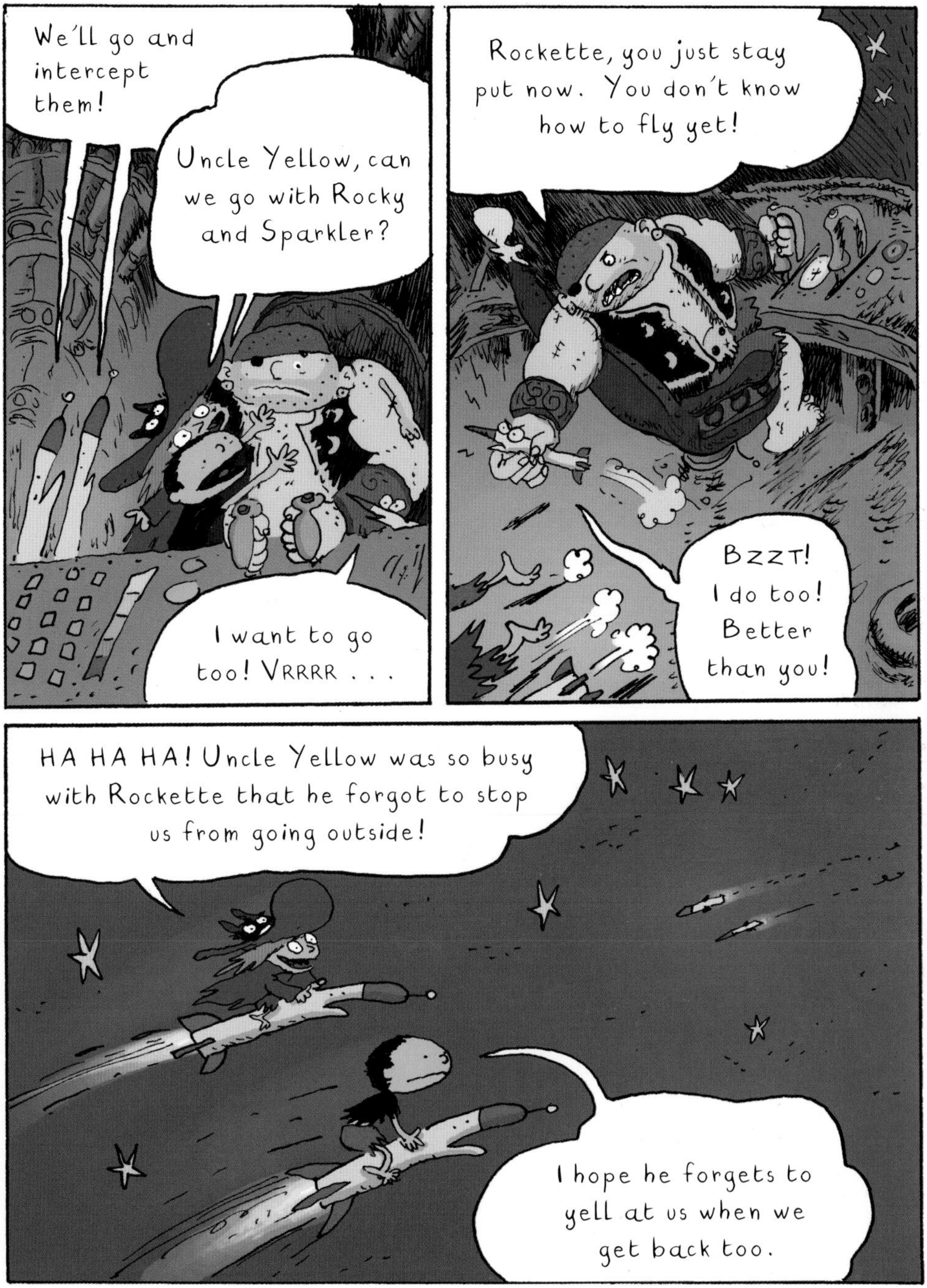
We'll go and intercept them!
Uncle Yellow, can we go with Rocky and Sparkler?
I want to go too! VRRRR . . .
Rockette, you just stay put now. You don't know how to fly yet!
BZZT! I do too! Better than you!
HA HA HA! Uncle Yellow was so busy with Rockette that he forgot to stop us from going outside!
I hope he forgets to yell at us when we get back too.

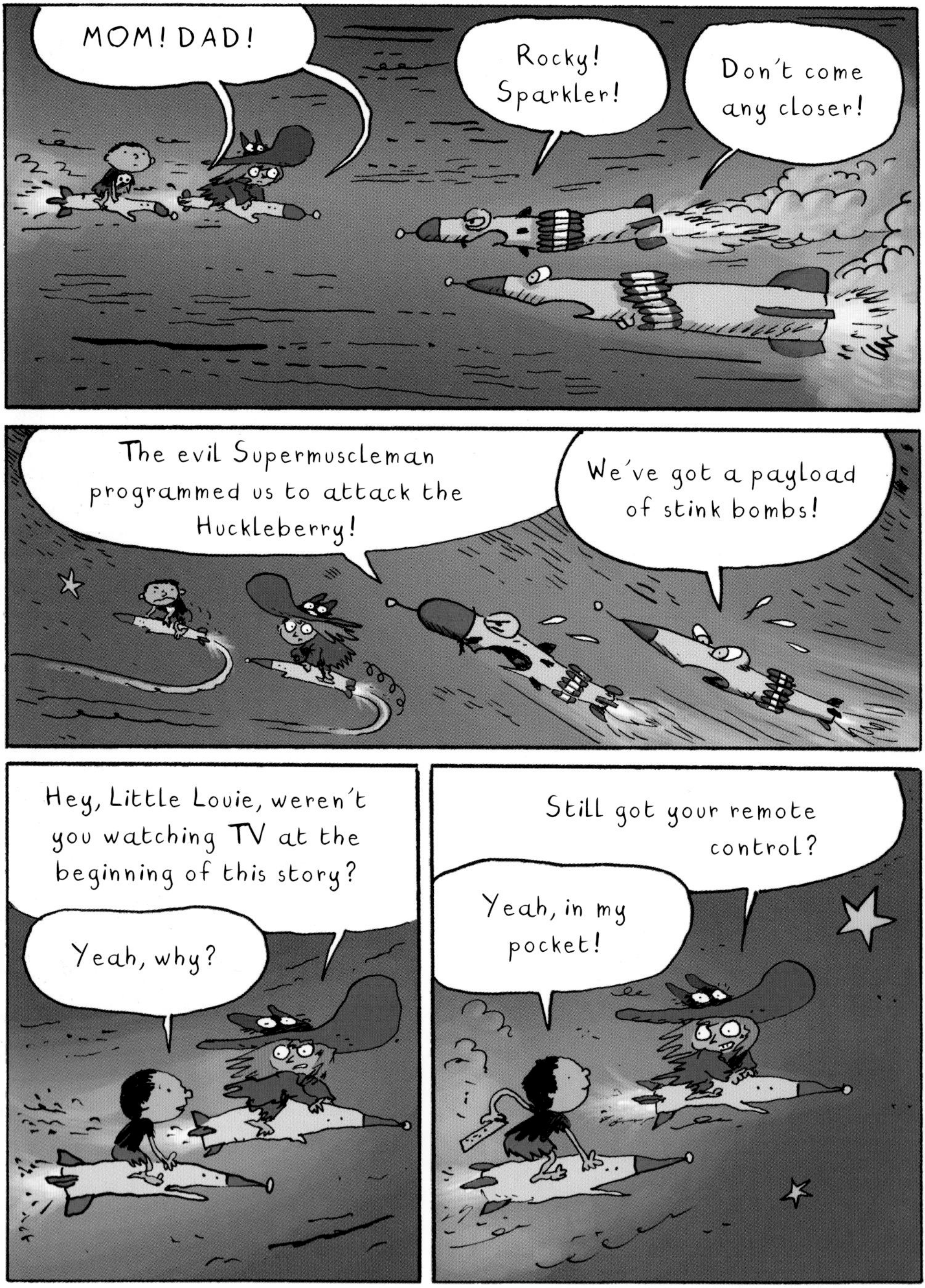
MOM! DAD!
Rocky! Sparkler!
Don't come any closer!
The evil Supermuscleman programmed us to attack the Huckleberry!
We've got a payload of stink bombs!
Hey, Little Louie, weren't you watching TV at the beginning of this story?
Yeah, why?
Still got your remote control?
Yeah, in my pocket!

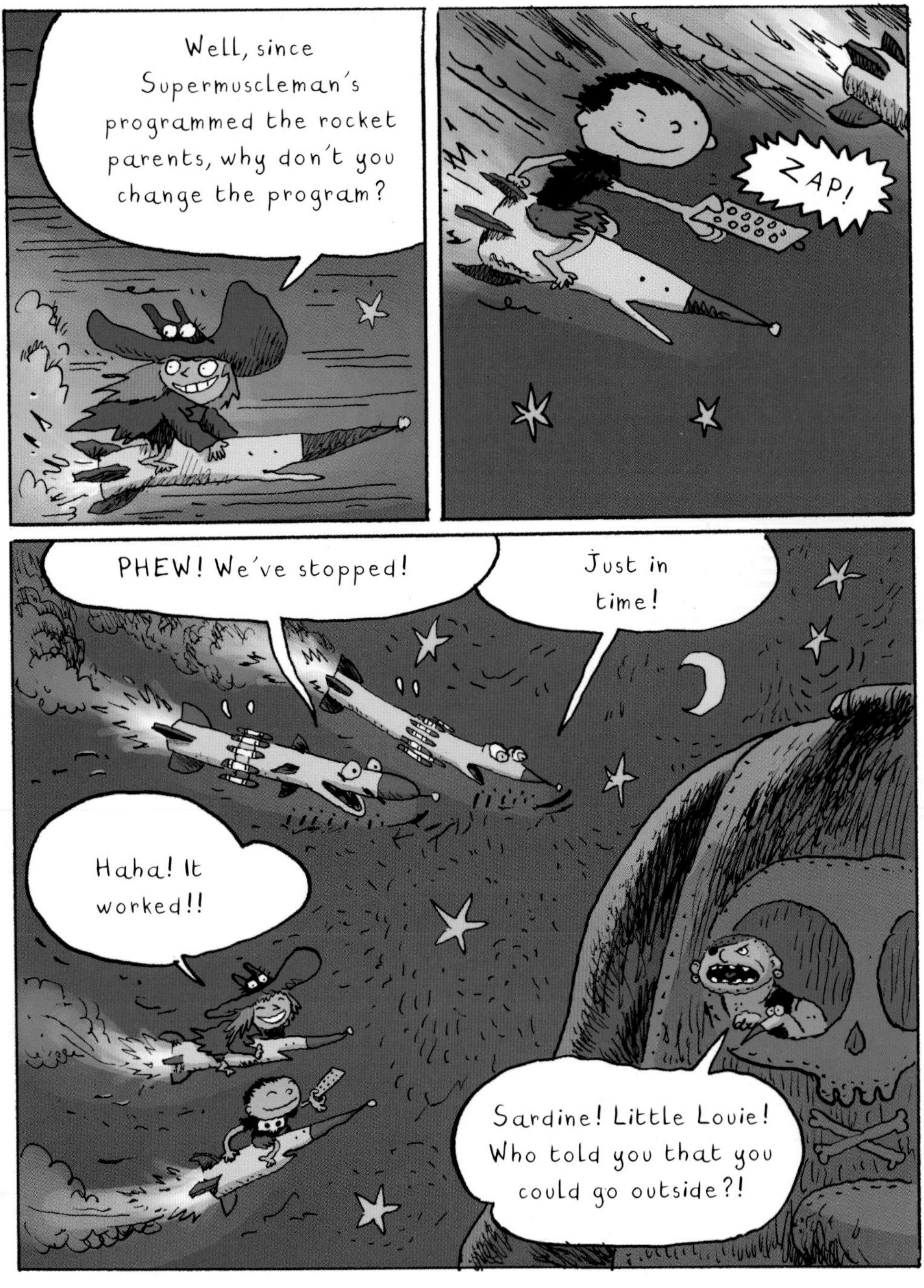
Well, since Supermuscleman's programmed the rocket parents, why don't you change the program?
ZAP!
PHEW! We've stopped!
Just in time!
Haha! It worked!!
Sardine! Little Louie! Who told you that you could go outside?!

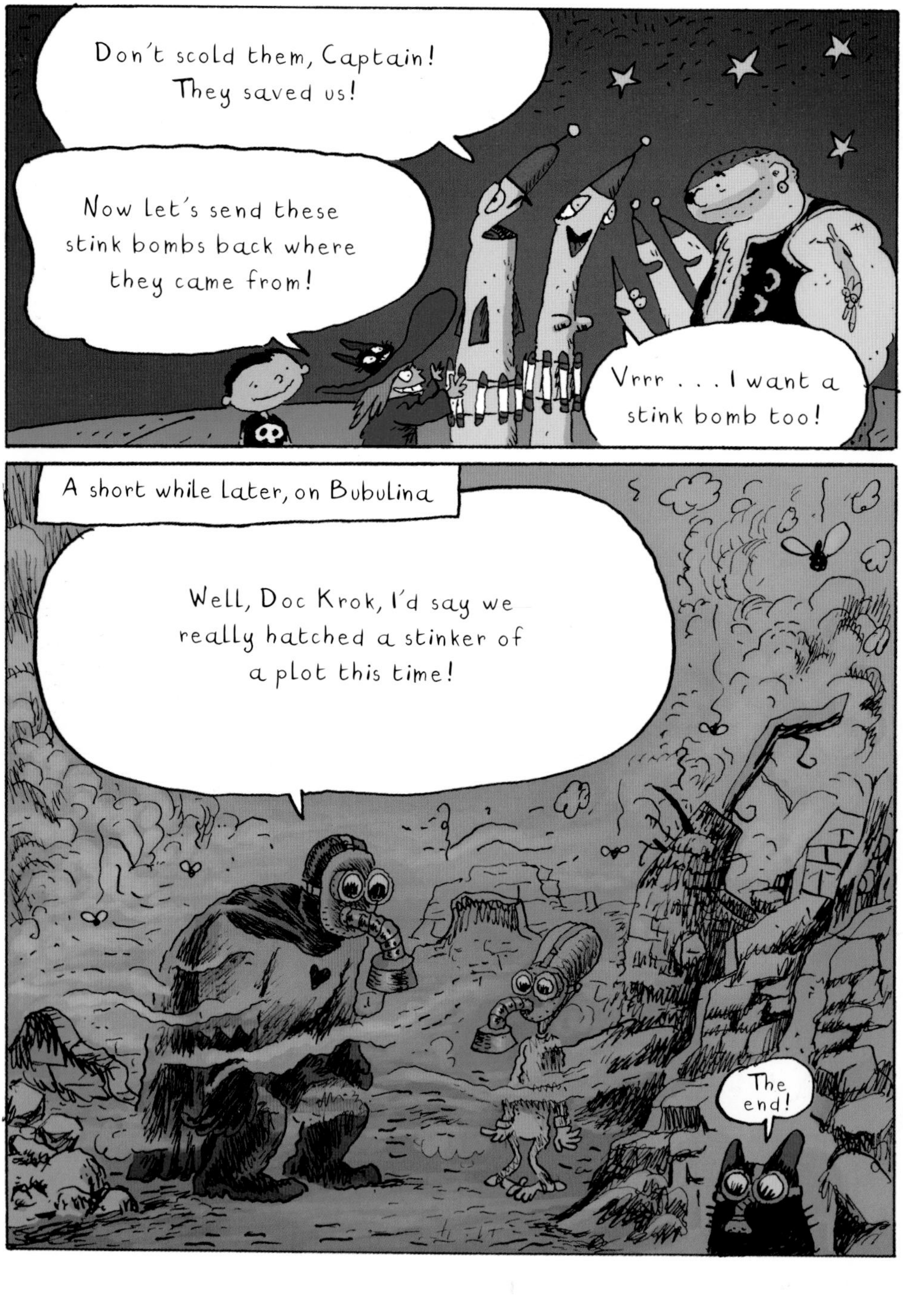
Don't scold them, Captain! They saved us!
Now let's send these stink bombs back where they came from!
Vrrr . . . I want a stink bomb too!
A short while later, on Bubulina
Well, Doc Krok, I'd say we really hatched a stinker of a plot this time!
The end!

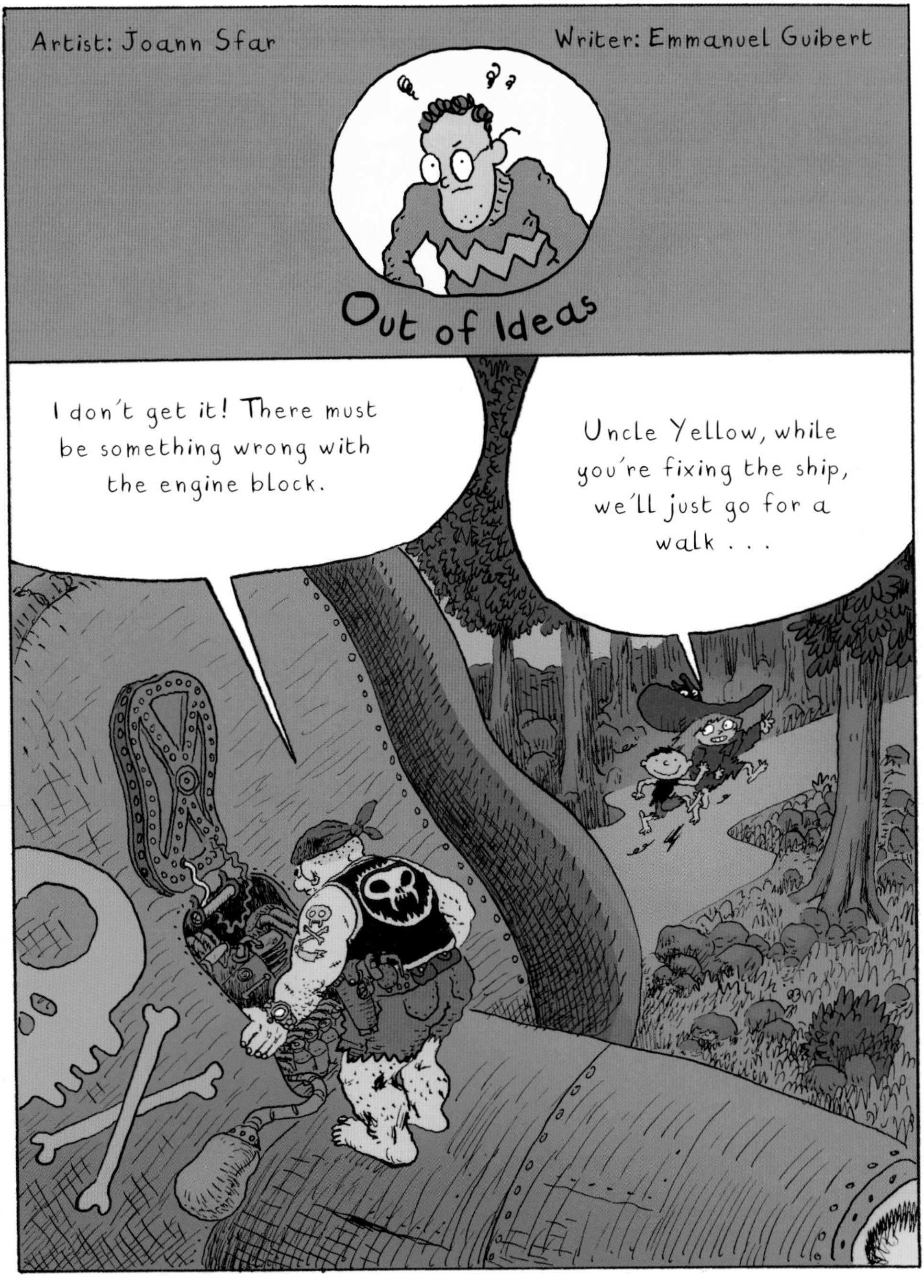
Artist: Joann Sfar
Writer: Emmanuel Guibert
Out of Ideas
I don't get it! There must be something wrong with the engine block.
Uncle Yellow, while you're fixing the ship, we'll just go for a walk . . .

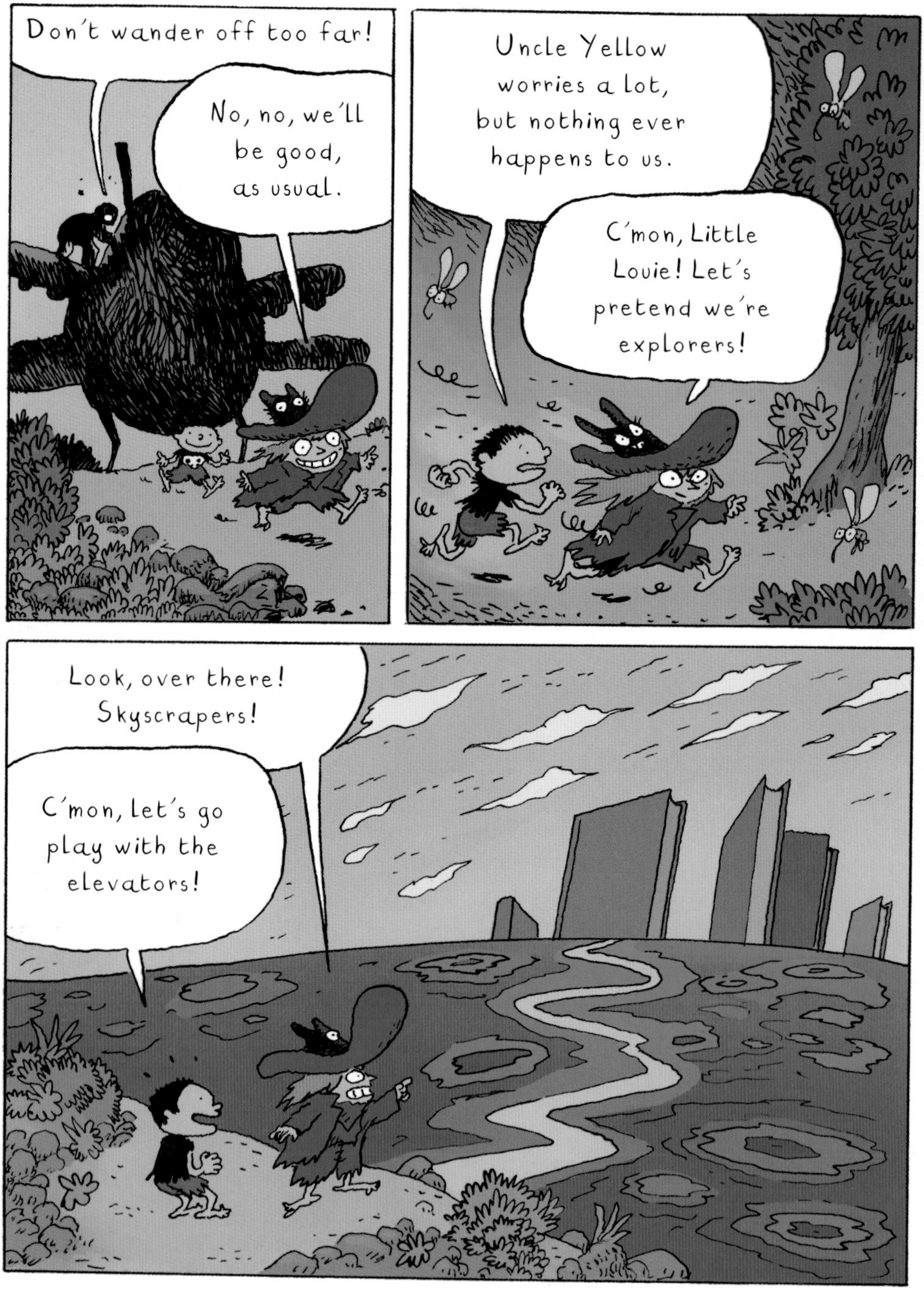
Don't wander off too far!
No, no, we'll be good, as usual.
Uncle Yellow worries a lot, but nothing ever happens to us.
C'mon, Little Louie! Let's pretend we're explorers!
Look, over there! Skyscrapers!
C'mon, let's go play with the elevators!

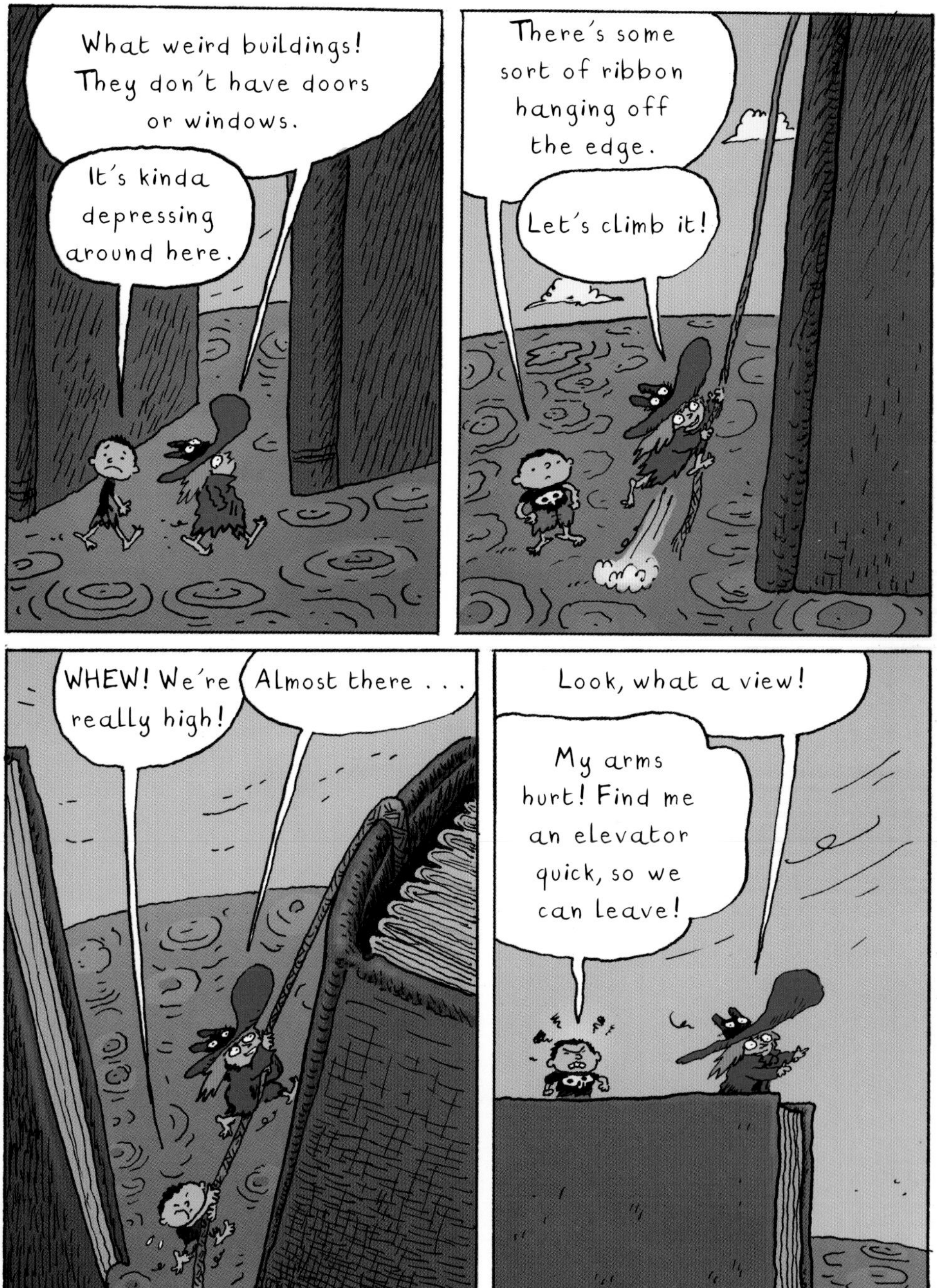
What weird buildings! They don't have doors or windows.
It's kinda depressing around here.
There's some sort of ribbon hanging off the edge.
Let's climb it!
WHEW! We're really high!
Almost there . . .
Look, what a view!
My arms hurt! Find me an elevator quick, so we can leave!

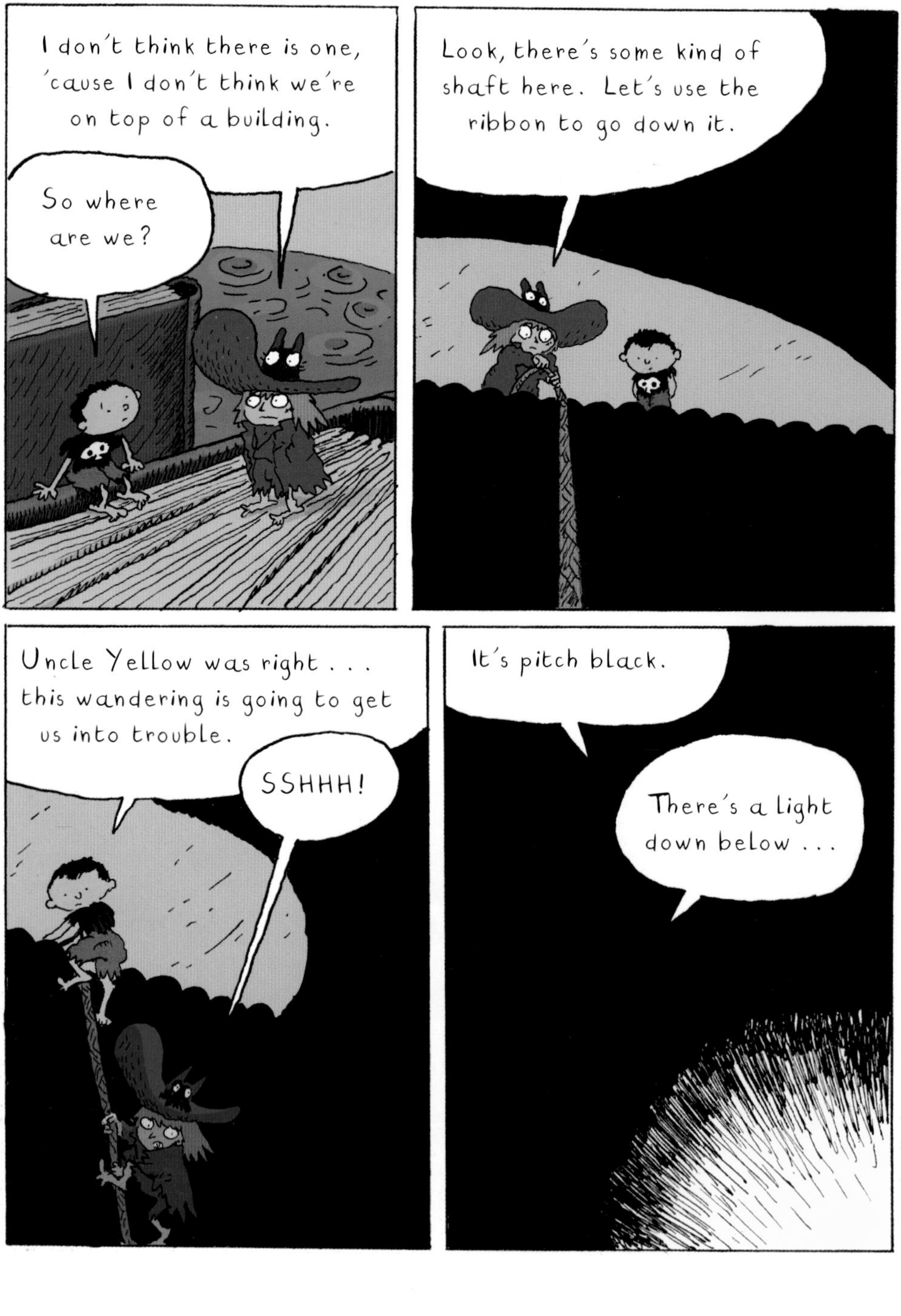
I don't think there is one, 'cause I don't think we're on top of a building.
So where are we?
Look, there's some kind of shaft here. Let's use the ribbon to go down it.
Uncle Yellow was right . . . this wandering is going to get us into trouble.
SSHHH!
It's pitch black.
There's a light down below . . .

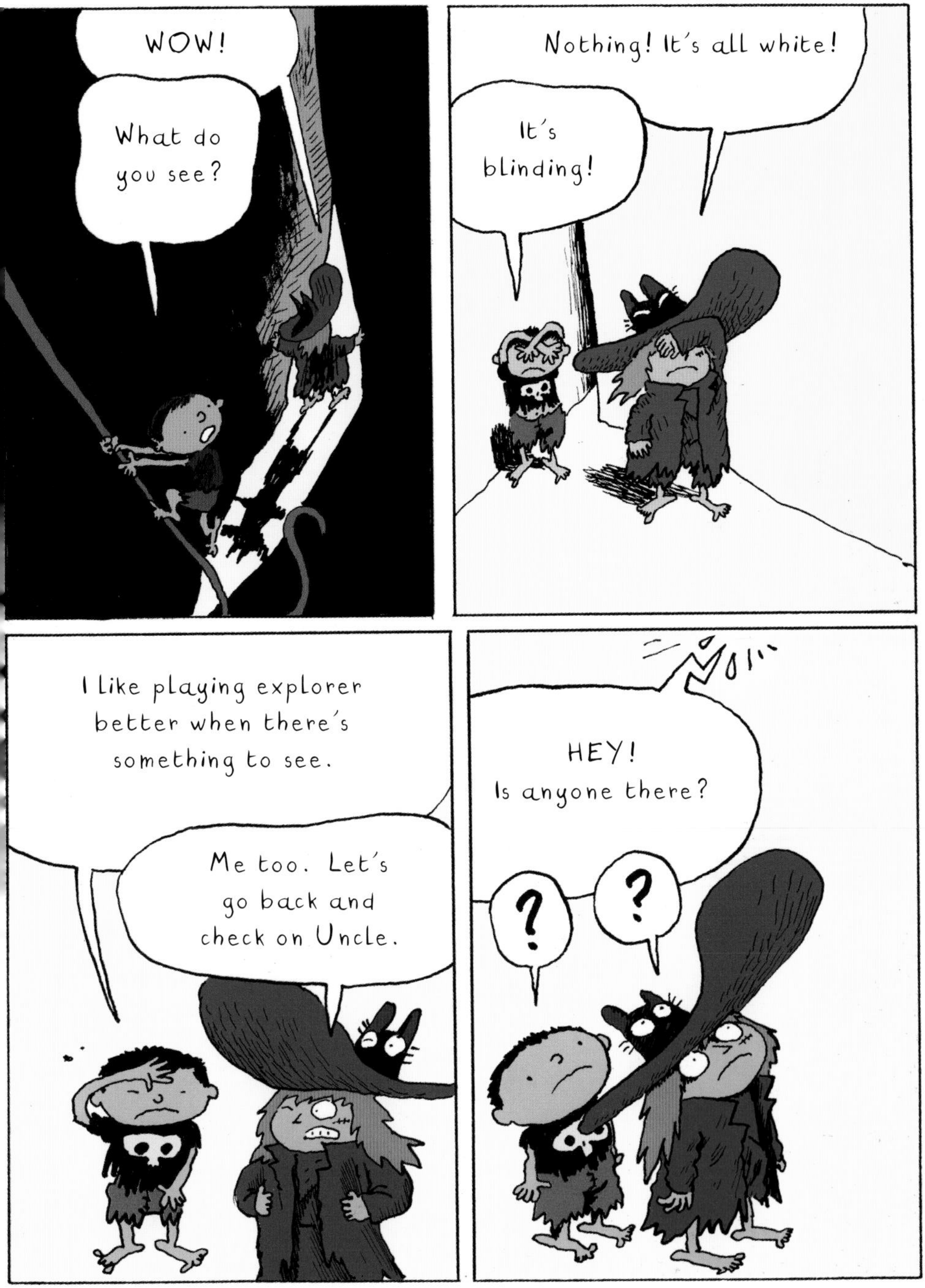
WOW!
What do you see?
Nothing! It's all white!
It's blinding!
I like playing explorer better when there's something to see.
Me too. Let's go back and check on Uncle.
HEY! Is anyone there?
?
?

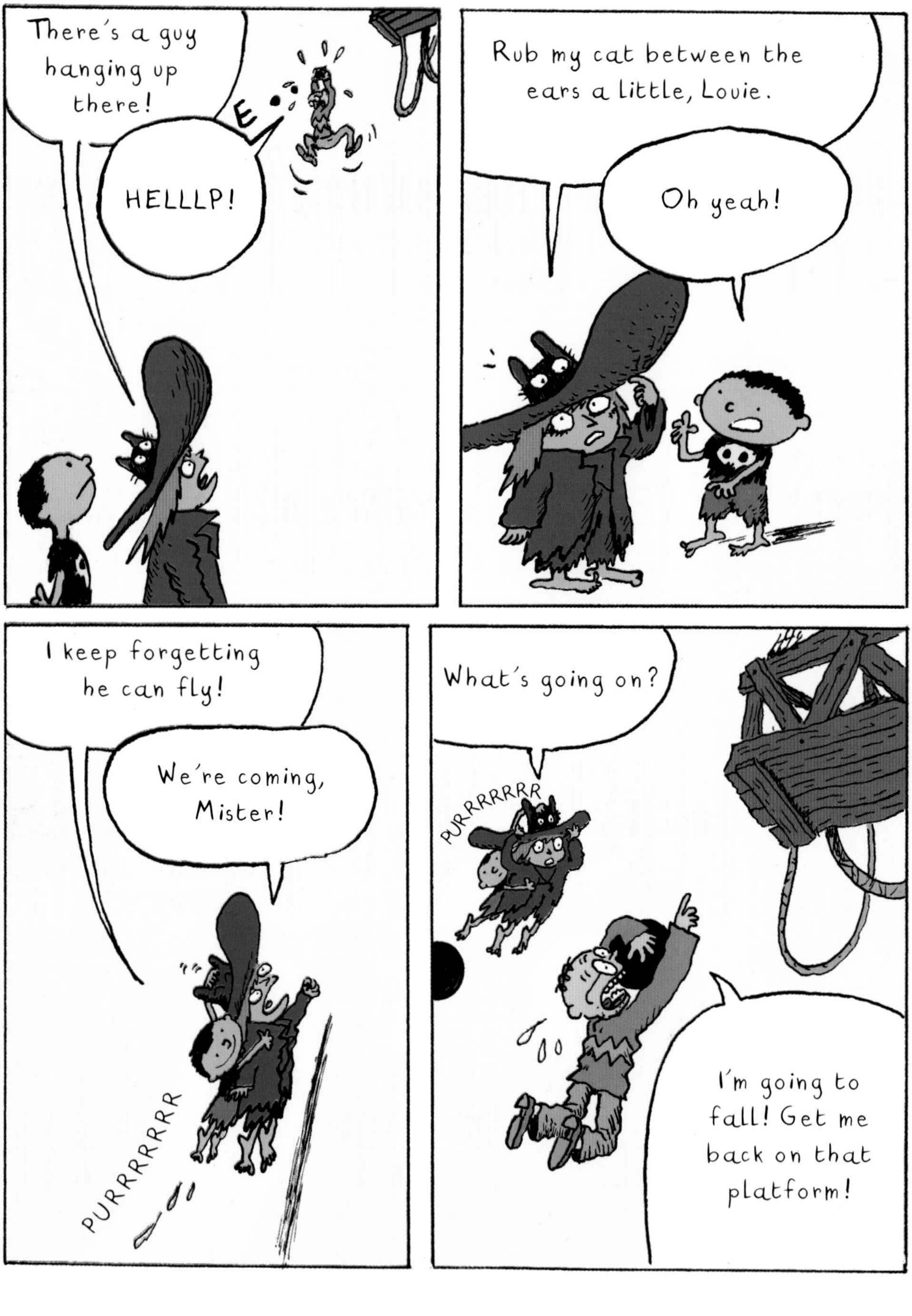
There's a guy hanging up there!
HELLLP!
E
Rub my cat between the ears a little, Louie.
Oh yeah!
I keep forgetting he can fly!
We're coming, Mister!
PURRRRRRR
What's going on?
PURRRRRRR
I'm going to fall! Get me back on that platform!

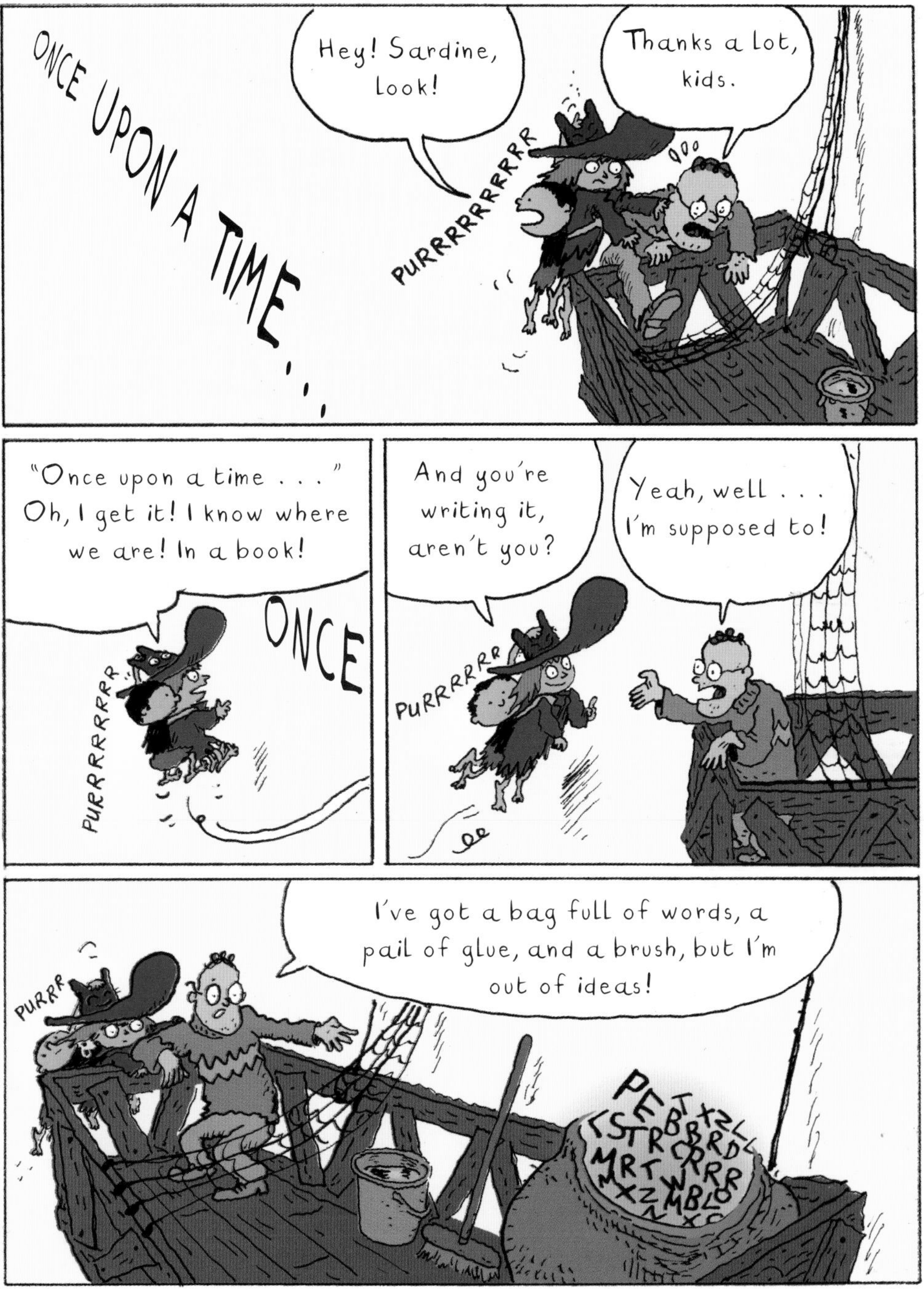
ONCE UPON A TIME . . .
Hey! Sardine, look!
PURRRRRRRRRR
Thanks a lot, kids.
"Once upon a time . . ." Oh, I get it! I know where we are! In a book!
ONCE
PURRRRRRRRR
And you're writing it, aren't you?
PURRRRRRR
Yeah, well . . . I'm supposed to!
I've got a bag full of words, a pail of glue, and a brush, but I'm out of ideas!
PURRR

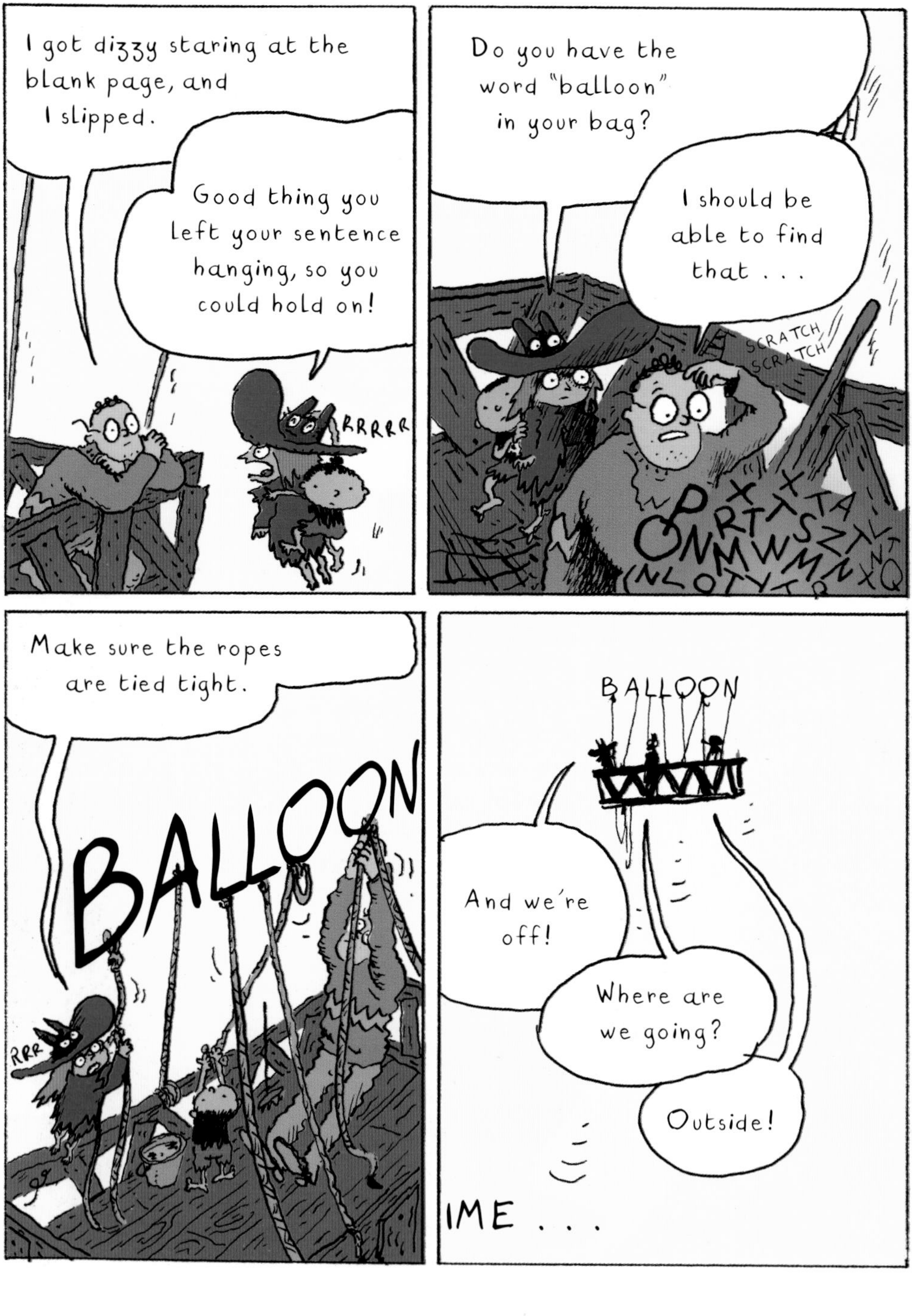
I got dizzy staring at the blank page, and I slipped.
Good thing you left your sentence hanging, so you could hold on!
RRRRR
Do you have the word "balloon" in your bag?
I should be able to find that . . .
SCRATCH SCRATCH
Make sure the ropes are tied tight.
BALLOON
RRR
BALLOON
And we're off!
Where are we going?
Outside!
IME . . .

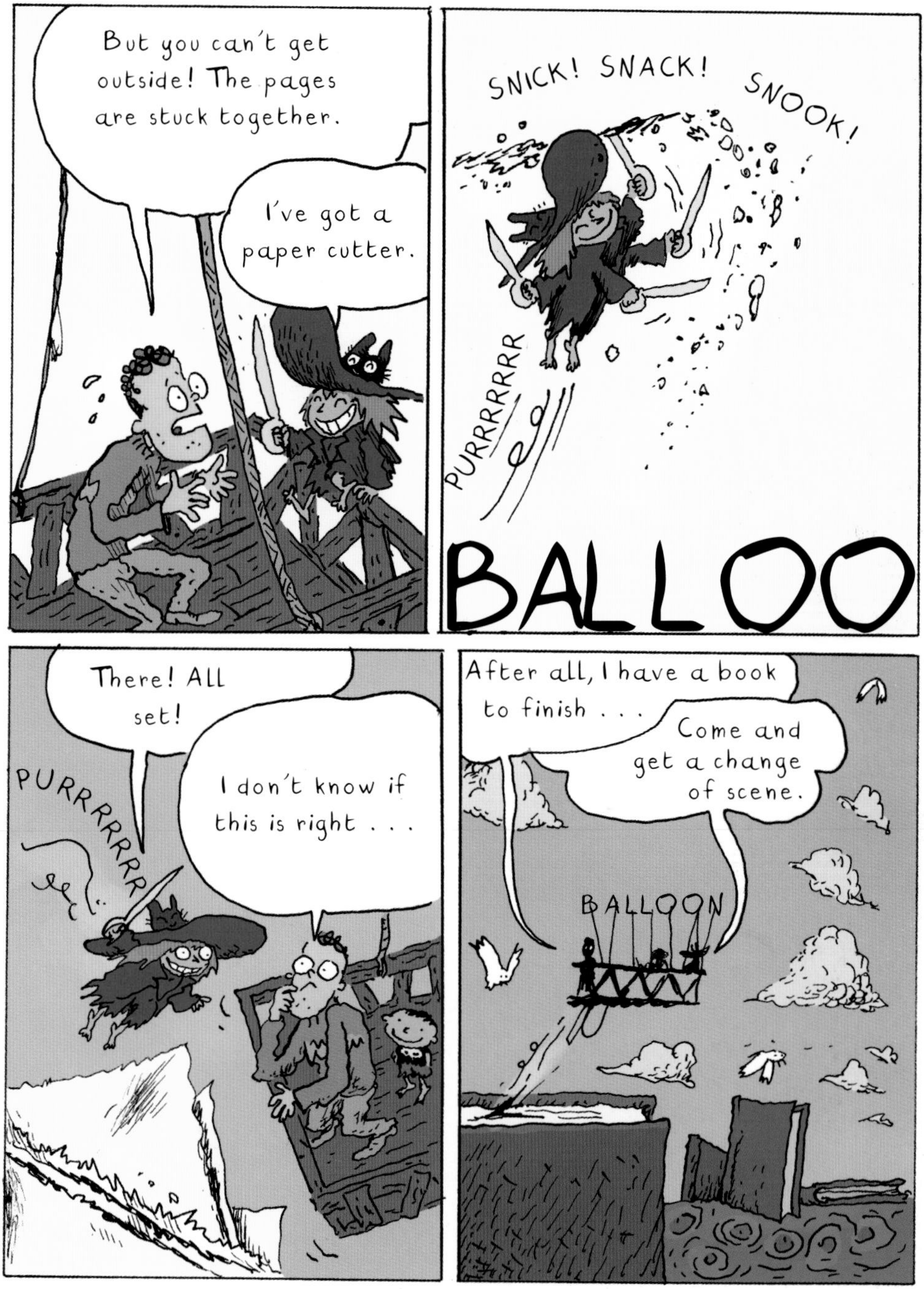

But you can't get outside! The pages are stuck together.
I've got a paper cutter.
SNICK! SNACK!
SNOOK!
PURRRRRRR
BALLOO
There! ALL set!
PURRRRRRRR
I don't know if this is right . . .
After all, I have a book to finish . . .
Come and get a change of scene.
BALLOON

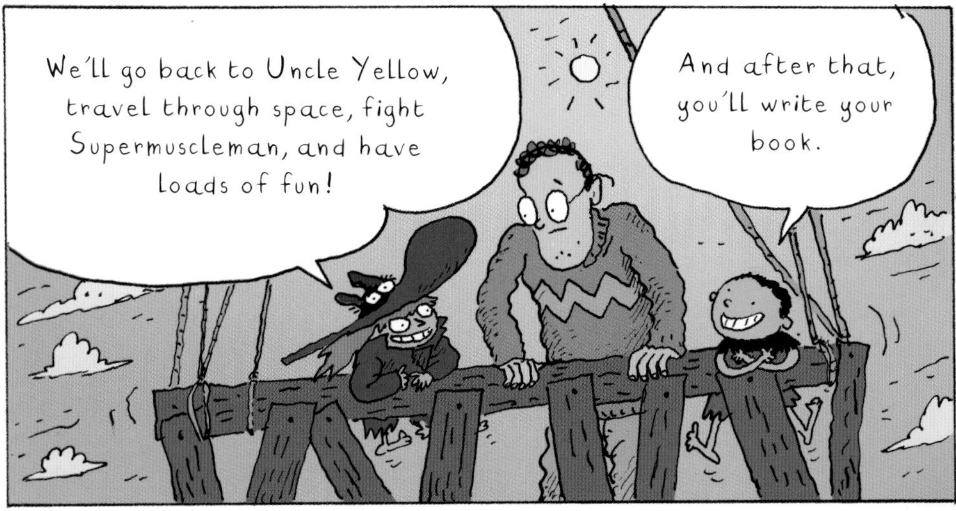
We'll go back to Uncle Yellow, travel through space, fight Supermuscleman, and have loads of fun!
And after that, you'll write your book.

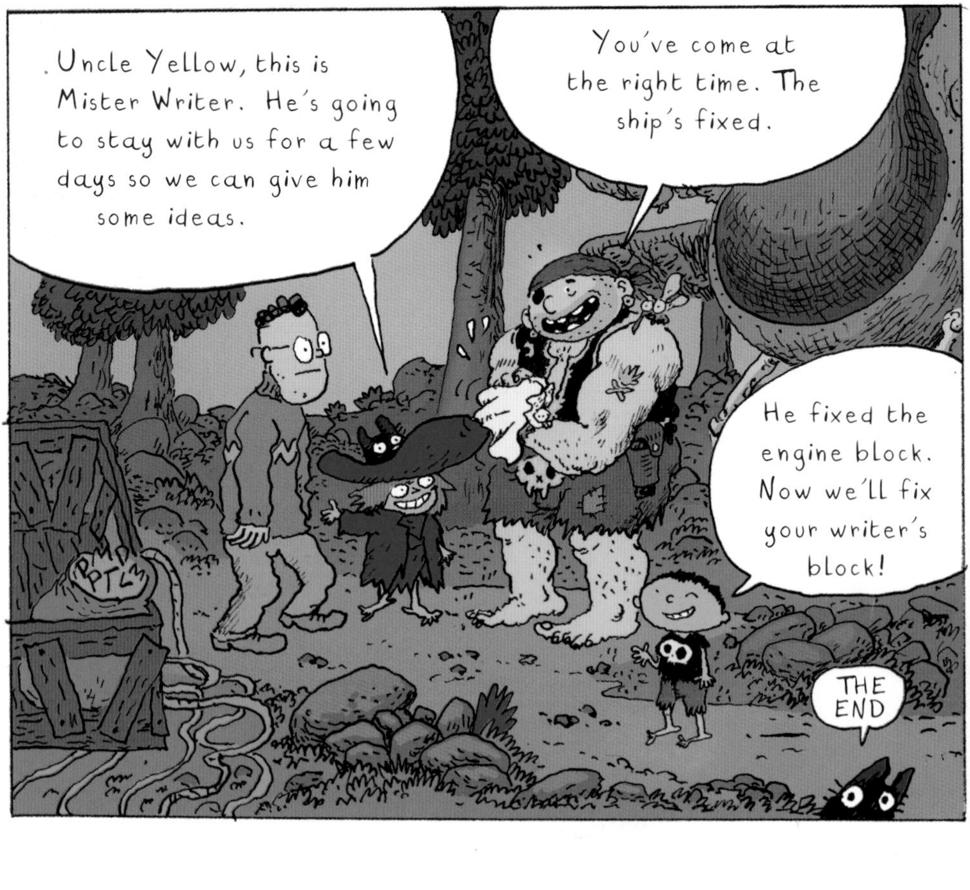
Uncle Yellow, this is Mister Writer. He's going to stay with us for a few days so we can give him some ideas.
You've come at the right time. The ship's fixed.
He fixed the engine block. Now we'll fix your writer's block!
THE END

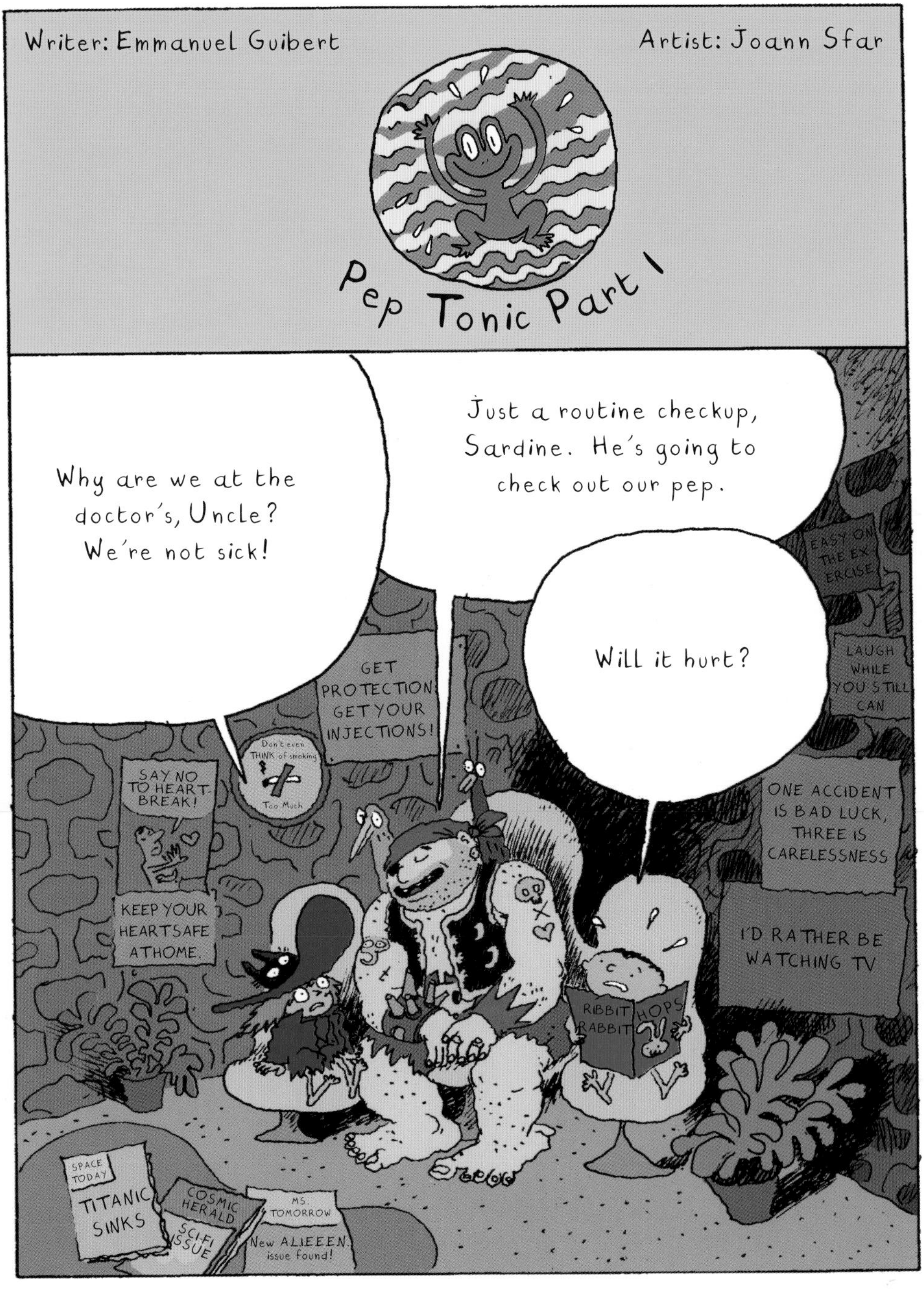
Writer: Emmanuel Guibert
Artist: Joann Sfar
Pep Tonic Part 1
Why are we at the doctor's, Uncle? We're not sick!
Just a routine checkup, Sardine. He's going to check out our pep.
Will it hurt?
GET PROTECTION: GET YOUR INJECTIONS!
Don't even THINK of smoking Too Much
SAY NO TO HEART-BREAK!
KEEP YOUR HEARTSAFE ATHOME.
EASY ON THE EXERCISE
LAUGH WHILE YOU STILL CAN
ONE ACCIDENT IS BAD LUCK, THREE IS CARELESSNESS
I'D RATHER BE WATCHING TV
RIBBIT RABBIT HOPS
SPACE TODAY
TITANIC SINKS
COSMIC HERALD
SCI-FI ISSUE
MS. TOMORROW
New ALIEEEN issue found!

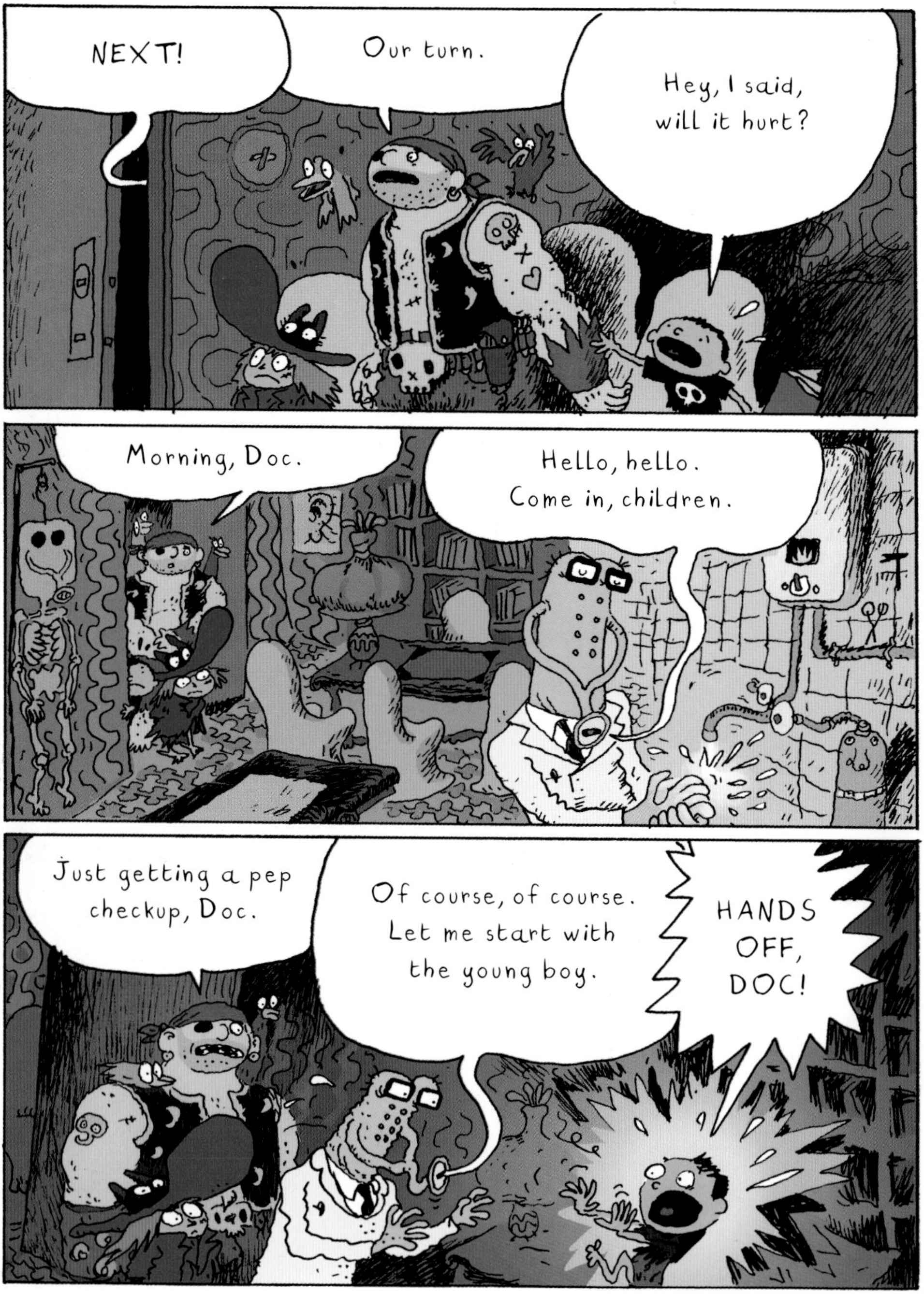
NEXT!
Our turn.
Hey, I said, will it hurt?
Morning, Doc.
Hello, hello. Come in, children.
Just getting a pep checkup, Doc.
Of course, of course. Let me start with the young boy.
HANDS OFF, DOC!

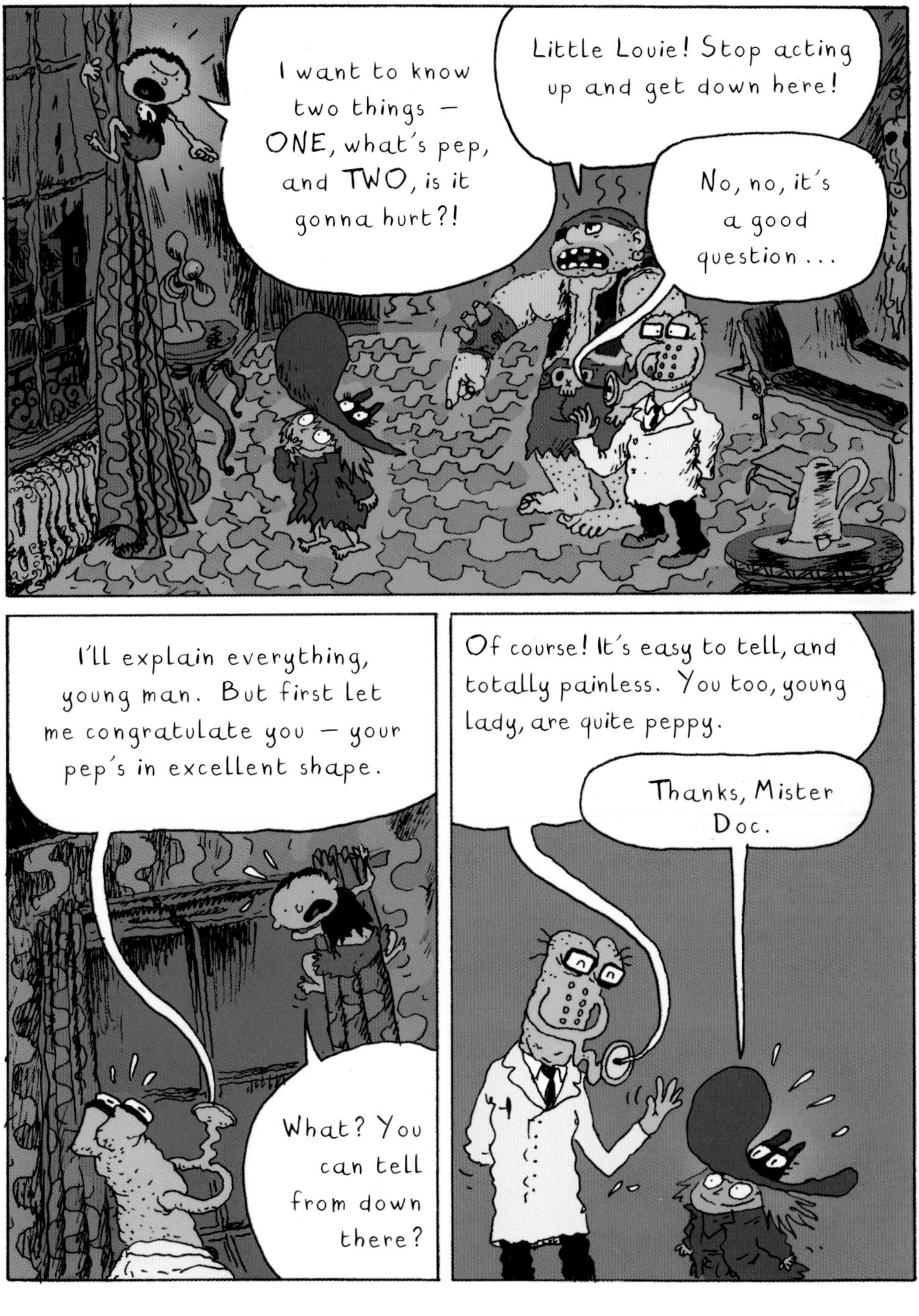
I want to know two things — ONE, what's pep, and TWO, is it gonna hurt?!
Little Louie! Stop acting up and get down here!
No, no, it's a good question...
I'll explain everything, young man. But first let me congratulate you — your pep's in excellent shape.
What? You can tell from down there?
Of course! It's easy to tell, and totally painless. You too, young lady, are quite peppy.
Thanks, Mister Doc.

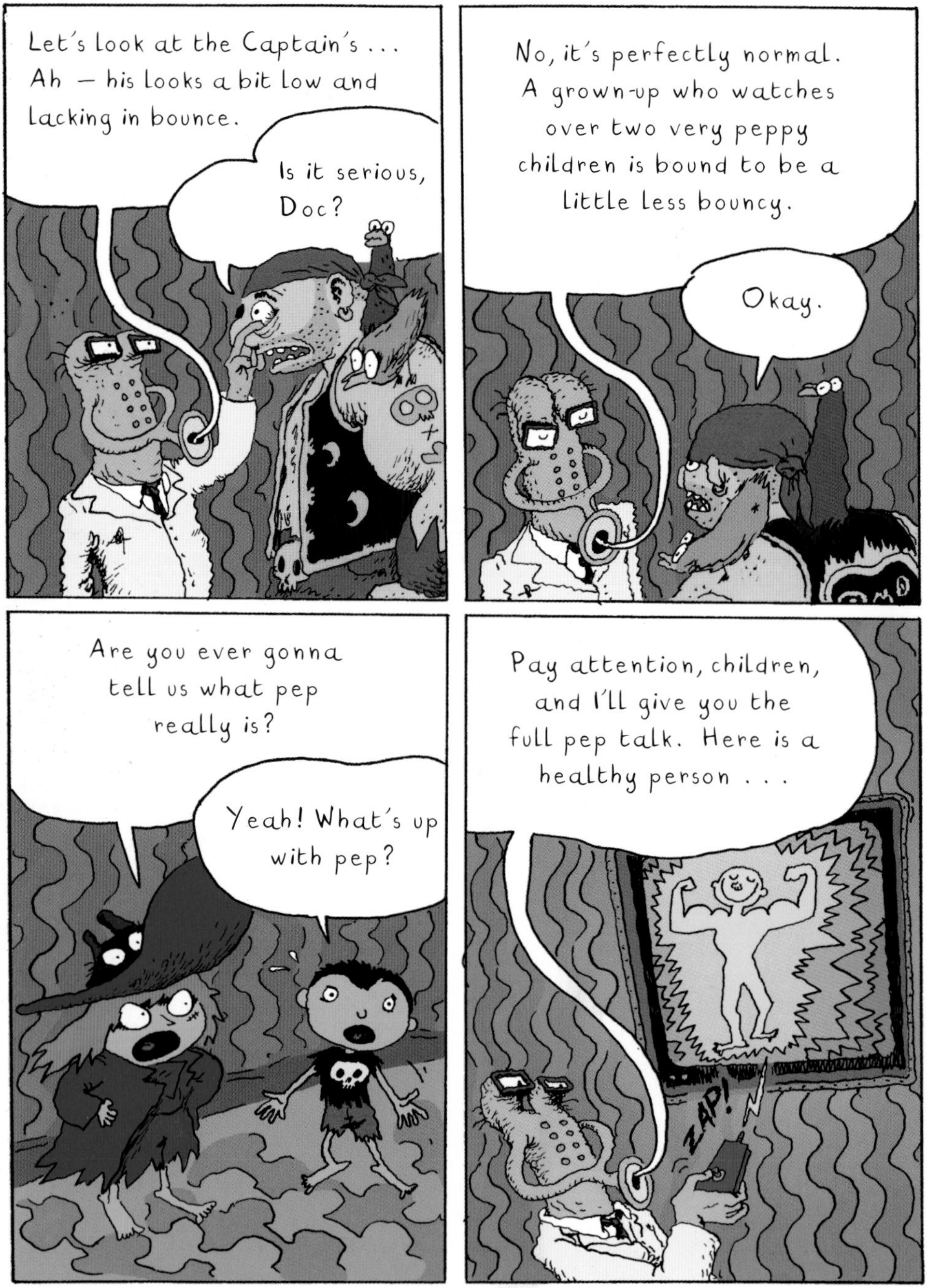

Let's look at the Captain's . . . Ah — his looks a bit low and lacking in bounce.
Is it serious, Doc?
No, it's perfectly normal. A grown-up who watches over two very peppy children is bound to be a little less bouncy.
Okay.
Are you ever gonna tell us what pep really is?
Yeah! What's up with pep?
Pay attention, children, and I'll give you the full pep talk. Here is a healthy person . . .
ZAP!

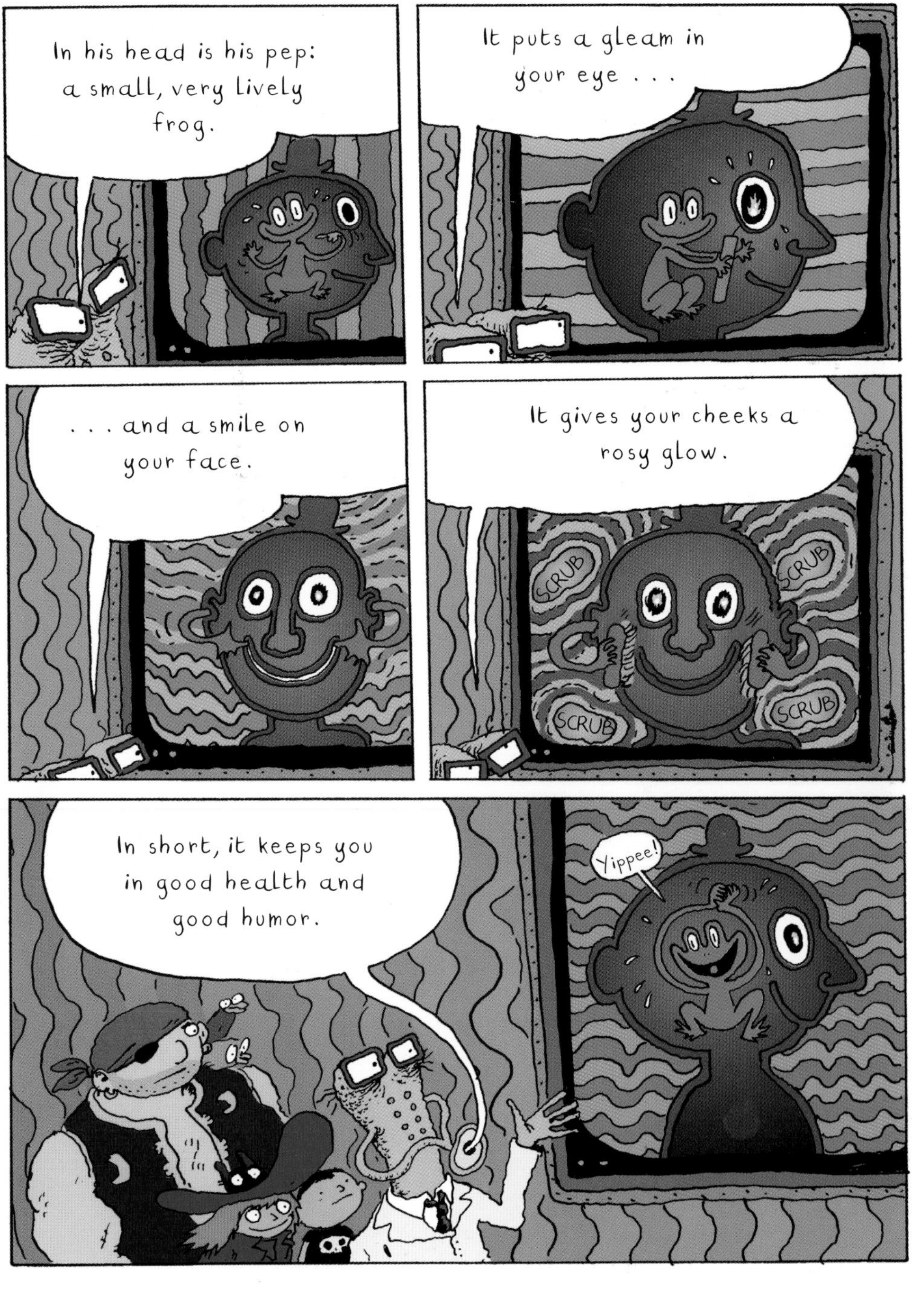

In his head is his pep: a small, very lively frog.
It puts a gleam in your eye . . .
. . . and a smile on your face.
It gives your cheeks a rosy glow.
SCRUB
SCRUB
SCRUB
SCRUB
In short, it keeps you in good health and good humor.
Yippee!

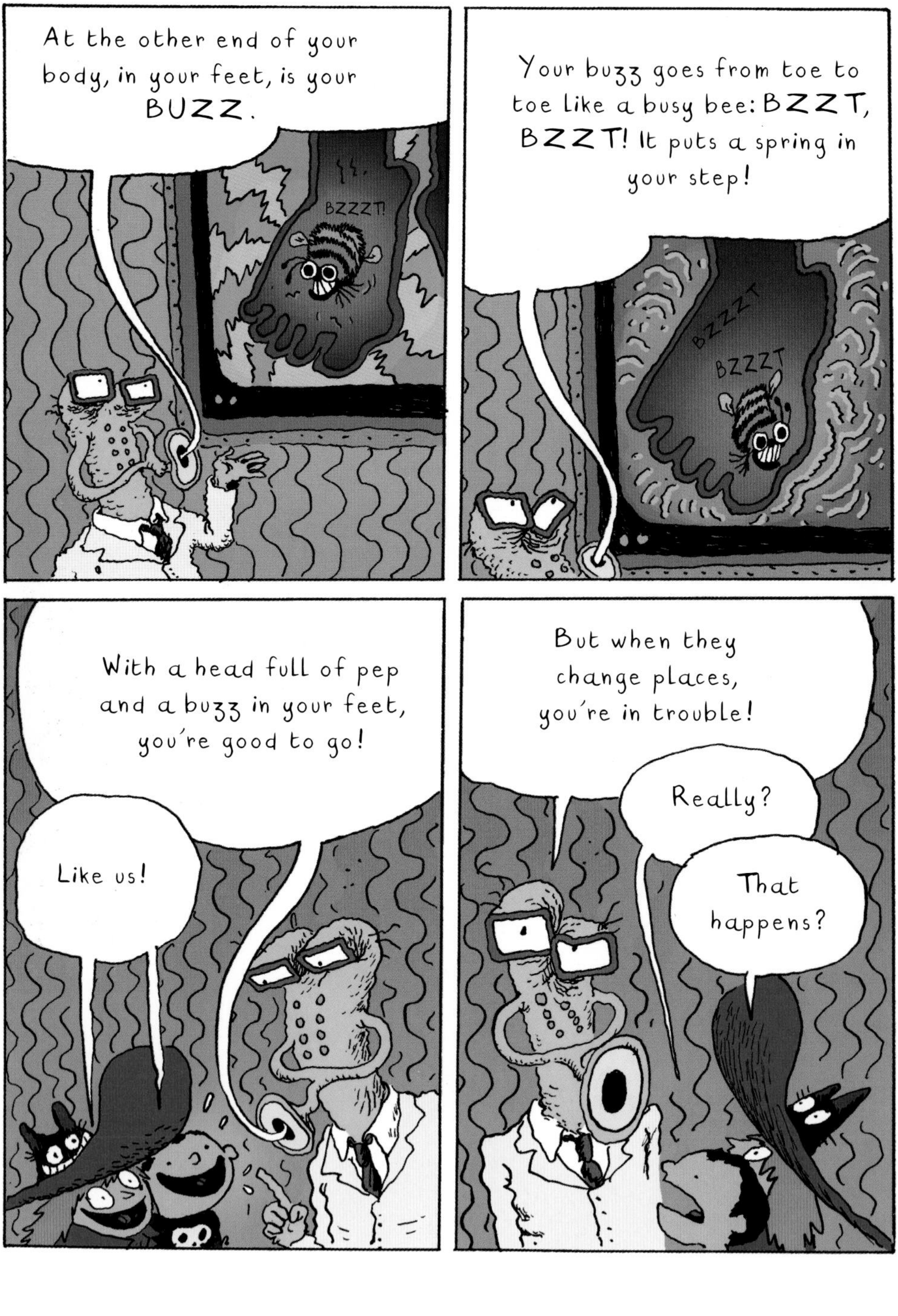
At the other end of your body, in your feet, is your BUZZ.
BZZZT!
Your buzz goes from toe to toe like a busy bee: BZZT, BZZT! It puts a spring in your step!
BZZZT
BZZZT
With a head full of pep and a buzz in your feet, you're good to go!
Like us!
But when they change places, you're in trouble!
Really?
That happens?

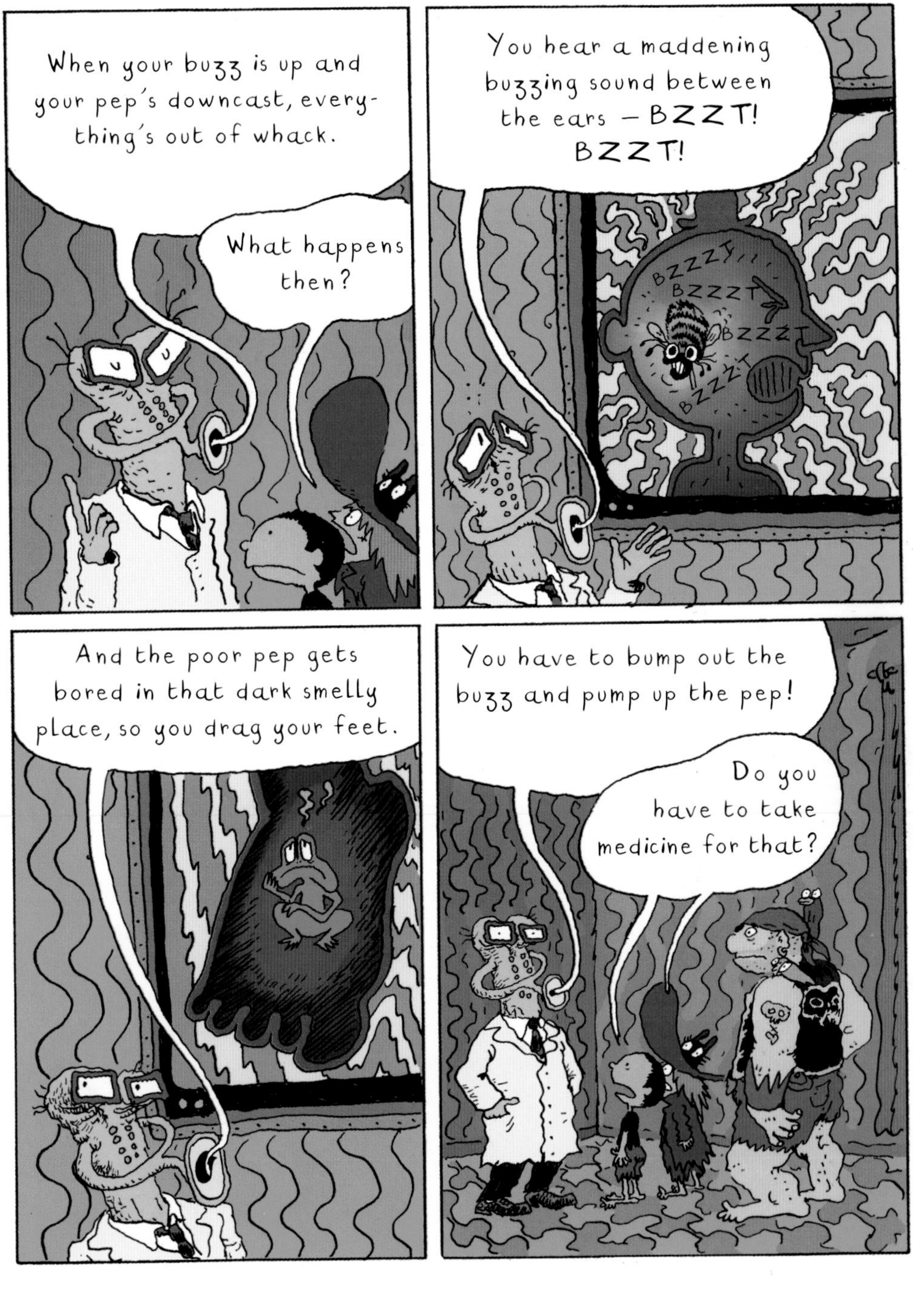
When your buzz is up and your pep's downcast, everything's out of whack.
What happens then?
You hear a maddening buzzing sound between the ears — BZZT! BZZT!
BZZZT
BZZZT
BZZZT
BZZZT
BZZZT
And the poor pep gets bored in that dark smelly place, so you drag your feet.
You have to bump out the buzz and pump up the pep!
Do you have to take medicine for that?

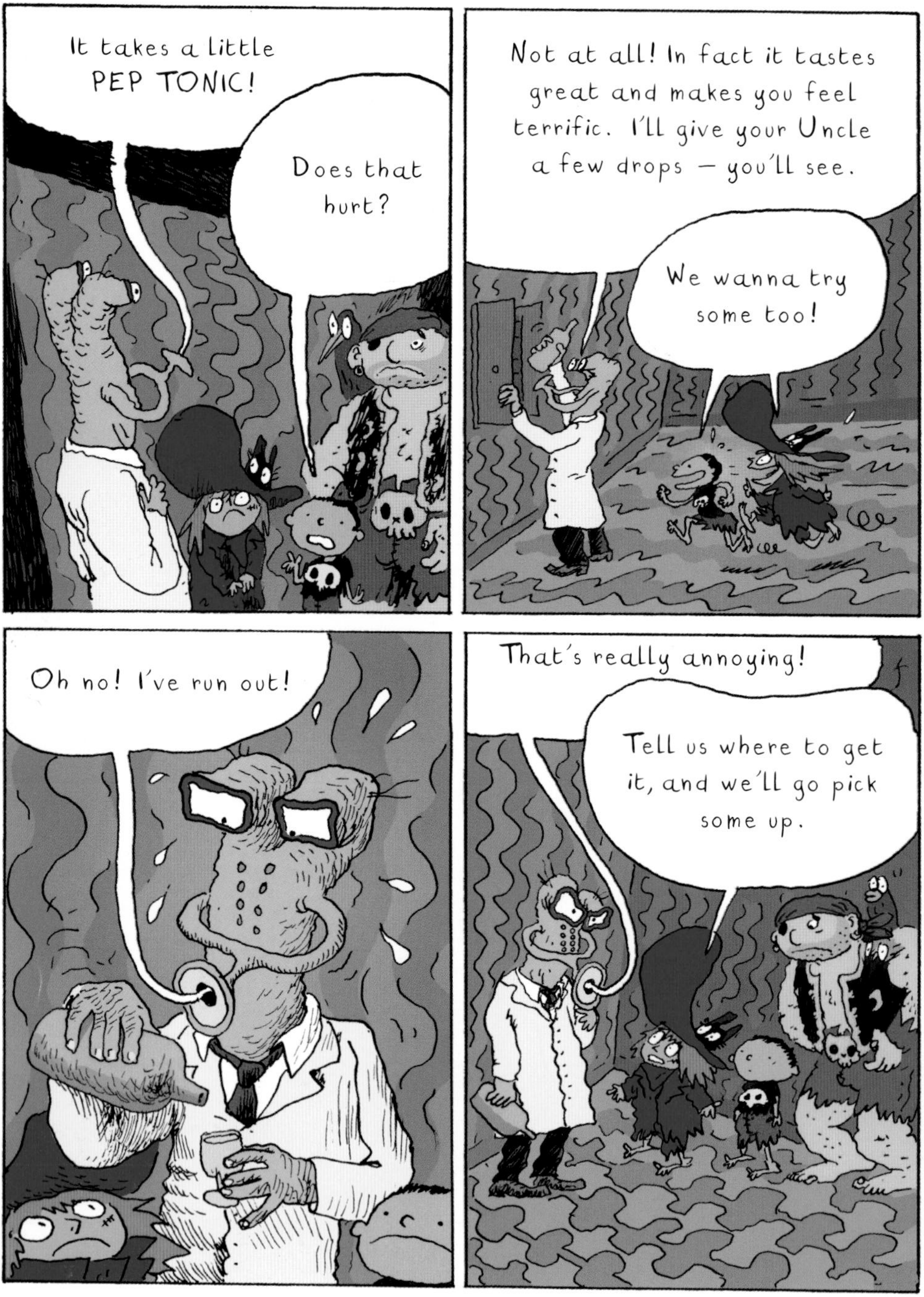
It takes a little PEP TONIC!
Does that hurt?
Not at all! In fact it tastes great and makes you feel terrific. I'll give your Uncle a few drops — you'll see.
We wanna try some too!
Oh no! I've run out!
That's really annoying!
Tell us where to get it, and we'll go pick some up.

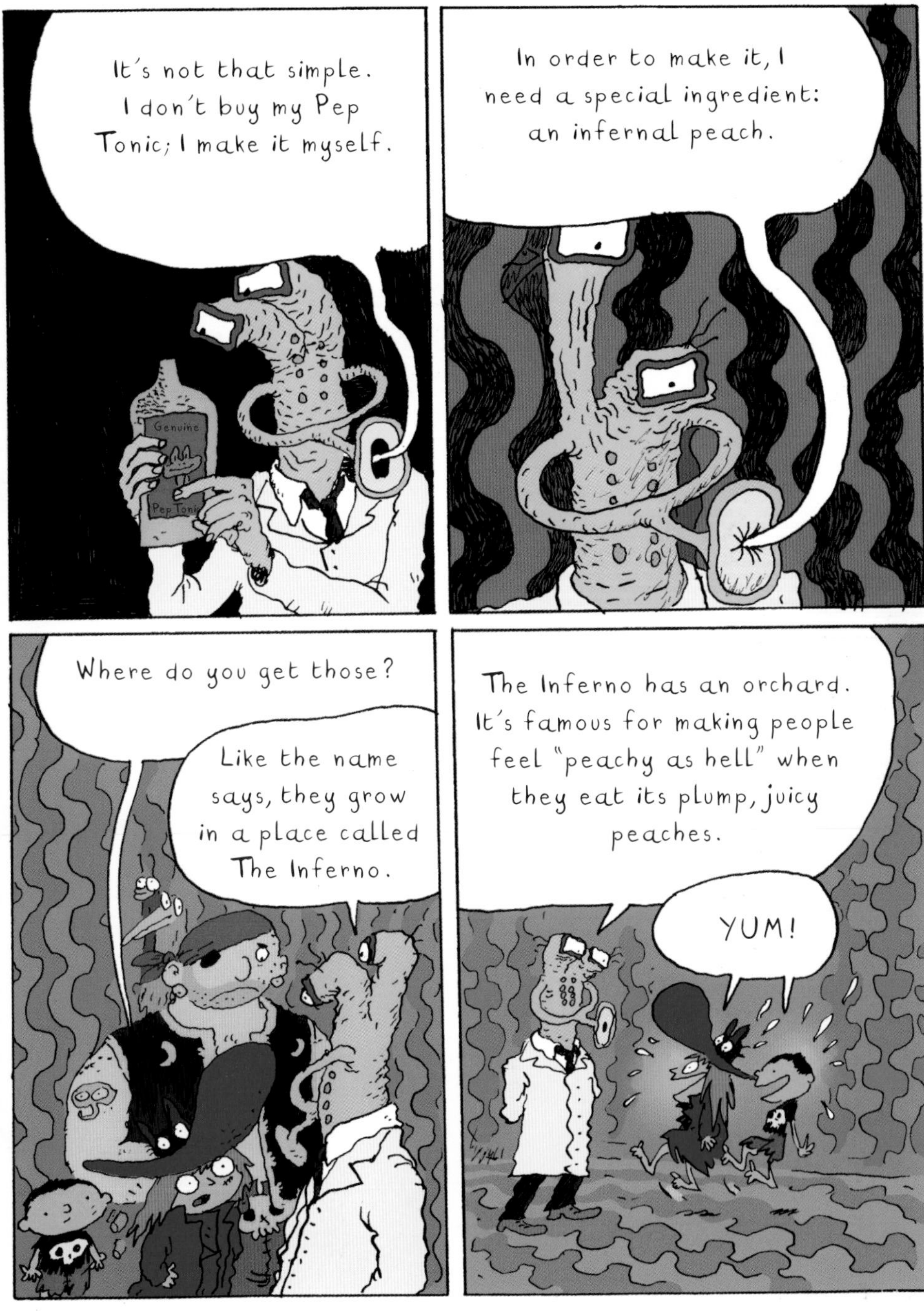
It's not that simple. I don't buy my Pep Tonic; I make it myself.
Genuine
Pep Tonic
In order to make it, I need a special ingredient: an infernal peach.
Where do you get those?
Like the name says, they grow in a place called The Inferno.
The Inferno has an orchard. It's famous for making people feel "peachy as hell" when they eat its plump, juicy peaches.
YUM!

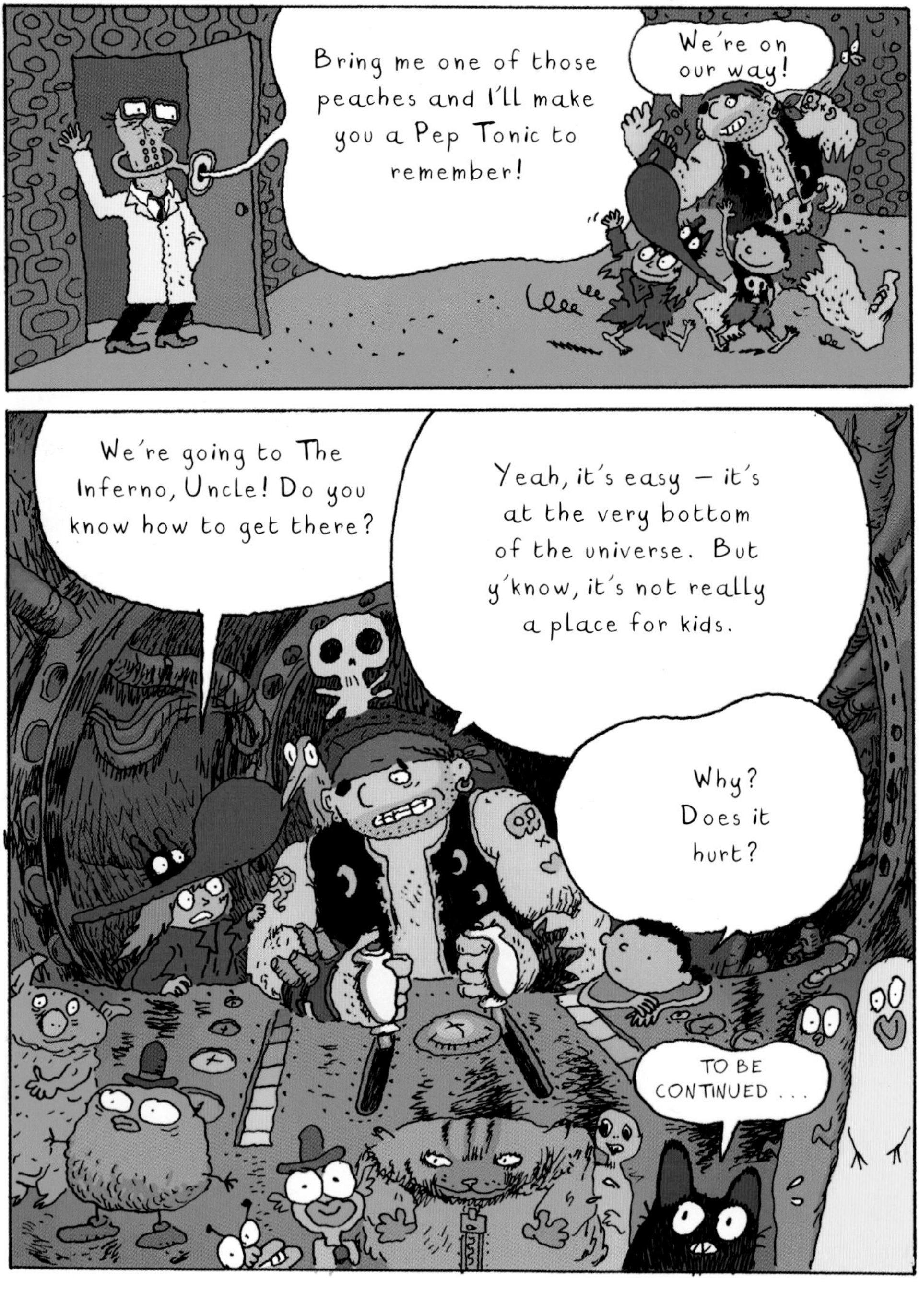
Bring me one of those peaches and I'll make you a Pep Tonic to remember!
We're on our way!
Weee
We're going to The Inferno, Uncle! Do you know how to get there?
Yeah, it's easy — it's at the very bottom of the universe. But y'know, it's not really a place for kids.
Why? Does it hurt?
TO BE CONTINUED . . .

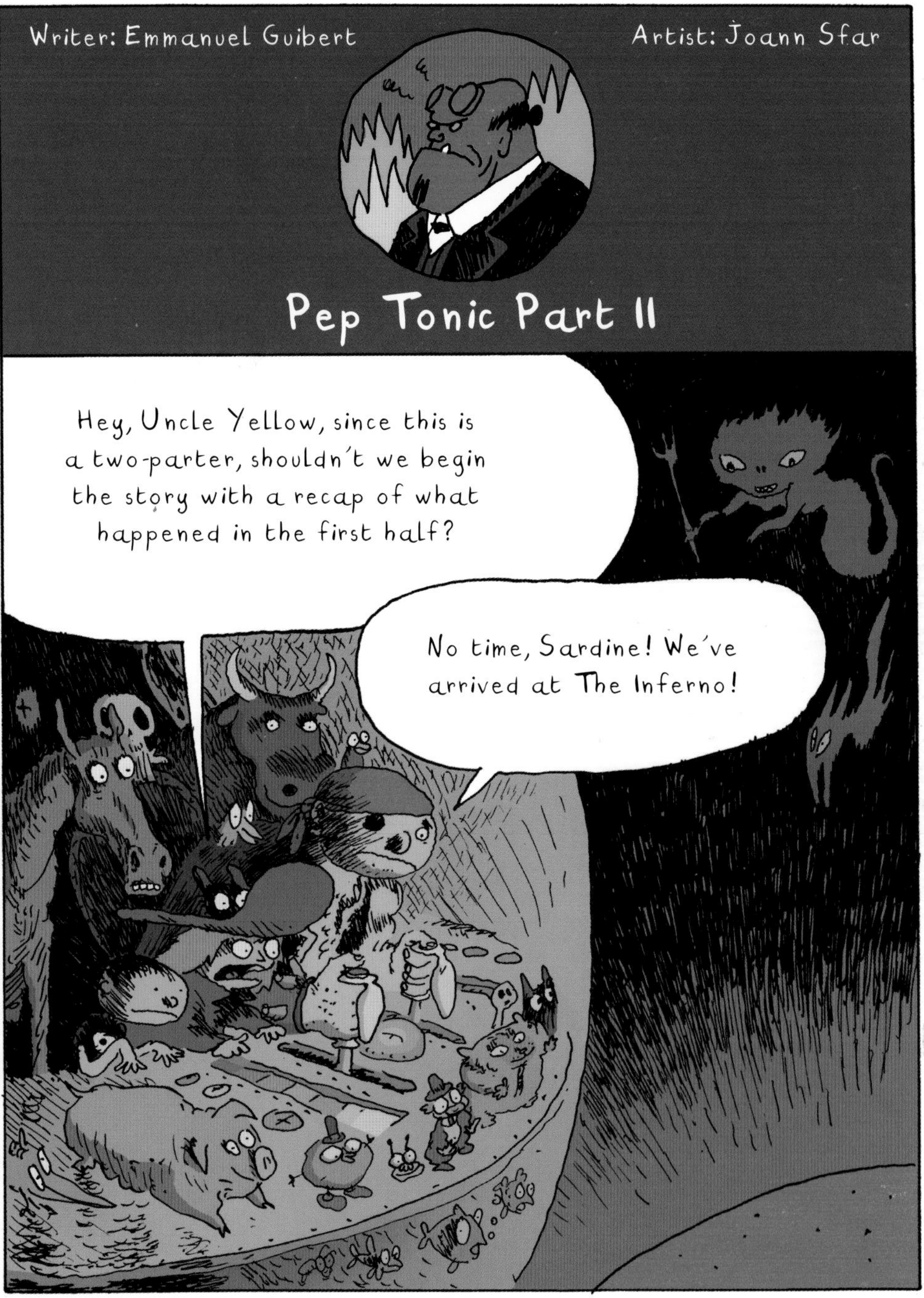
Writer: Emmanuel Guibert
Artist: Joann Sfar
Pep Tonic Part II
Hey, Uncle Yellow, since this is a two-parter, shouldn't we begin the story with a recap of what happened in the first half?
No time, Sardine! We've arrived at The Inferno!

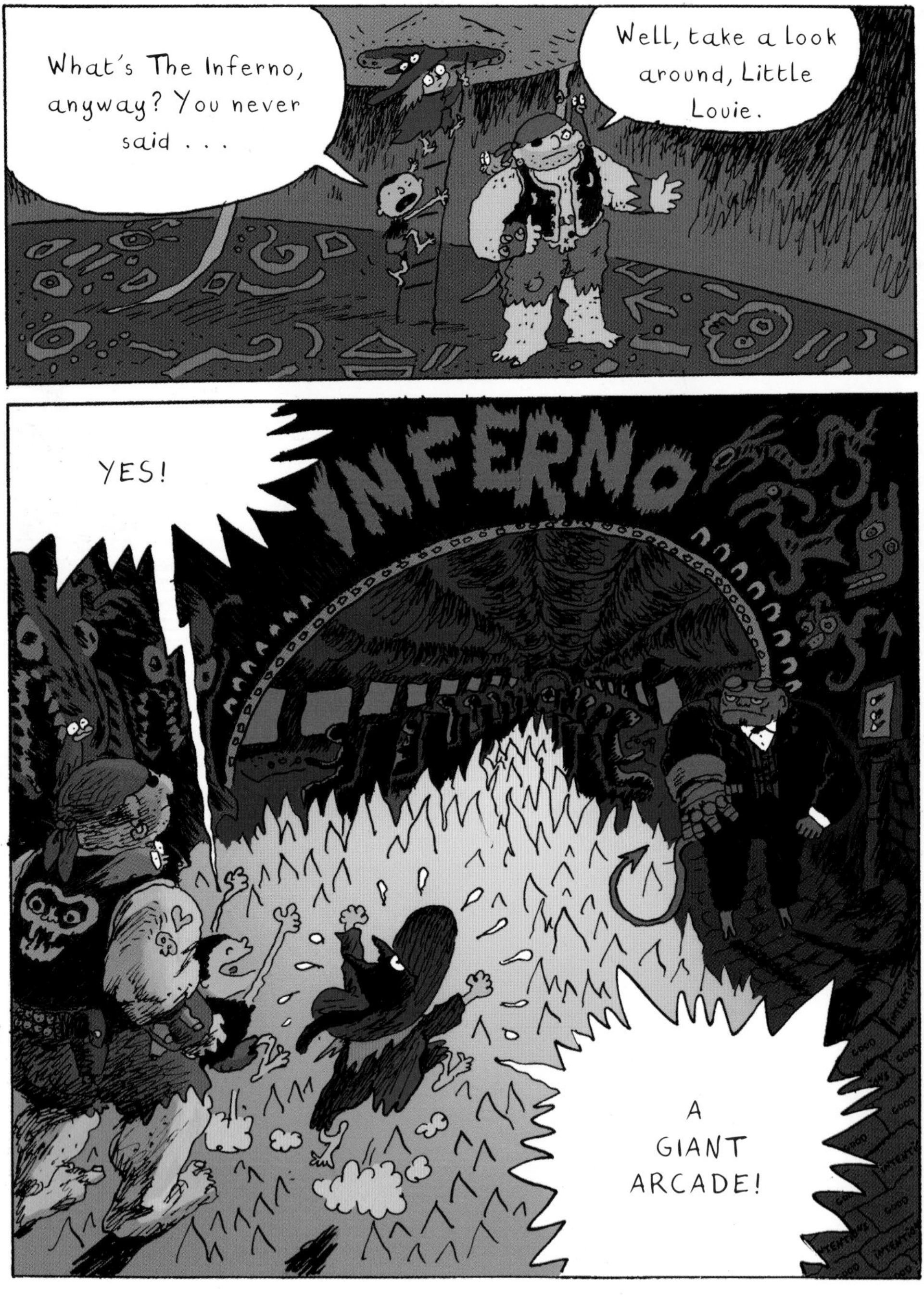
What's The Inferno, anyway? You never said . . .
Well, take a look around, Little Louie.
YES!
INFERNO
A GIANT ARCADE!

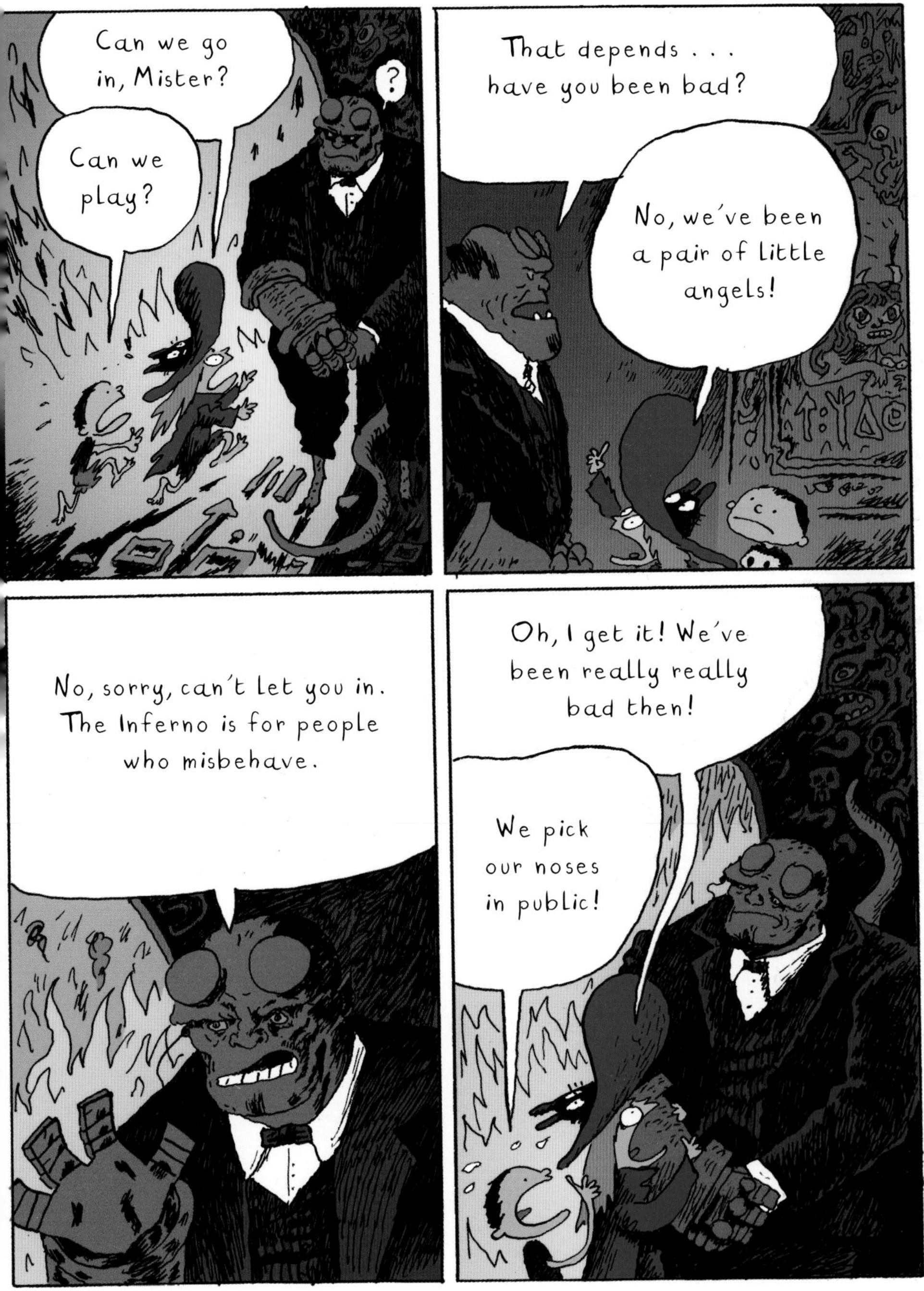
Can we go in, Mister?
Can we play?
?
That depends . . . have you been bad?
No, we've been a pair of little angels!
No, sorry, can't let you in. The Inferno is for people who misbehave.
Oh, I get it! We've been really really bad then!
We pick our noses in public!

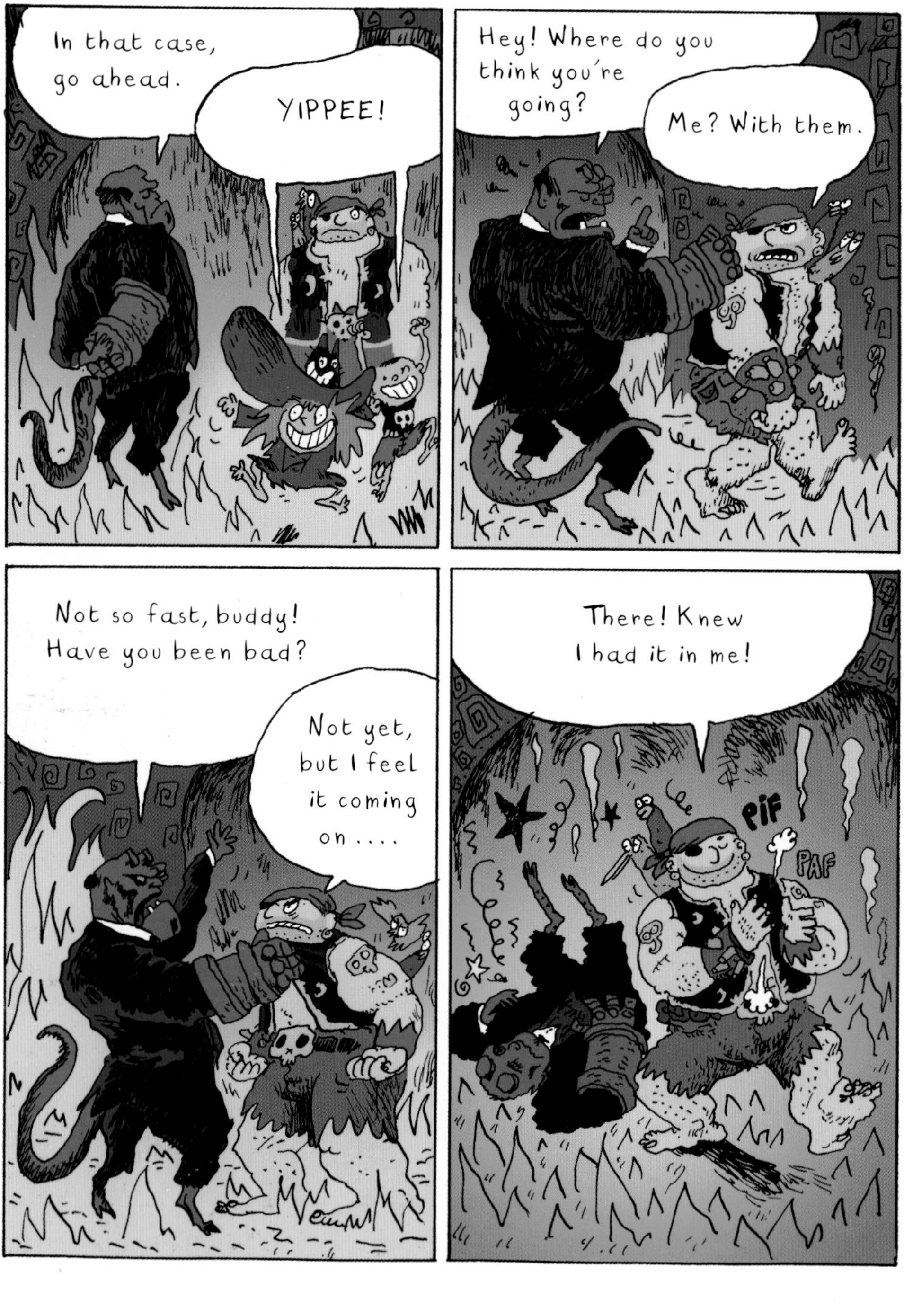
In that case, go ahead.
YIPPEE!
Hey! Where do you think you're going?
Me? With them.
Not so fast, buddy! Have you been bad?
Not yet, but I feel it coming on....
There! Knew I had it in me!
PIF
PAF

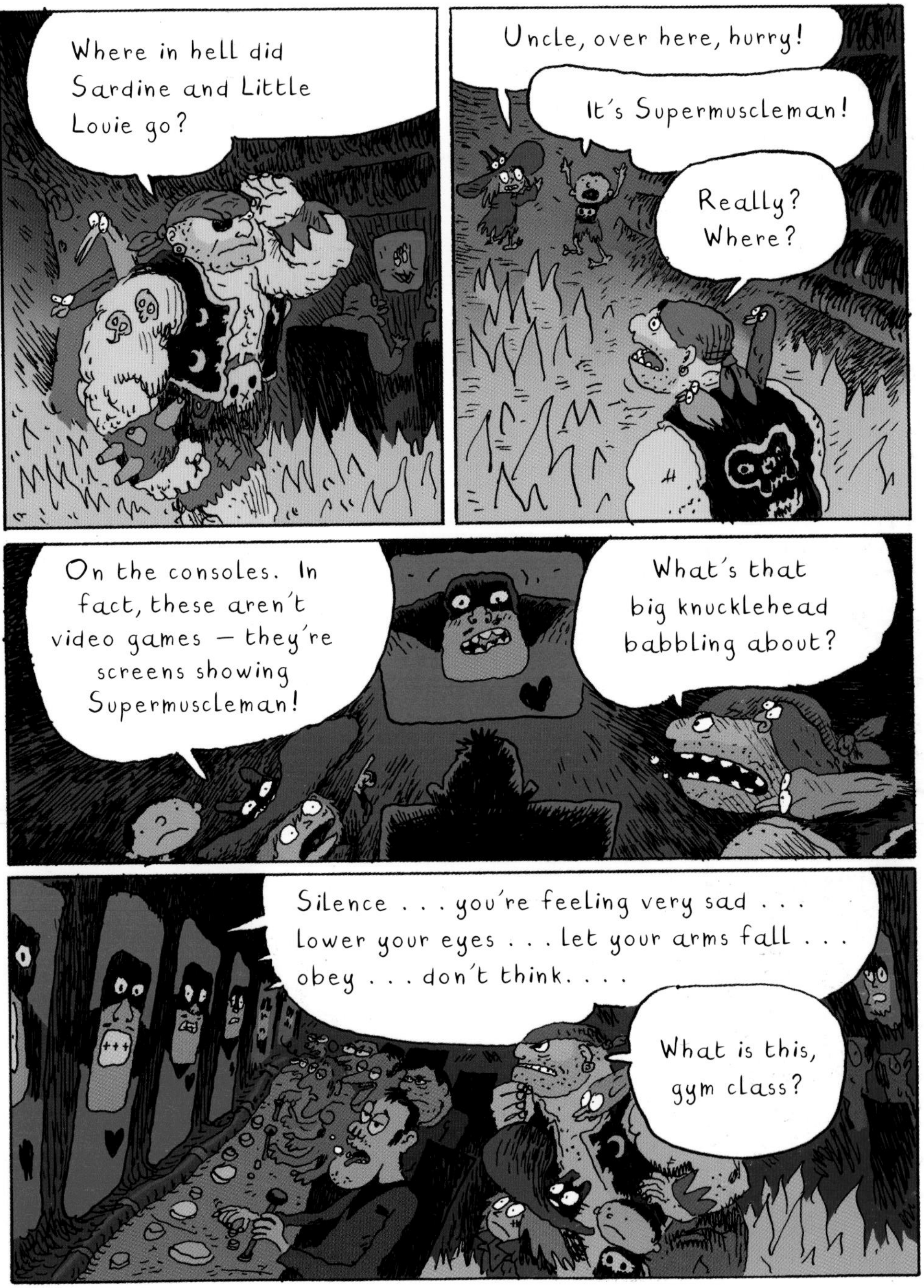
Where in hell did Sardine and Little Louie go?
Uncle, over here, hurry!
It's Supermuscleman!
Really? Where?
On the consoles. In fact, these aren't video games — they're screens showing Supermuscleman!
What's that big knucklehead babbling about?
Silence . . . you're feeling very sad . . . lower your eyes . . . let your arms fall . . . obey . . . don't think. . . .
What is this, gym class?

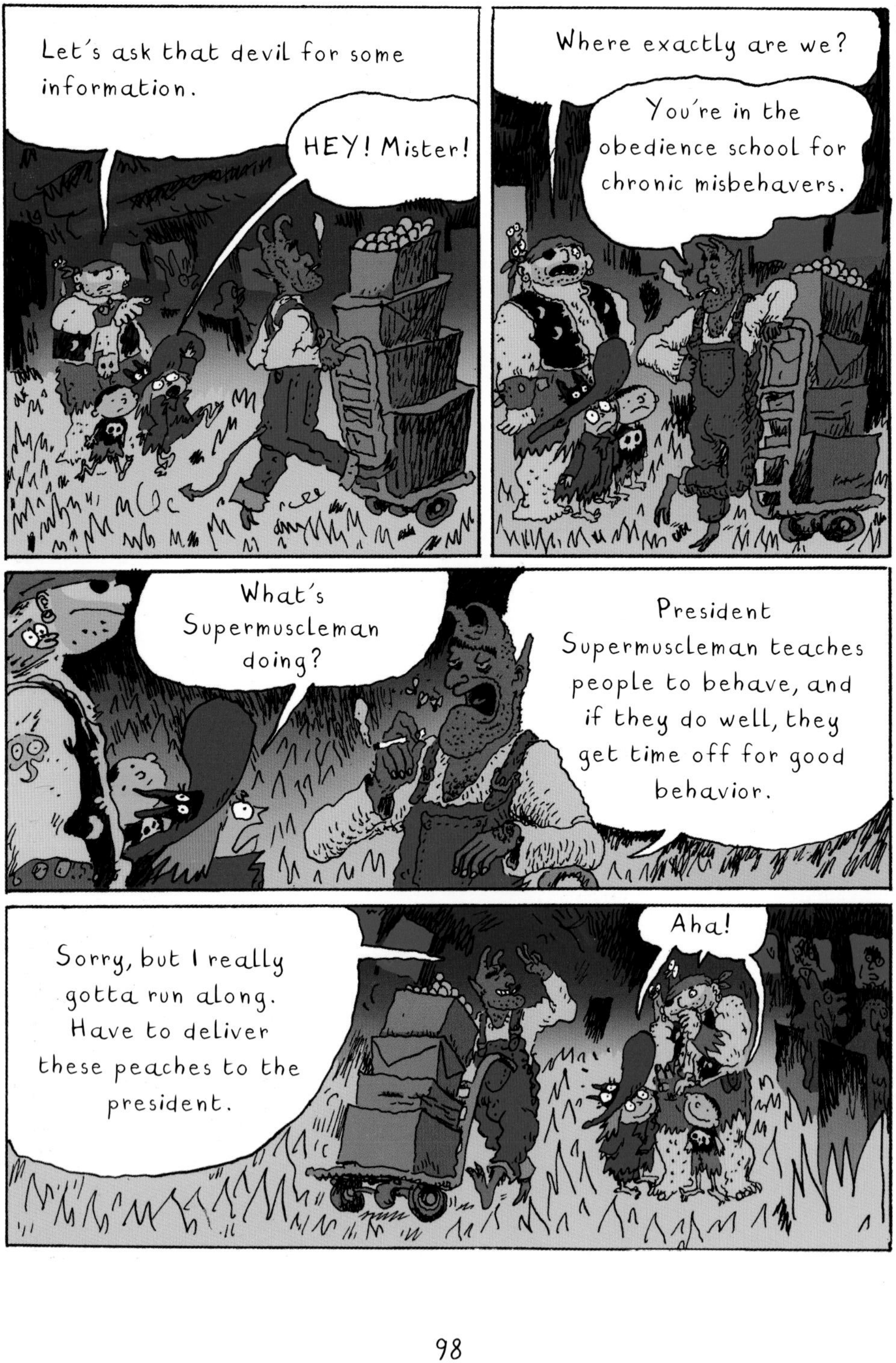
Let's ask that devil for some information.
HEY! Mister!
Where exactly are we?
You're in the obedience school for chronic misbehavers.
What's Supermuscleman doing?
President Supermuscleman teaches people to behave, and if they do well, they get time off for good behavior.
Sorry, but I really gotta run along. Have to deliver these peaches to the president.
Aha!

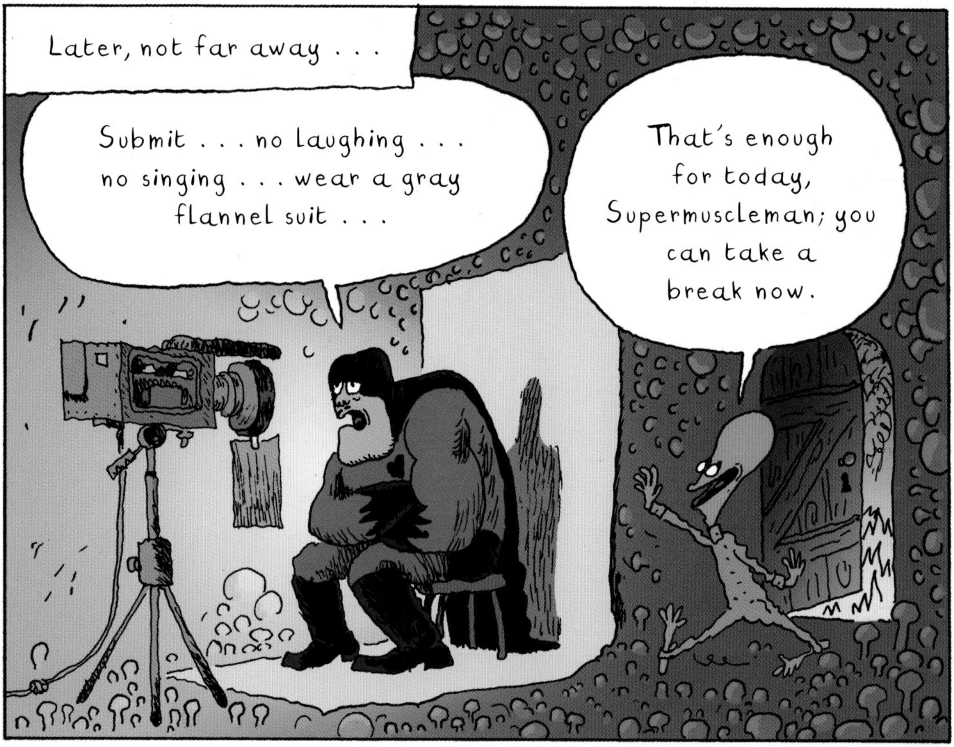
Later, not far away . . .
Submit . . . no laughing . . . no singing . . . wear a gray flannel suit . . .
That's enough for today, Supermuscleman; you can take a break now.

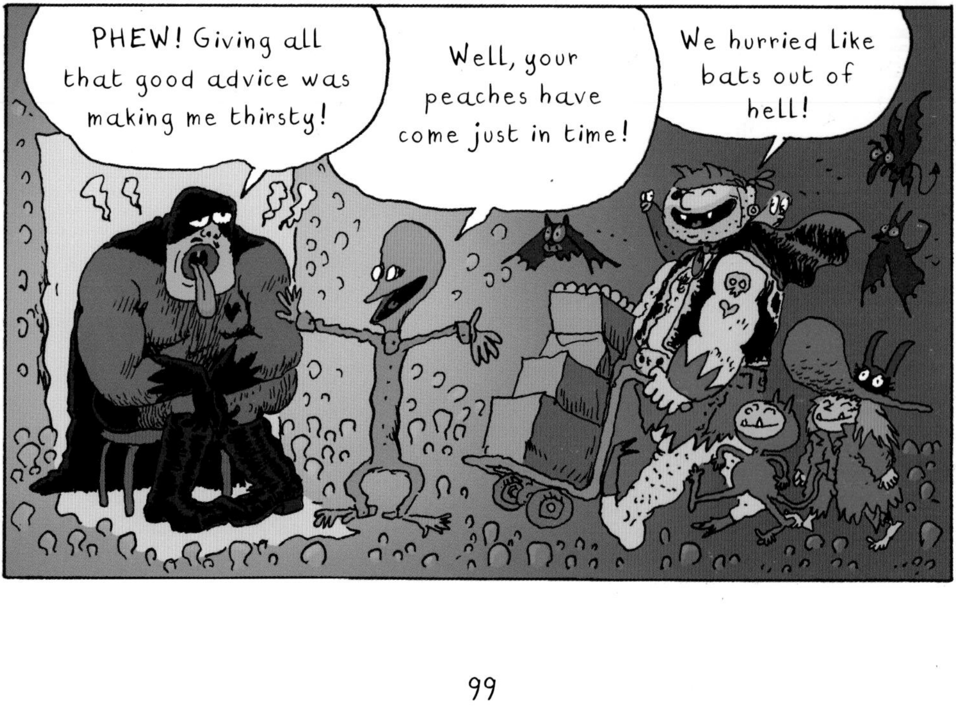
PHEW! Giving all that good advice was making me thirsty!
Well, your peaches have come just in time!
We hurried like bats out of hell!

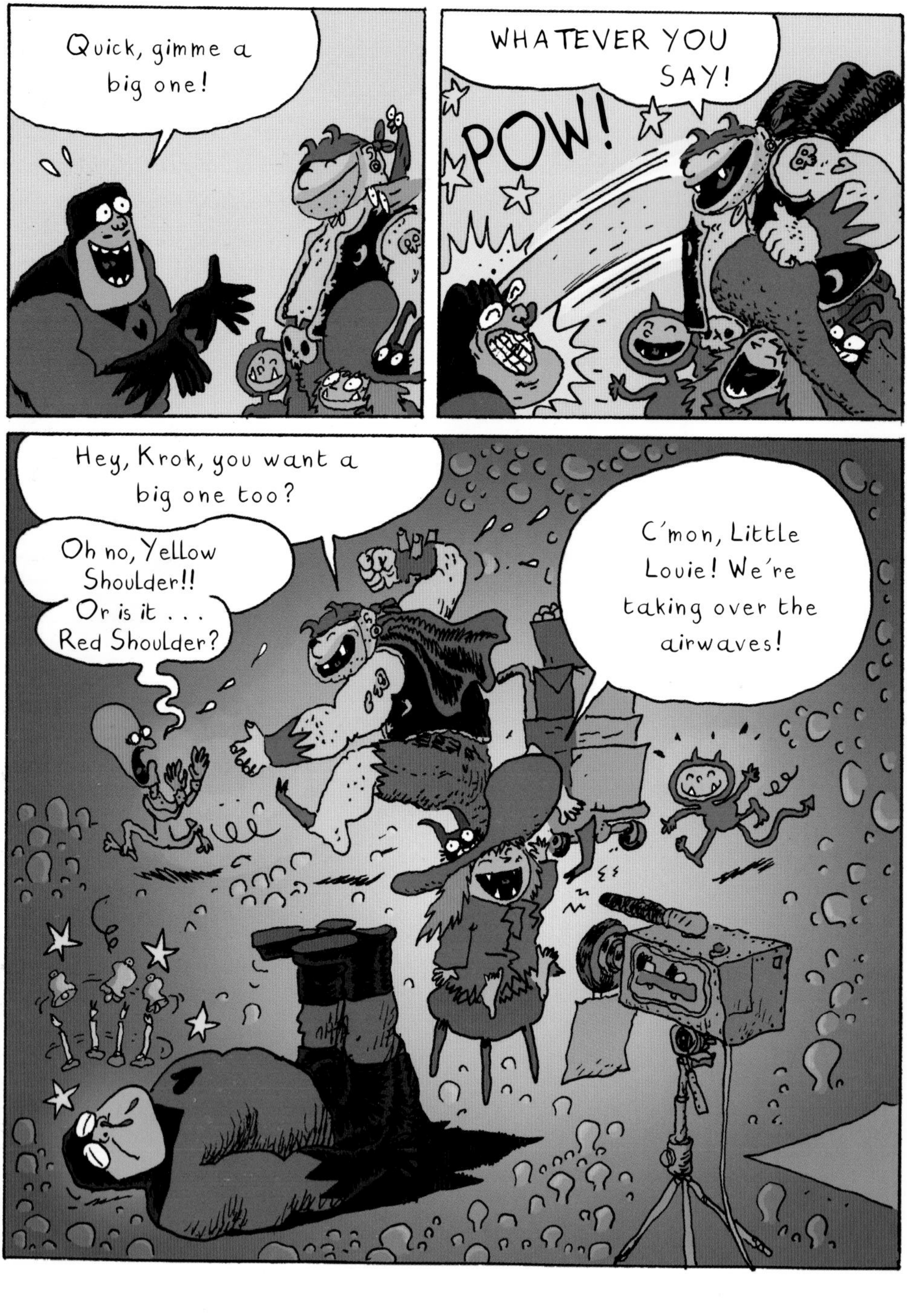
Quick, gimme a big one!
WHATEVER YOU SAY!
POW!
Hey, Krok, you want a big one too?
Oh no, Yellow Shoulder!! Or is it . . . Red Shoulder?
C'mon, Little Louie! We're taking over the airwaves!

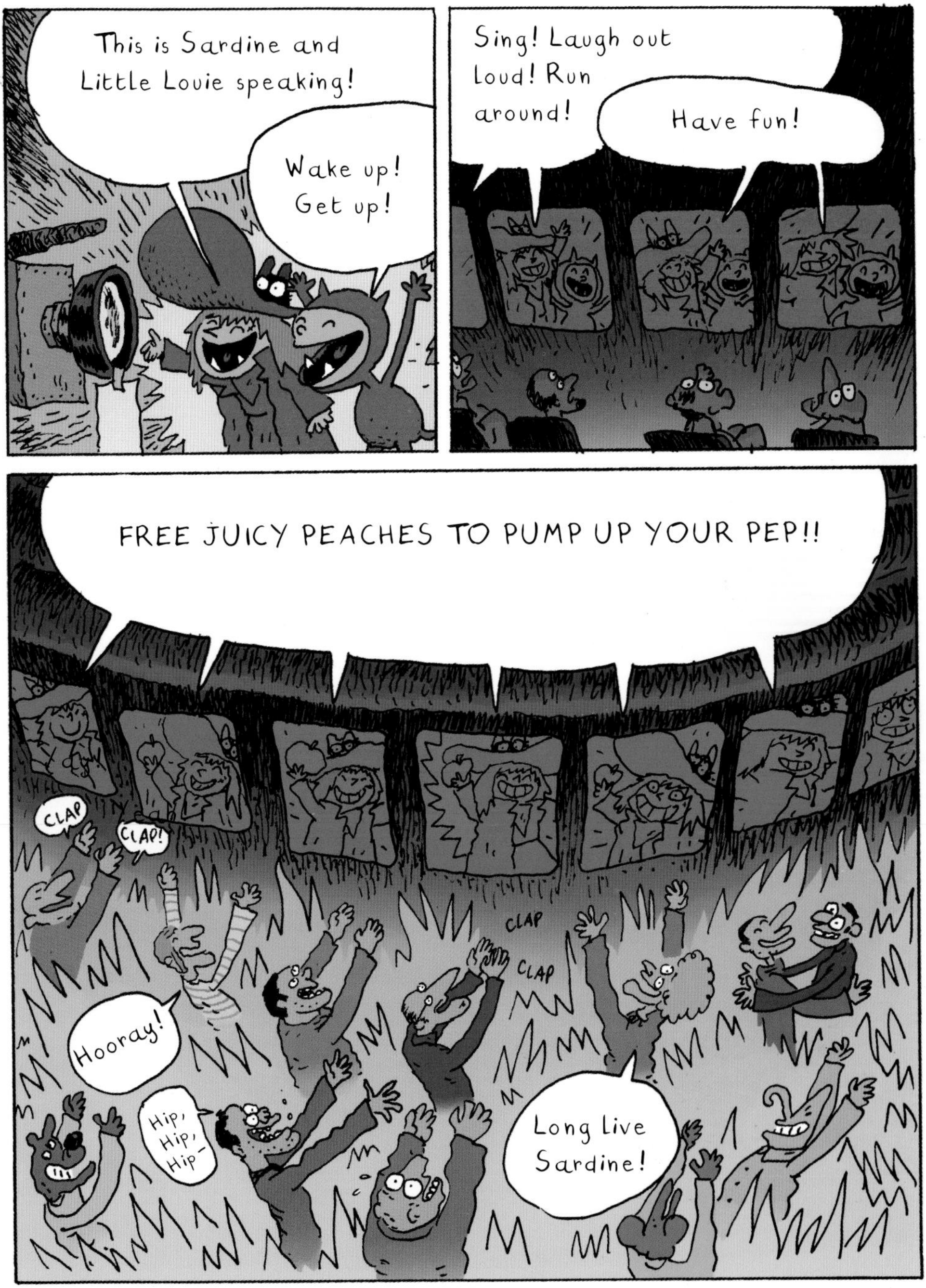
This is Sardine and Little Louie speaking!
Wake up! Get up!
Sing! Laugh out loud! Run around!
Have fun!
FREE JUICY PEACHES TO PUMP UP YOUR PEP!!
CLAP
CLAP!
CLAP
CLAP
Hooray!
Hip, Hip, Hip-
Long Live Sardine!

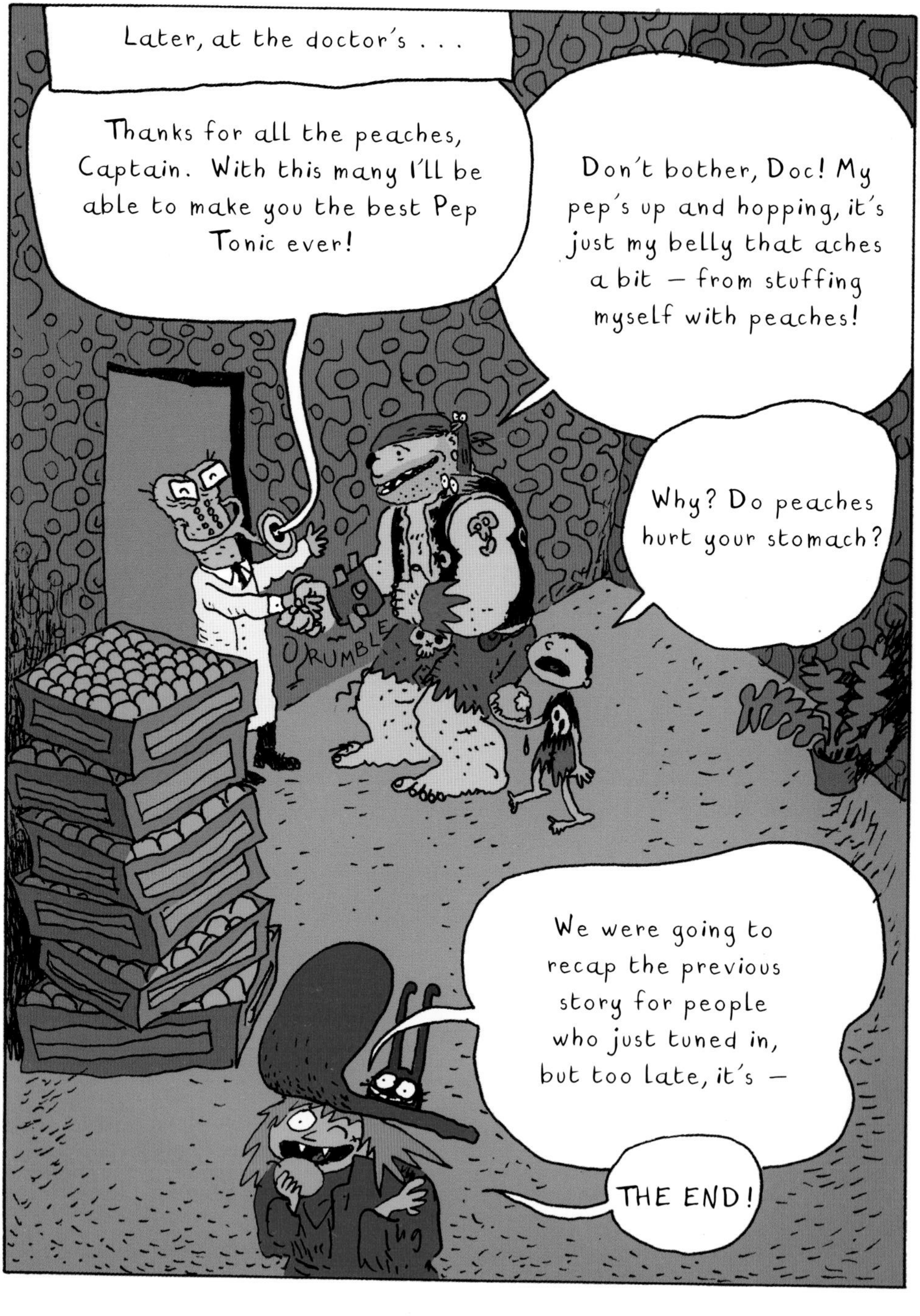
Later, at the doctor's . . .
Thanks for all the peaches, Captain. With this many I'll be able to make you the best Pep Tonic ever!
Don't bother, Doc! My pep's up and hopping, it's just my belly that aches a bit – from stuffing myself with peaches!
Why? Do peaches hurt your stomach?
RUMBLE
We were going to recap the previous story for people who just tuned in, but too late, it's –
THE END!

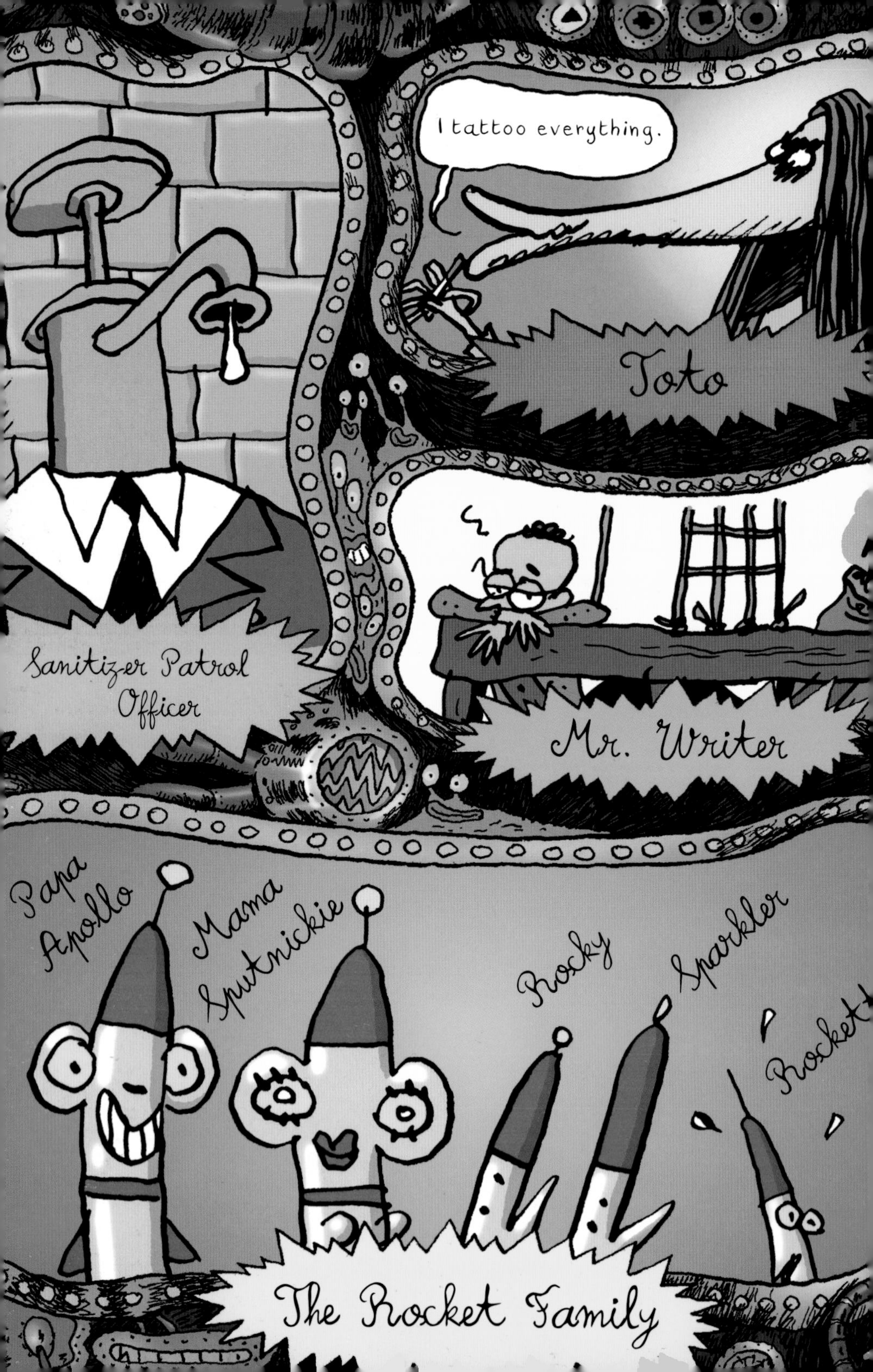
I tattoo everything.
Toto
Sanitizer Patrol Officer
Mr. Writer
Papa Apollo
Mama Sputnickie
Rocky
Sparkler
The Rocket Family

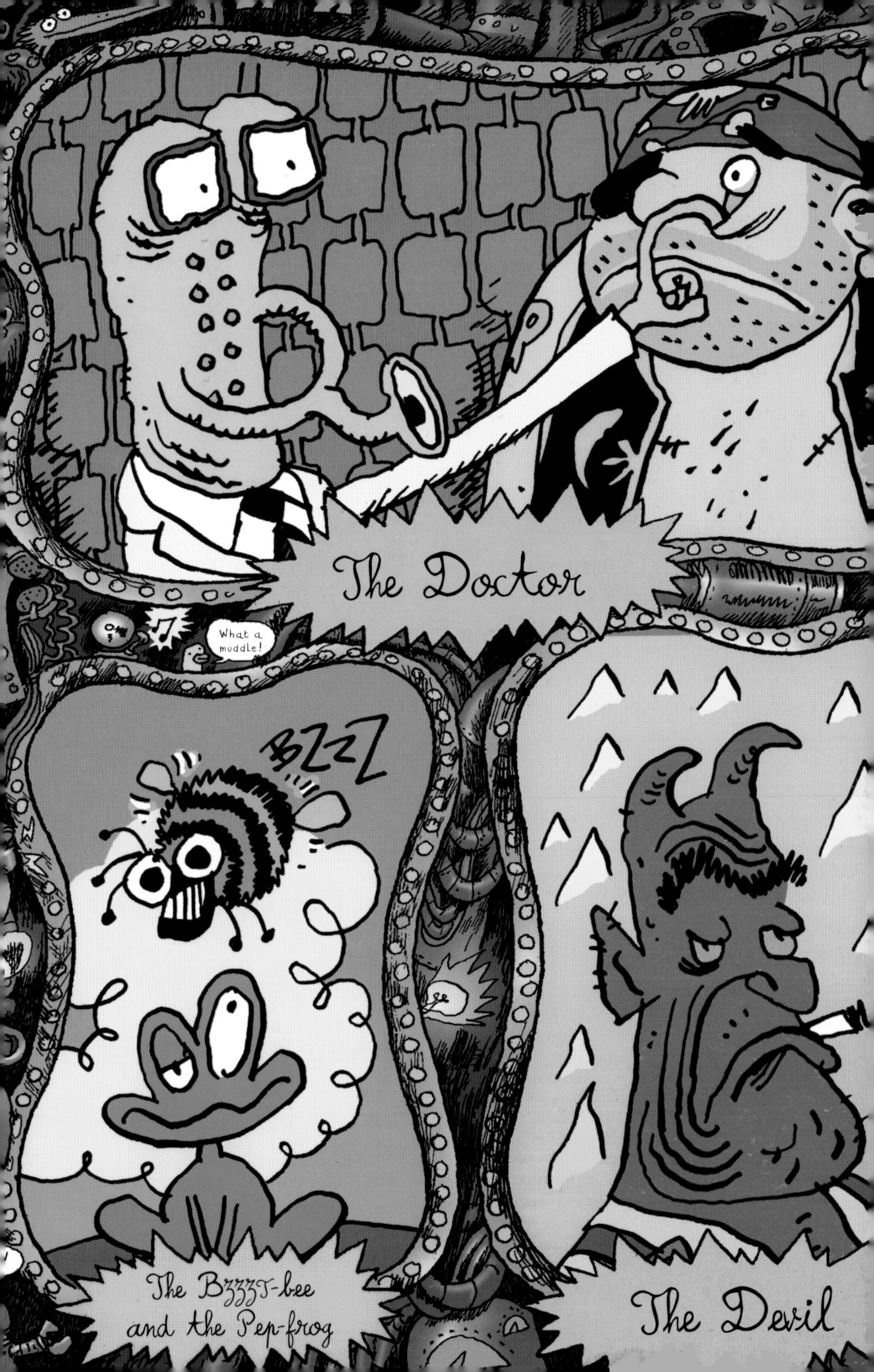
The Doctor
What a muddle!
BZZZ
The BZZZT-bee and the Pep-frog
The Devil

## First Second

New York & London

Copyright © 2003 by Emmanuel Guibert and Joann Sfar
English translation copyright © 2007 by First Second

Published by First Second
First Second is an imprint of Roaring Brook Press, a division of
Holtzbrinck Publishing Holdings Limited Partnership
175 Fifth Avenue, New York, NY 10010

Distributed in Canada by H. B. Fenn and Company Ltd.
Distributed in the United Kingdom by Macmillan Children's Books, a division of Pan Macmillan.

Originally published in France in 2003 under the titles *Sardine de l'Espace: Les tatouages carnivores*
and *Sardine de l'Espace: La grande Sardine* by Bayard Éditions Jeunesse, Paris.

Library of Congress Cataloging-in-Publication Data

Guibert, Emmanuel.
Sardine in outer space / Emmanuel Guibert and Joann Sfar ; translated by Sasha Watson ; colorist, Walter
Pezzali ; letterer, François Batet.– 1st American ed.
p. cm.
Translations of stories originally published separately in French.
ISBN-13: 978-1-59643-129-4 (v. 4)
ISBN-10: 1-59643-129-6 (v. 4)

1. Graphic novels. I. Sfar, Joann. II. Title.
PN6747.G85A2 2006
741.5'944–dc22
2005021790

First Second books are available for special promotions and premiums.
For details, contact: Director of Special Markets, Holtzbrinck Publishers.

First American Edition August 2007

Printed in China

1 3 5 7 9 10 8 6 4 2

Some fine offerings from First Second for young readers of graphic novels...

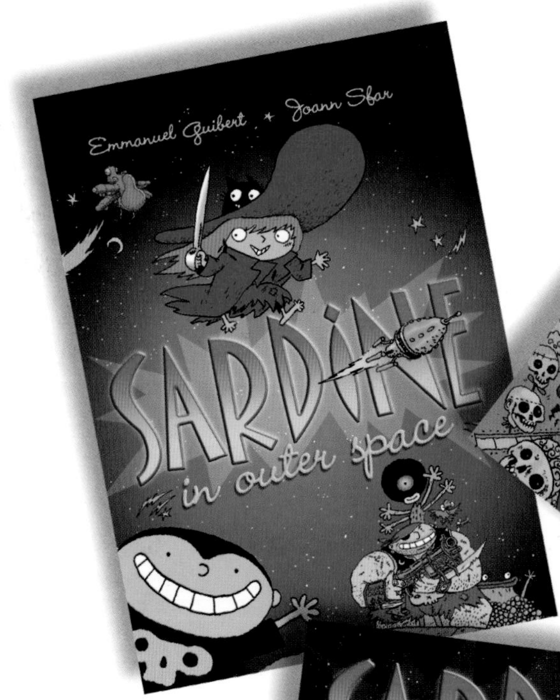
Emmanuel Guibert ★ Joann Sfar
SARDINE
in outer space

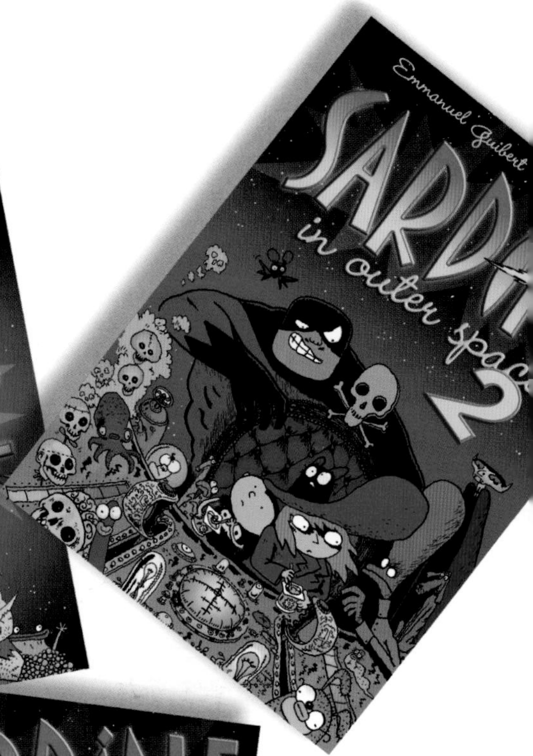
Emmanuel Guibert
2

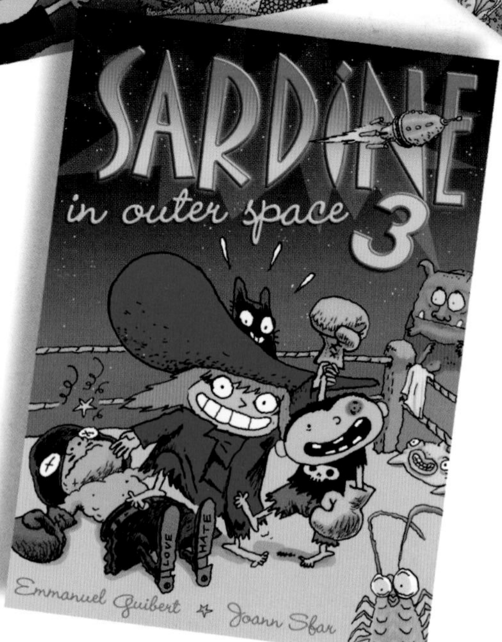
SARDINE
in outer space 3
LOVE
HATE
Emmanuel Guibert ★ Joann Sfar

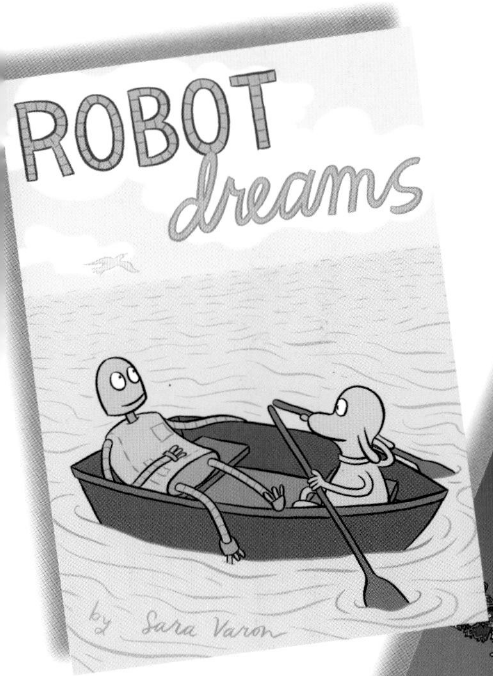
ROBOT
dreams
by Sara Varon

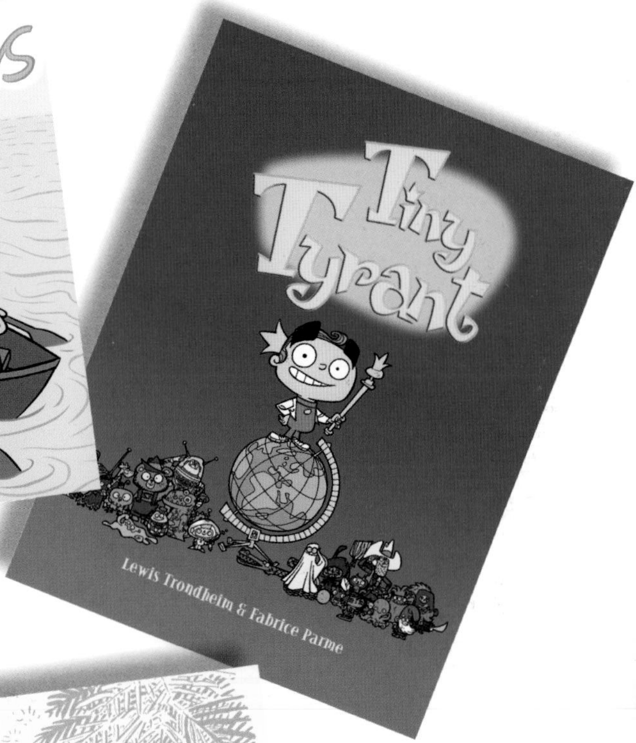
Tiny
Tyrant
Lewis Trondheim & Fabrice Parme

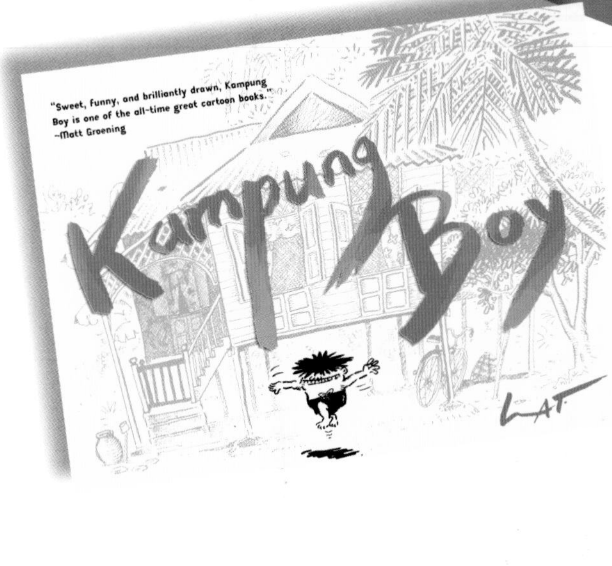
"Sweet, funny, and brilliantly drawn, Kampung Boy is one of the all-time great cartoon books."
–Matt Groening
Kampung
Boy
LAT

And lots more to discover at

**www.firstsecondbooks.com**